Where the Heart Leads

By Ally McGuire

2023

Butterworth Books is a different breed of publishing house. It's a home for Indies, for independent authors who take great pride in their work and produce top quality books for readers who deserve the best. Professional editing, professional cover design, professional proof reading, professional book production—you get the idea. As Individual as the Indie authors we're proud to work with, we're Butterworths and we're *different*.

Authors currently publishing with us:

E.V. Bancroft
Valden Bush
Addison M Conley
Michelle Grubb
Helena Harte
Lee Haven
Karen Klyne
AJ Mason
Ally McGuire
James Merrick
Robyn Nyx
Simon Smalley
Brey Willows

For more information visit www.butterworthbooks.co.uk

CATALOGING INFORMATION
ISBN: 978-1-915009-35-7
CREDITS
Editor: Nicci Robinson
Cover Design: Nicci Robinson & Ally McGuire
Production Design: Global Wordsmiths

Acknowledgements

My first romance novel—I didn't think I'd make it, but with the help of my wonderful wife and the team at Global Wordsmiths, I have. I'd like to thank my editor, Nicci; you were gentle with my dream of writing a romance—until you weren't because I needed a kick in the pants. Thank you for your perfect approach to my little artist child. Thank you to Margaret Burris for proof reading and catching the Britishisms that have somehow slipped unnoticed into my America psyche, and I very much appreciate your willingness to work for the love of it. And thank you to my lovely team of ARC readers for being willing to take their precious time to review my book.

And lastly, thank you to the readers who are taking a chance on a new romance author like me. I know there's a lot of competition out there, so thank you, and I hope you find your faith is rewarded within these pages.

Dedication

To my amazing wife,
who never lets me give up.

Chapter One

"I MEAN, SERIOUSLY. HOW can he expect me to go cycling with my new implants? It's not like these butt cheeks were cheap. I don't want them deflating just because he wants me to go riding up some trail." The woman tossed her long hair over her shoulder and motioned in the vague area of her extremely high buttocks.

Finn Montoya nodded. Sensible. No one wanted deflated butt cheeks. She drew a stick figure with a decidedly droopy butt and scribbled the words below it.

Finn sat in a booth against the wall where she could see everyone who came in, watch who sat down, who didn't, and where she could still hear snippets of conversation from the people waiting for their specialty coffees, overpriced teas, and absurdly named pastries. At Urth Café, there was never a lack of every facet of humanity. Well, not every facet. The Beverly Hills spot didn't exactly tailor itself to those who didn't have ten bucks to spend on a drink they could have made at home. But in a way, that was even better. Unlikable people made for great characters, and she loved writing down the lines of decidedly unempathetic, unintelligent, and often unbelievable things people said. It was a world away from reality, her own little bubble of the surreal.

She sipped her latte, which had come with an intricate peacock created in foam, and she doodled stick people with thought bubbles over their heads as she continued to listen to the conversations around her.

"And then his mother told me that if I didn't shop at boutique stores, I'd look like every other wife he's had. I told her I wasn't going to be caught dead in secondhand, smelly clothes. And you know what she said? She said I was an uneducated snob. Isn't that an oxymedicine or ironic or something?"

Finn drew a male-looking stick figure surrounded with wives all wearing the same T-shirt with Ironic Oxymedicine written on the front. How many wives had he had? And why did women keep marrying him even though they had to know his track record before they walked down the aisle? It was morbidly fascinating, this world of the elite and oblivious.

The morning rush calmed, and she set aside her doodle pad and took out the dominos with numbers and letters in primary colors on them. She smiled at the barista who put another latte down on the table beside her, since hers was covered with tiles.

"Working out plot points again?" Delia asked.

"Trying to. Or maybe coming up with my own language. I haven't decided yet." Finn tilted her head. "New lipstick?"

Delia pursed her purple-black lips. "I like the way the boob joggers look at me when they see it. Like I puked in their new sneakers."

Finn grinned. "Boob joggers?"

"You know, the ones who wear really tight tank tops with more cleavage than top, and they look like they're going running, but if they did, their boobs would be doing all the running because they'd flop right out of those tops." Delia made hand gestures to underscore her meaning.

"Boob joggers. Got it." She sipped the latte after appreciating the palm leaf design in the foam. "Thanks for this."

The door opened, and Delia gave her a quick salute before heading back behind the counter.

Finn continued to sip as she looked at the newcomers. The woman was tall and Hollywood beautiful, though she tried to hide it beneath a baseball cap and shades. Sunglasses inside was always a tell. Why didn't celebrities know that by now? The kid with her, about twelve or so, had that slouchy *wish I was anywhere else* kind of look. When the woman, presumably her mother, put her hand on her shoulder, the kid shrugged it off and moved out of reach. The woman's chest moved as though she'd sighed deeply.

They went to order, and Delia seemed at ease with them. She joked with both mother and daughter, who seemed to lighten up a bit with the banter. Delia beckoned the kid over and was showing her how to create the shapes in the foam when a few more customers came in. The kid shoved her hands in her pockets and moved back toward her mother, who was busy paying.

Finn frowned when she saw someone in the line take a photo and show it to the person behind them. More phones came out, and the people surged closer, and when one called out to the woman, who turned, it quickly opened the flood gates. The others began to surround her.

"Angie! Angie! Can we take a selfie?"

The movement was subtle, but Finn saw the woman, Angie, apparently, gently push her daughter behind her, out of the way of the cameras and pressing crowd. The kid's jaw clenched tight as she stood close to the counter. She pushed her glasses up her nose and wrapped her arms around herself, wrinkling the Rolling Stones T-shirt she was far too young to be wearing unironically.

And then it got worse, and Finn watched with avid curiosity. If there'd been popcorn, she'd be eating it by the handful.

Someone with a professional camera and a sense of entitlement pushed through the crowd and shoved the camera practically up against the woman's nose. They asked all kinds of questions in such a rush that they couldn't possibly expect an answer to any of them. The door opened, and several more entitled camera people pushed in.

The woman said something to Delia, who looked a little overwhelmed, and she nodded and hurried into the office. The harassed woman looked around, seemingly at ease, but when she met Finn's gaze, there was no doubting the worry in her eyes. Finn looked at the kid, who seemed to be breathing quickly, and understood. She motioned at the tiles on the table and then glanced at the kid and back to the woman, who gave an infinitesimal nod.

Finn got up and moved toward the counter, near where Delia had been showing the kid the foaming technique. "I'll bet you a nickel I can beat you at a word game."

The kid looked at her like she was crazy, then at the table that Finn motioned to.

"We'll stay right where your mom can see you, but you'll be out of this shitstorm."

The kid looked surprised and then grinned. Damn. She probably shouldn't swear like that when talking to a kid.

"I'm really good at words. You're on." The kid backed up, keeping her head down so her lanky brown hair fell over her eyes, and dropped into a chair beside Finn.

They went to the table and sat.

"You're used to dodging them. That was impressive," Finn said as she spread out the tiles.

"You should see me climb a fence or throw mud at them when they're looking in the windows." The kid picked up a tile. "My name's Luna. How do we play?"

"I'm Finn." She explained the simple rules, and they began to play. Out of the corner of her eye, she watched the woman smile, take photos with fans, and answer questions with coy answers that weren't answers at all. And she kept her body turned in such a way that she never took her eyes off Finn and her daughter.

Finn kept a tally of the score in her doodle pad and saw when Delia came over and said something to the woman. She backed away, holding up her hands but still smiling.

Delia came over to Finn's table. "Plan B in action, Luna." She raised her eyebrows. "We're in motion."

Luna sighed. "I don't have any nickels. Sorry."

Finn groaned. "I've been cheated." She stood so she was in front of Luna, blocking her from view. "I'll have to see you out, young grifter. I shan't allow you to swindle any other good patrons of this establishment." She made a subtle shooing motion.

Luna rolled her eyes, but her grin gave her away. "You're so weird."

"You have no idea." Finn followed Luna and Delia out the staff-only back door. It opened to the alley, where a black limo waited. Luna slouched her way to the open car door.

"Thanks for the game, weirdo Finn." She pushed her glasses up her nose again.

Finn raised her chin imperiously. "And thank you for the challenge, grifter Luna."

The café door opened again, and Luna's mother came out. Her persona was gone, and in its place was an expression that looked tired and harried. "I'm so sorry. Thank you so much for helping us out." She held out her hand. "I'm Angie Davis."

The name didn't ring a bell, though it obviously should have. Finn shook her hand, which was soft and gentle. "Finn Montoya. And it was no problem."

Luna stuck her head out of the car. "Mom, I owe Finn five nickels. I lost five games in a row, but I'll beat her next time."

"You were betting with my child?" Angie asked, blinking a little quickly.

A cameraman came around the corner of the alley and began to jog toward them. Finn backed away. She had no desire to be caught on film. "It keeps things interesting."

Angie shook her head and got in the car. She slammed the door and lowered the window. "Here, as a thank you."

She was holding out a hundred-dollar bill, and Finn laughed loudly. "I sat and played a game. I didn't teach her how to read Coptic."

The car started rolling and Angie dropped the bill, letting it flutter into the air. "Thanks again," she called, and the window went up before the camera guy managed to get there.

He stopped and looked at Finn as though deciding whether she was interesting or not. She stared at the bill, which was getting soggy thanks to a puddle of something of the gelatinous, once-edible variety, mixed with a little engine oil for good measure. The camera guy shrugged and headed back to the street, and Finn reached down and plucked the bill from the ooze. Holding it in front of her, she went back inside to her table.

This was the weirdest city in the world.

Chapter Two

"No, Claire. I told you, I don't care who's producing or directing. I'm not doing a horror film. That's final." Angie paced the immaculate white kitchen, enjoying the feel of the cold floor under her bare feet as the El Niño winds blew warm air through the open patio doors.

"But it's a spoof horror film. It's meant to be ironic, dark humor." Claire's voice was getting higher. "They really want you." She let out a mildly dramatic sigh. "Every actor takes some crap movie roles. It's part of the game. And it'll keep your name out there."

Angie pinched the bridge of her nose and leaned against the central worktop. "You don't need to remind me that the roles are going to dry up at some point, Claire. It's why I let you bully me into doing film after film with no breaks." She opened her eyes and looked out at the pool, where Luna was flopping around on a banana shaped raft, alone as usual. "I keep promising Luna I'll take time off, but it never happens."

"You'll have plenty of time off if you turn down the roles I send you." Claire's tone softened. "Seriously, babe, I get it. But it's my job to throw as much as I can at you, while I can. You know how this business is."

"No one knows better." Angie watched as Luna flopped onto her stomach on the warm cement and put her iPad on the grass where she could see it without having to bend funny. "But I'm worried about her."

"And you know better than anyone how resilient kids are too." There was a voice in the background. "Okay, I have to go. I'll tell them no-go on the horror, and I'll be in touch with the next offer. Love you."

She hung up before Angie could say anything else. She set the phone on the counter and continued to watch Luna. She tried her best to keep her daughter out of the limelight. If Luna had been interested in acting, it would've been different, but she seemed to hate pretty much everything that came with her mom's career. Of course, she was at the age where nothing was good enough, no matter what it was, but still. It would have been nice to hear her say she'd enjoyed one of Angie's movies. She thought for sure that Luna would have liked the adventure romance, which included plenty of stunts that Angie had done herself. But per usual, she'd rolled her eyes and refused to watch it at all. She'd even refused to go to the premiere, saying she hated all the cameras and how she was expected to smile and care what designer she was wearing. It didn't help that the social media trolls were ruthlessly unkind when it came to Luna's skinny frame and glasses.

At the café the other day, Angie hadn't let it show, but she'd come near to panicking when the crowd had pressed so close. No one knew that Luna had anxiety attacks, especially in large groups. She'd thought they'd be safe going to the place that she and Luna had been to a few times before, and where Luna went on her own occasionally, but she should have known better and just had someone go pick it up for them, the way she usually did. She'd hoped for some normal time with her daughter, but this life wasn't built for normal.

Thankfully, that handsome woman had stepped in. For the life of her, she couldn't remember her last name, but she did recall that her first name was Finn, which was unusual. There had been something about her, about the detached but curious way she'd watched what was happening that had made Angie okay with allowing Luna to sit with her. And since she'd been able to keep an eye on them the whole time, she'd been able to do what she needed to with the paps. It would have been nice to just grab Luna and head straight out, but she had a new film being released in three weeks, and the marketing build-up was essential.

Questions about whether or not she had anything romantic with her co-star and what kind of chemistry they had always made her inwardly flinch. It was worse when Luna was there having to listen to that stuff too. As uncomfortable as it could make Angie, she had no doubt it was way worse for Luna. Hence the reason she rarely took her out in public.

The phone rang, and she sighed when she saw who it was. "Hey, Jim. What's up?"

"Is that any way to greet the love of your life?" he said and laughed. "Don't answer that."

A headache, one that always seemed to appear when her kind-of ex called, started behind her left eye. "Rough day. What's going on?"

"I saw the pics of you in the café, and it made me think of you and Luna. I wanted to check in, see how you're doing."

"She's by the pool. I can go get her—"

"No, that's okay. Don't bug her." His laugh this time sounded a little forced. "I'm sure she doesn't want to talk to me."

Angie shook her head at his intentional obtuseness. "I'm not surprised you think that. Why are you really calling?"

He cleared his throat. "I heard you were up for that horror role in Gustavi's next movie. Are you taking it?"

"No. Why?"

"Well, Theresa would really love the chance, and if you're going to turn it down, maybe you could put in a good word for her?"

Now the headache was in full force. "You want me to put in a word for your current girlfriend?"

"Well, it's not like she's your competition, is it?"

She winced at the tiny bit of venom in his tone. He would've been agreeable to play the happy couple, but the one night of drunken fumbling that had resulted in Luna had been more than enough for her. She'd come out as a lesbian a month after Luna was born and had never looked back. But she did her best to keep her dating life as private as possible and away from the cameras.

She knew the game, and a leading lady in romantic comedies had to be believable. If she was always out with a hot woman on her arm, no one would buy into the happy ever after of the movies she'd become the poster woman for.

"I'll let Claire know that Theresa is interested. But I can't do anything more than that. Is that all?"

"Totally. Thanks so much, Angie. Seriously."

There was a squeal in the background. Apparently, Theresa had been listening in. "Yup. No problem. Have to go." She ended the call and got herself a glass of water to take up to her room. It was time for some quiet. Maybe when she woke, everything would have sorted itself out. That's how it worked in the movies anyway.

Chapter Three

"Nickels?"

Finn leaned her elbows on the bank counter. "Nickels. One hundred dollars' worth, please."

The bank teller continued to look confused, almost offended, by the odd request. No doubt as society headed toward a cashless, electronic existence, asking for cash, especially change, could be considered something worth calling security over for. Fortunately, the teller just grumbled as she brought over the bag of change.

"Is it really so strange?" Finn hefted the bag. "Surely there are plenty of stores who need change all the time."

The teller shrugged. "Sure. But they ask for a specific variety, and they have a business account. Regular people don't need change. They try to get rid of it."

"Well, maybe one day I'll open a business account." Finn held aloft the bag. "Until next time."

"So weird."

Finn heard the words spoken as she walked away, and they made her smile. Far from being hurt by it, she reveled in people finding her out of the ordinary. If nothing else, she was memorable for more than the nanosecond society gave to most things or people these days, and that meant something.

She took the bag out to her car and put it in the box she had labeled and ready to go with a brief letter inside. It was addressed to Angie Davis's agent. She had no idea why she felt the need to do it. But Luna's pinched expression, the white in her knuckles, the way she tried to make herself smaller... Finn knew those feelings all too well. And she knew what came with them too. Anxiety, the feeling of being alone, of being a prop for good photos. It stole something from your soul.

She took the box to the post office and sent it next day delivery. The kid shouldn't have to wait to be told she wasn't alone in the world, that someone had seen and remembered her.

Once that errand was done, she got on the freeway and headed toward Long Beach. She never grew tired of the giant, multi-lane roads full of people heading to a zillion different destinations. It was a far cry from the place she'd grown up, and when she'd moved to LA years ago, she'd promised herself she'd never complain. Things could be, and had been, far worse.

She got off the freeway and parked at the El Dorado Nature Center. It was a strangely placed little nature reserve, set between the freeway and a shopping center. But as she strolled over to meet her group, she breathed deeply and let the scent of nature fill her. Well, nature and some wafting car fumes.

"Welcome, fellow Winger."

Finn's eyebrow twitched, but she managed to keep a straight face. "Always nice to see you and the other Wingers."

Gertrude Brice was the unofficial leader of the Wing Watchers, a post she took seriously. At eighty-seven, she outpaced many of the younger members, even on the steeper hikes. Her blue eye shadow, shock of wild white hair, and yellow hiking pants made her a perfect person to lead their bird watching expeditions, especially as she so resembled the little blue tits she'd seen in a birding magazine. Her enthusiasm and knowledge didn't hurt either.

"Finn, we have a bet going." Gertrude motioned at the milling group behind her. "I say you're a spy. Pam says you're a fancy chef of some kind." She rolled her eyes. "And Jim says you're a gigolo. Which is it?"

Finn shook her head and bent to whisper in Gertrude's ear. "If I were a spy, I couldn't very well tell you, could I?" She winked and straightened. "And I make a mean grilled cheese for the women I manage to get to take care of me."

There was a moment of silence before the general grumbling started.

Gertrude gave out a bark of laughter and slapped Finn on the back. "There's nothing like a good mystery woman. Keep 'em guessing, that's what I say." She turned and held up her bright red paddle in the shape of a hummingbird. "Now, we're going to head west. Today, watch out for the red-winged blackbird, bushtits, green herons, and maybe even a hooded oriole."

She set off, and the rest of the group followed. As usual, Finn lingered in the back. She wasn't a birdwatcher. Sure, she liked them. They were beautiful and made pretty music. But she lacked the avid desire to catch them doing their bird things in their bird habitats. What she really liked was being with a group of people who were far more interested in the world around them than they were in her. Of course, it was a close-knit group, and they shared aspects of their lives on every expedition. When asked about her life, Finn gave each person a different answer, ranging from failed astronaut to elementary school linguistics teacher. Hence, the betting. The truth was no less dramatic but far less fun. It was better to keep things light.

"I miss pineapple."

She looked over at Steven, who had fallen into step beside her. His bald head was extra shiny today and reflected the green canopy above them. "That's an interesting thing to miss. I'm pretty sure you can find it in places other than Hawaii."

He stuffed his hands in his pockets, his binoculars bouncing on his concave chest. "I had to give it up. Ate so much of it when I was on vacation that my body rejected it. Face swelled up like one of those bloated fish."

"Puffer fish?" she asked unhelpfully, while trying to picture his rather skeletal face in an allergic reaction. It might make him look a little less like the personification of death, sans cloak and scythe.

"Yup. That's the one. And boy, did it go right through me. Had to rush to the bathroom and hardly left it for a full day. Then I tried pineapple juice when I got back, and BAM! Same thing happened again." He shook his head, looking truly sad about his lack of bromelain and vitamin C.

"Hawk!" Gertrude held up her red hummingbird sign and stage-whispered, stopping the group behind her who all brought up their binoculars and aimed them in the same direction.

Finn was busy considering the deleterious nature of eating too much pineapple and left the bird-spying to the others. They'd stand there and stare at it for some time, something she'd learned on the other adventures with them. She took a seat on a nearby bench and let her thoughts roam. It was a good way for stories to begin coming together, with awkward plot questions or character issues working themselves out naturally in her subconscious.

Steven plonked down next to her. "Why do you come?"

"What do you mean? Birds." She waved vaguely toward the trees.

"Come on. You're as interested in birds as I am in sports that include a ball of any kind." He tilted his head and looked a little like a bird himself. "What's the real reason?"

She wasn't about to expose the real reason, but she'd get as close as she could. A genuine question deserved a genuine-ish answer. "I like being around people, but having a focus other than the usual small talk is better than sitting in a restaurant and trying to find stuff to say."

He scuffed at the ground with his worn hiking boot. "So you don't like getting close to people?"

She didn't answer. She didn't have one that wouldn't lead to more questions.

Gertrude waved her sign when the hawk got tired of posing for the group and flew off. "Onward."

Finn followed the group, grateful that Steven didn't seem to have anything more to ask, though she would've welcomed more of his pineapple-esque stories. Stuff like that was perfect fodder for books.

By the end of the two mile stop-start walk, Gertrude declared the day a raging success. They'd seen all four of the birds on her list, as well as a few others which were an unexpected delight.

"Remember that our next walk is in Knickerbocker Canyon. Wear proper hiking shoes and bring sunscreen. Especially you, Steven. We don't want that shiny dome of yours competing with the sun like it did last time."

The group laughed and dispersed. Finn got back in her truck and headed to the gym, feeling nicely emptied of the worry and stress she'd built up over the lack of words flowing for her new book.

But that peace dissolved when she got home later and found another letter requesting her RSVP for the award ceremony. Like a frustrated teenager, she shoved it under the other mail, including the latest copy of *Railroad Fun* magazine. If they kept bothering her, maybe she'd have to move. In fact, maybe she should just take off without leaving a forwarding address.

She'd done it before. She could do it again.

Chapter Four

ANGIE LAY ON THE couch, scanning the pre-release reviews Claire had sent over. So far, so good. Most of the reviews raved about it being sweet and funny, poignant but uplifting. Those were the reviews her movies usually got, and she was happy with them. One review said the romantic characters had the chemistry of seaweed, which left her irked as well as bewildered. What kind of chemistry did seaweed have, after all? And how did that translate to a relationship?

Long ago, she'd found that the downfall of all creative people was reviewers. Opinions formed based on personal preference and an occasional desire to come across as witty were often unnecessarily cruel and almost never useful. Fortunately, she wasn't one to take them to heart for the most part. As long as the good outweighed the bad, she stayed happy.

She rolled off the couch and stretched. Claire had sent over some casting calls she thought Angie might be interested in auditioning for, and she'd need to decide soon enough. But the last film had been a rough three months of nearly constant work, and it had come right after another film. She was ready for a short break before she dove into the next one.

"Nice to see you home." Helen, who had been Luna's nanny since the day Angie had brought her home from the hospital, ambled in.

Angie watched as Helen got herself a drink. She looked stiff, older than Angie remembered. "Are you okay, H?"

Helen slid onto a dining table chair and tapped the table with her water bottle. "Sit with me."

Angie joined her, a sense of foreboding rising. "Is it a health thing? What can I do?"

Helen took her hand and squeezed it. "Nothing like that, honey. But we've always been up front with each other, and I have something to say."

"Is it Luna? Has she done something to upset you?" She tried to think of any incidents over the past week. "I know she can be difficult right now—"

"Stop, Angie. Listen."

Angie took a breath. "Sorry. Go ahead."

Helen nodded. "I'm retiring, Angie. Luna is a wonderful child, and she's a lot less work than she used to be. But she's also going to want to start going out more and having a life of her own, and I'm not going to be able to keep up with that pace."

Angie's stomach dropped. "But you're all she's ever known. You're family."

"I am, and that won't ever stop. You'll both be able to get hold of me if you need me. But I've only got a few decades left, and it's time I did some things on my bucket list." Helen looked out at Luna, who was in her usual spot by the pool, reading a book. "Last week, I saw a message on her phone. It specifically *un*invited her to the Jeffersons' kid's party because she's a nerdy loner and no one likes her." She made air quotes with her fingers as she said it.

"Those little shits. How dare they?" Angie stood and reached for her phone on the counter. "I'll tell Miranda—"

"No, you won't." Helen pointed to the chair, her eyebrow raised in that don't-give-sass way of hers.

Angie sat. "But it isn't okay."

"No. It isn't. But it's part of a bigger problem, Angie." She took a drink of her water and continued to watch Luna. "She's lonely. You're filming all the time. She doesn't have anything in common with the kids she's met at that fancy rich kids' school, and you don't take her on set often enough for her to meet the kids of the other actors who *do* bring them on set."

Angie flinched, feeling chastened. "I'm trying to keep her away from it all. You know what I went through."

"I do. But the world has changed, Angie. It's moved on, and you need to as well, for Luna's sake. And including her in your world instead of keeping her on the outside of it would help."

They were silent for a while, letting the hum of the fridge and the gentle wind moving the blinds be the only noise. "I hear you. I do," Angie said. "And after my next film, I'll take a long break. She and I will go away. Maybe I'll take her to Paris so she can see the Louvre like she's always wanted to." She laughed. "I can see how she's different from other kids. What twelve-year-old wants to hang out in a museum?"

Helen sighed and shook her head. "Time is precious, darling. Anyway, I'm happy to do some interviews for my replacement, but when I've narrowed it down, I want you and Luna to make the final choice."

Angie nodded, and her eyes welled up. "Life isn't going to be the same without you."

"Nope. You'll miss me." Helen smiled and pulled her into a hug. "But I'm not going off to die. You can call me any time you want." She let go and stood. "Now, I'm going to have a talk with Luna. I imagine we'll have some slammed doors and silent treatments for a few days. Prepare yourself."

Angie nodded but didn't say anything. She watched as Helen settled on the lounger beside Luna's. She started talking and Luna sat up, her eyes wide. Her hands started going as she clearly argued against Helen's decision, then she was up and running into the house.

Angie tried to stop her, but Luna flashed by and thundered up the stairs. The door slammed and seventies rock music made the walls vibrate.

Helen came back in. "Endings and beginnings. Life is full of 'em."

***

The following day, a package arrived from Claire, along with a note. *Weirdest thing you've ever been sent, and that's saying something. x C*

Inside was a folded sheet of paper with Luna's name on it, along with an enormous bag of nickels.

$100 equals 2000 nickels. I've taken the five you owed me. You now have 1,995 nickels to put toward further rematches, should you ever wish to try to beat me again.

The wonderfully weird Finn

It wasn't often that Angie could say she was baffled. But this was, indeed, baffling.

Luna came in, sullen and silent as predicted, and her gaze fell on the nickels. She frowned and plucked the letter from Angie's hand, and her frown slowly turned into a grin. "So weird."

"Weird is right. Who sends a child money in the mail and says, 'Come play a game with me?'" Angie dropped the nickels back in the box. "As if I'd let my daughter go meet up with a stranger like that."

Luna rolled her eyes. "As if you have any idea what I do every day, or care for that matter." She pulled a soda from the fridge.

"Luna, that's not fair. You know I care."

Luna stopped and stared at her. "We both know I was a mistake. One night with a guy because you were drunk. You didn't want me, and you still don't." She shrugged as though the words weren't shards of glass flung into the air. "Whatever. I can do my own thing and stay out of your way."

It hurt to breathe. Angie started toward her but Luna backed up a step, like an animal that didn't want to be touched. "Honey, you weren't planned, that's true. But you're the best thing to happen to me. You're—"

Luna huffed and turned away. "Save the acting for the cameras, Mom." She ran upstairs without giving Angie a chance to try again.

She sank onto the couch and put her head in her hands. What an awful thing for Luna to think, to feel. What kind of mother was she to allow it to get to this point? Her beautiful, intelligent, whip-wit daughter was lost, and it was Angie's fault. Somehow, after the next film, she had to make it right.

Chapter Five

FINN CLOSED HER EYES so she didn't try to jab her spoon into them to yank the ideas from her recalcitrant brain. The characters were there. Shadowy, maybe, but they'd take true form when she began to write. But goddamn it, the plot wasn't coming. Just when she thought she had it down, she poked a million needle-sized holes in it until it fell to the floor like much-used tissue.

"Your drawings are as weird as you are."

She opened her eyes to find Luna standing beside the table with a sack of nickels dangling from her hand. She was looking at Finn's doodle book of stick figures, one of which featured a figure with a penis hat and a thought bubble that read, *I can totally fix everything wrong with you.* She quickly shut the book and then smiled at Luna.

"Ah, young grifter. You got my invitation to a new duel." She glanced past her, but the celebrity mother was nowhere to be seen.

Luna shook her head and sat, plonking the nickels on the table. "I'm not playing two thousand games with you."

"Nor would I ask you to. I have other things to occupy my time. Important things." She tapped on the drawings. "As you can see." She set the notepad aside, then took out the letter-tile game.

Delia brought over a steaming hot chocolate topped with cream and a giant marshmallow, as well as a fresh latte for Finn, even though she hadn't ordered one. She winked as she set them down. "Don't get rowdy, you two. I don't want to have to throw you out on your asses."

Luna slurped the whipped cream off her hot chocolate, leaving a mustache behind. "As long as you throw us both out, and you don't go easy on her because she's old."

"Oh, don't you worry. I'd toss her out and then you, so you'd have a soft landing." Delia whistled as she went back behind the counter.

Finn frowned. "I'll have you know I'm not soft at all. I'm like a brick wall."

"A brick wall before it becomes brick. Like when it's still sand, maybe." Luna began to scramble the tiles as she'd seen Finn do the last time.

"Hi. I'm Helen."

An older woman clearly with Luna held out her hand, and Finn shook it.

"Luna said you had a standing date to play, and she didn't want to be rude and not show up." Helen's eyes twinkled as she looked at Finn seriously. "True?"

Finn glanced at Luna, who pushed her glasses up her nose and continued to look at the tiles. "Unquestionably true, dearest Helen. Luna promised me a rematch, and to save her reputation, she needs to beat me at some point, though it may take her a thousand games to do so. Would you like to join us?"

She didn't miss the way Luna stiffened slightly.

"No, but thank you. I'm going to sit right over there and enjoy my coffee and a magazine." Helen lightly touched Luna's head and didn't react when she ducked away.

They played without chatting for the first two games, and Finn saw that Helen sat a few tables over to keep an eye on them. It wasn't surprising that Luna had a chaperone, obviously, and Finn was glad to see it. It also made her smile to see that Helen was reading a copy of *Spirit and Destiny* magazine.

"Thanks." Luna placed her tile. "For this."

Finn placed her tile. "Yeah. No problem." She nodded toward Helen. "Bodyguard?"

Luna glanced over and smiled. "Kind of. The actual bodyguard is outside with the driver. Helen is my nanny." She said it with a really bad accent, probably meant to be British. "But she's leaving me too."

Finn noted her final word and felt for the kid. "People do that. But then other people show up. They come and go."

The tile hit the table a little harder than before. "I hate it. Change sucks."

"It does." She moved a tile, knowing it was the wrong one. "It's scary and can make you feel all wobbly inside."

Luna's hand stilled. "I call it the jellies."

Finn nodded. "Red? Or green?"

She put her tile down. "Brussel sprout."

"That's disgusting." She grinned inwardly when Luna took advantage of her wrong move and slid the tile that would win the game into place, even though she didn't know it yet.

"Exactly. Like the jellies. Disgusting and something I don't want." Her voice trembled slightly. She hesitated and scanned the table. "Hey. Hey! I won, didn't I?" She looked up, her smile wide. "I totally beat you."

Finn frowned and studied the table. "Well, cover me with ash and call me a chimney sweep. You did."

Luna looked puzzled and then shook her head. "You owe me a nickel."

Finn pulled out a little coin pouch, took out a nickel, and handed it over with a flourish. "Your winnings."

Luna blew on it, then tucked it in her pocket instead of dropping it in the bag full of nickels. "This one is special, so I'll keep it somewhere else."

"Excellent. Nice T-shirt, by the way."

Luna looked down at her shirt as though to analyze it. "I like really old music. Other kids think it's stupid, but I think those old songs are way better. They tell stories instead of just repeating the same stupid phrase over and over again."

Finn flinched at the idea of Blondie being "really old music," but at least the kid had good taste. "Vintage shirts like that must be hard to find."

Luna mixed the tiles and started again. "I make them myself. I got a digital printing machine, and I load up whatever photos I really like of the best bands."

Finn put her tile down. "Wow. I was delivering newspapers on my bicycle at your age. Impressive." She'd never actually owned a bicycle, but it seemed like an encouraging thing to say.

Luna's brow furrowed. "How old *are* you? Who gets a newspaper?" She shook her head like it didn't matter. "Anyway. Like I said, the other kids think it's stupid." She pushed her glasses up her nose.

"I think it's awesome. Would you make me one?"

Luna looked up from the game and glanced at Finn's plain black top. "I won't put anything stupid on it."

"Well, that's good to know. I'm not a fan of looking stupid." Finn put her tile down. "What about Tracy Chapman?"

Luna's eyes lit up. "She's so awesome. I love 'Fast Car.'"

Helen came over and put her hand on Luna's shoulder. "Sorry, kiddo, but it's time for your lesson."

Luna looked briefly disappointed. "Okay."

"Oboe? Elvish? Finnish? Bass guitar?" Finn asked, scooping the tiles into their bag.

Luna shook her head. "Skateboard. I'm getting lessons from the best, and I'm already pretty good."

Finn smiled. Of course it would be something cool. "Have fun on your wheels."

Luna smiled and waved, and Helen followed her out. The bodyguard opened the door and walked beside her to the car, where a driver waited with the engine running.

As much fun as it had been with Luna, the visual of a life Finn had left behind made her uncomfortable and her mood dipped. She needed to get herself together.

She gathered her things and headed home and groaned softly when she saw who was sitting on her porch in the rocking chair.

She nearly backed out of the drive again, but when she caught his eye, he tilted his head like he knew what she was thinking. "Fine," she said out loud, if only to convince herself.

"You flew a long way for nothing, amigo." She passed him on the porch and went inside.

"You call getting to see my closest and oldest and only friend nothing?" Pablo Ramirez, her friend since elementary school, came in behind her and swung her into a hug.

She batted at his head. "Put me down, you big oaf." When he set her back on her feet, she hugged him hard and then pushed him away. "There. Now go home."

He lowered himself into her overstuffed chair and sighed happily. "I am home."

She brought him a beer and settled on the couch. "Not in a million years. Having you in the house would be like having a pet bear. Loud, smelly, hairy, and eats way too much." She took a swig of beer. "Not to mention the shedding. Do you shed?"

"Where have you been? I've been waiting forever." He ignored her chatter, as he always had.

She grinned. "Playing word dominoes with a twelve-year-old kid who reminds me a lot of you."

"And you've officially become the saddest thing of all." He put his hand to his chest. "That's what your life has come to? Playing games with kids?"

"Seriously, Pablo." She set her beer on the table. She wasn't about to explain how she saw her own messed up childhood in the kid's eyes. "I love you more than I love my morning coffee, but why are you here? Is something wrong?"

He scratched at his chin, a tell that he was nervous. "I didn't know if you wanted to know, but I needed to come tell you in person." He set his beer down and looked at her, all levity gone from his expression. "Your abuela passed away yesterday."

She sat back, the wind knocked from her. "How?"

"In her sleep. No pain. Just..." He waved his hand gently in the air. "Gone."

That was something, at least. She nodded but couldn't find anything to say. She wasn't even sure what to feel. He shifted, and she focused on him.

"I was the one who found her, and this was in her bedside table."

He handed her an envelope with her name in an almost illegible scrawl on the front. She stared at it, unable to touch it. "What could she possibly have had to say to me? And why were you the one to find her?"

He set the envelope on the table, a silent, mysterious bomb waiting to go off and send familial shrapnel into her soul.

"I grew really close to her after you left. After—"

She shot him a warning glance and he shrugged.

"After everything that happened, she stopped talking to your whole family. Your dad, sisters...no one. But you know how much she liked me, and all that time we spent with her after school and in the summer."

She wasn't sure when she started to cry, but he moved quickly to her side and pulled her into an embrace. Being held like this had become foreign, but she relaxed after a minute and let the wave crash over her.

The last link to her old life, the one person in her family who had truly loved her, was gone.

Chapter Six

ANGIE LEANED BACK IN the chair and stretched, trying to unknot the knots that wove like a braid from her shoulder blades to the back of her skull. "How do casting agents do this for a living? If I have to hear one more person tell me which of my films is their favorite, I'm going to break something."

Helen snorted. "Casting agents do it for a particular film, not to watch over the well-being of their child. The stakes are a bit higher here."

Angie rolled her neck and looked at Helen. "You could stay..."

Helen pushed a page in front of her. "This is the final candidate today, and I agree the others weren't right. I'll stay on until we find the right person."

Angie sighed. "Who's next?"

"Karen Richards."

Angie picked up the paper and scanned it, but it looked much the same as the others. "Let's finish, and then I can tell you I'm too busy to do this again for the next five years, so you have to stay with us."

Helen let the next nanny-contender in.

This one, like most of the others, was in her late twenties. Unlike the others, who had come dressed like they were going to be backup dancers in a music video, this one wore a long, flowing skirt, simple sandals, and a loose tank top. Her smile looked genuine.

"Hi, Karen. Nice to meet you." She shook the young woman's hand and was pleased at the firm handshake.

The interview went well from there. Karen was likable, interesting, had a good education, and was native to LA, which meant she knew the areas and how things worked in a city as varied and traffic-jammed as any city could be. After a half hour conversation, Angie looked at Helen. "Maybe we should introduce Karen to Luna?"

Helen nodded and left the room, and a moment later they came back in together.

Luna sat at the table, her hands folded in front of her. "I understand you're applying to be my new nanny." She said the word with the same kind of venom she usually reserved for cauliflower. "What is your favorite band, and why?"

Karen tilted her head, looking thoughtful. "That's a tough one. I like all types of music. But I guess I'd have to say Lady A for band, and Carrie Underwood for single singer."

Luna frowned suspiciously. "Country music?"

"The best for telling great stories. I love a good cry. And the drama in them is amazing."

Luna stayed silent for a moment, staring at her, and then finally nodded and held out her hand. "Welcome to our house."

Karen looked surprised and shook Luna's hand. "Glad to be here."

Luna left the room, and Angie smiled. "I guess that's that. Helen and the agency will help you with all the non-disclosure agreements and such, and you can talk to Helen about when you want to start. I assume you'll want to shadow her to learn the ropes?" She couldn't fathom a stranger coming in and asking a ton of questions.

"That would be great, if you're good with that, Helen?" she said, and the excitement was evident in her eyes.

Helen walked Karen out, talking along the way, and Angie let out a sigh of relief. She'd been a little worried about hiring someone so young, but as Helen said, it would be good for Luna to have someone around who looked more like an older sister than a nanny. It was already hard enough on Luna having bodyguards out with her.

Angie's phone rang, and she picked it up. "Hey, Claire. I'm

sorry, I haven't had a chance to look at—"

"Open your email. Right now. Now, now, now."

Angie held Claire's high-pitched excitement away from her ear and pulled her laptop toward her. She opened her email, and her breath left her in a whoosh. "Really? Is it real?"

"Really for real. You have to be at the studio at ten for the audition, but you're the one they want, so it's in the bag. Who's your favorite agent in the whole world?"

Angie laughed and wiped away tears of disbelief. "You. I'll send you a whole box of those donuts you like. In fact, if I sign this contract, I'll buy you the donut shop itself."

"Please. More than one of those a year, and I'll have to move back to Nebraska and become the farmer's wife I was meant to be." Claire told someone else she'd be right there. "I have to run. Call me the moment you leave the audition tomorrow." She made a kissy sound and ended the call.

Angie leaned back in her chair and read the email again. She'd wanted to star in a movie with Hollywood's most amazing leading lady, Elodie Fontaine, since she was a little girl. In the script she scanned, she'd be playing Elodie's daughter as they moved to Japan, along with Angie's on-screen daughter. It would still have plenty of funny parts, but there was an underlying seriousness to it that would push her into new territory.

This could finally put her firmly into the running for an award if it went well.

She stood and ran her hands through her hair. She wanted to jump around, laugh, shout, share...but there was no one to share it with.

Deflated, she carried her laptop to the living room and poured a glass of wine. She'd spend the evening reviewing the script and character so she could read for the part as though it was already hers.

Helen came in and sank into the couch with a soft groan. "I'm too old for this." She looked at Angie and smiled. "What has you so excited?"

Angie laughed. "Can you tell?"

"There's a flush to your cheeks and your eyes sparkle when you're really happy. What is it?"

Angie told her the big news, and Helen hugged her tightly. "I'm so happy for you, darling. What a wonderful opportunity." She sat back down and poured herself some wine from the bottle Angie had left on the table. "Have you told Luna yet?" She didn't make eye contact, instead watching the wine as she swirled it in the glass.

Angie deflated the rest of the way. "Not yet. I won't until I know for sure that I have the part."

"And if you get it? You'll be filming away, I assume?"

Angie sighed and took a long drink of her wine. "Most likely. The director is one who likes authenticity whatever the cost." She burrowed down into the plush pillows for the hug she needed. "Any advice?"

Helen continued to swirl her wine rather than drink it. "I think she's smart, and she knows who she is. I think you ask her what *she* wants this time, instead of thinking you know what's best."

"But I'm her mother. *Shouldn't* I know what's best?"

Helen laughed and finally took a sip of her wine. "I'm afraid that title doesn't confer on you a way to know what someone else wants, even if that someone is your daughter. Maybe especially if it's your daughter."

"Her birthday is coming up too. I have no idea what to do for her. I know the other kids are having huge, lavish parties. One of the Sanders' kids had a racetrack built around the property and had cars brought in for all the kids to use. And I heard that Colin Smith took his ten-year-old and twenty of her friends on a river cruise down the Seine, and Wolfgang Puck cooked them their meals." She shook her head in bewilderment. "I'd do any of that for Luna if I thought it was what she wanted. But after what you told me about her lack of friends..." The thought brought tears to her eyes.

"Again, Angie, talk to her. Ask her what she wants." Helen set the half-empty wine glass on the table and stretched. "I'm off to bed."

Angie gave her a half smile as she left and then went back to reading the script. She'd discuss the film, as well as Luna's birthday, with her the following day. Maybe there'd be reason for them both to be excited.

***

"Listen to me, you cockwaffle of a potato," Gino Spinezzi shouted into the phone. "I told you what I wanted you to do, now get it done. Don't keep giving me excuses." He set the phone down and held his hands in a prayer position, his eyes closed, for a long moment.

Angie waited, keeping her eyes on the script as though she hadn't been listening to the shouting match. Beside Gino, who was the producer, Bert Forster, the director, looked so bored as to almost be asleep.

"Sorry, Angie," Gino said, opening his eyes and lowering his hands. "I can't stand incompetence. It costs money, and I feel like it shows disregard for the people working so hard on the film."

She smiled sweetly. "It's so nice that you worry about people's time that way." God forbid she ever got on his bad side. Being called a cockwaffle of any kind wasn't on her wish list.

"Should we do the read-through?" Bert sat up, looking more awake. "It's really just a formality, Angie. When we got the script, we agreed you'd be perfect for the part. It's outside your usual roles, but we can't picture anyone else doing it justice."

Her heart hammered at the praise. Both men had won numerous serious awards and worked with the best in the business. "I can't tell you what that means to me. Thank you."

The read-through began, and they asked for adjustments here and there, which they were happy with. They even gave her a scene that wasn't in the script and asked her to do a cold read, which she enjoyed. She could already feel the character coming to life in her.

"Fantastic." Gino looked at Bert, who nodded and continued to scribble on a notepad. "I think I speak for both of us when we say we'd love you to take this on, Angie."

Her stomach lurched, and she put her hands to her cheeks. "That's so amazing. Thank you so much."

Gino stood, holding out his hand, and then Bert startled and shot up as well, as though caught by surprise. "We'll send your agent the details, but if it's okay, I'd like to be able to contact you directly about scheduling. All this middle-man bullshit drives me crazy."

She laughed and scribbled her personal email address in Bert's notebook. "Any time you want to."

Bert shoved his hands in his pockets. "We'll do the table read in about two weeks. Okay?"

She would have said yes even if they'd said they'd start filming at midnight that day. "Absolutely. Thank you again."

The world passed in a blur, and she nearly missed her exit as she thought about who she'd be working with. When she pulled into the driveway, she simply sat in the car for a long time, considering the road that had brought her to this moment. A tap on the window made her jump.

"Mom? Have you locked yourself in the car?" Luna pointed. "There's a little button there that will unlock the doors."

Angie grinned and pressed her hands to the window. "The car has kidnapped me! It's taken on a life of its own. Save yourself!" She pulled the lever and dropped the seat back, so she disappeared from Luna's view. Luna's laugh made her smile. She heard it far too infrequently.

She put the seat back up and got out of the car. Wrapping her arm around Luna's shoulders, she said, "What do you say to pizza for dinner?"

Luna shook her head. "Can we have Thai? I'm craving spicy."

"Thai it is."

They went inside and Luna ordered from their favorite takeout place. "Seriously, why were you just sitting in the car?" Luna asked.

"I was thinking about my life."

Luna rolled her eyes. "Dramatic. And you weren't out there long enough to think about the whole thing. That would take years."

Angie threw a pen at her. "Rude. I'm not that old. I was thinking about how lucky I am to have a child I love, a job I love, and such a great home for us."

Luna's eyes narrowed. "What happened today?"

Angie sat at the table and motioned for Luna to join her. "I had an audition. And I got the part."

Luna didn't look impressed. "That happens all the time."

"This time is a little different. I get to work with Elodie Fontaine."

Luna looked impressed. "That's cool. I liked her in that *Catherine the Great* thing."

"Yeah, she was amazing in that. I've wanted to work with her all my life." Angie got up and poured herself a glass of iced tea and a large glass of milk for Luna, who always needed one when she ate spicy Thai food. "But enough about that for now. Let's talk about your birthday."

The doorbell rang, and the house manager came in carrying their bag of food. He gave a quick smile and left. No one ever interrupted if she and Luna were having dinner together.

She took out dishes and served, watching out of the corner of her eye as Luna played with her fork, spinning it on the table. When she sat down with their bowls, Luna didn't look up before she began to eat.

Angie left it quiet as they ate, then said, "Luna? Anything you want to do for your birthday? Did you want to have a party, or take friends somewhere?"

Luna pushed at her glasses. "I don't know. Maybe. Or maybe just skip it this year."

Angie slurped at a noodle, making Luna smile a little. "We're not skipping your birthday. Come on, there must be something you want to do."

Luna bit her lip and set her fork down. "Honest?"

"Honest."

"There's an archaeological dig going on in Turkey. They're uncovering another layer of Troy, and they've invited novices to come and help. I want to do that."

Angie was rarely speechless, but she was left with absolutely nothing to say. "For your birthday?"

Luna nodded enthusiastically. "That's the open weekend for novices. It would be so amazing."

"I don't... I mean, what about a party? Something closer to home? We could gather some of your friends and rent out Disneyland for the day."

"Why'd you ask me what I want if you want me to do something else?" Luna pushed her bowl away. "Why do you keep trying to make me like other kids?" She left the table and ran upstairs.

Angie rested her head in her hands. The beautiful start to the day had ended as it often did; she'd disappointed her daughter and ended up alone.

Chapter Seven

TODAY'S STICK FIGURE DRAWINGS included a woman who sat at the table closest to the café door. A perfectly average, normal-looking woman sat with her cup of coffee, watching as people walked in. But as they walked out, she asked if they wanted her phone number. When they said no, mostly looking either amused or befuddled, she didn't appear in the least fazed. She even offered it to a lesbian couple, after asking if they were, in fact, a lesbian couple. To which she replied, "Niiice," and then promptly offered them her number.

They declined. She kept sipping her coffee.

Another set of stick figures included a mother and child, both on their phones, texting other people about how lonely they were.

Finn sighed and closed the notebook, only to open the one she should be using more often. The one with the manuscript in progress, which was far from progressing in any direction at all. The story felt stunted, like it had some kind of word-rot spreading through it, infecting the characters and plot so they turned pallid and sickly looking. A two-hour session at the gym later might help bounce something out of her brain. At the very least, it would force her to concentrate on something other than plot holes.

The bag of nickels thunked onto the table, and Luna slid into the seat opposite. "What did you want to be when you grew up?"

No formalities. That would work. "When I was about seven, I wanted to play Mexican guitar in restaurant bands. At thirteen, I wanted to be a superstar singer. At eighteen, I thought I would be a psychologist."

Luna moved the tiles around and began the game. Over her shoulder, Helen and a younger woman sat talking. Helen caught her eye and waved, as did the younger woman.

"What do you want to be?" Finn asked, placing her tile.

Luna put her tile down with surprising force. "Who cares? Everyone else gets to decide, right? Who cares what I want?"

That was unexpected but not surprising, given the golden celebrity cage in which the child was growing up. But Finn, despite their odd arrangement, remained a stranger. It wasn't her place to give advice to someone else's child. Was it? She thought back to various movies and books where some outsider had become a mentor figure. There were plenty of examples to pull from. The question was, should she be the eccentric recluse or the wise wizard? She didn't have a beard—she wasn't quite that old—but she could definitely pull off eccentric recluse.

"The thing is," she said, moving her tile, "there will come a time when people can't make your decisions for you. And when that time comes, if you have a good idea of who you are and what you want, you'll be ready to take that next step."

Luna was silent as they played, and Finn let her think. She knew from experience that sometimes you simply needed time for things to sink in.

"Why did you change what you wanted to be? Are you a flake?" Luna finally said, smiling at Delia as she set down their hot drinks.

"I most certainly am not." Finn dipped her tongue in the foam of her cappuccino and stuck it out at Luna, who grimaced.

"Gross."

Finn sipped and thought. "I think we're always learning new things, and sometimes those things make us want to try them ourselves. When I was little, we had a few of my birthday parties in Mexican restaurants, and there was a mariachi band who walked around the restaurant playing. They always stopped and played for a long time at our table, and it made everyone happy. I wanted to make people happy too, so I wanted to do that."

Luna's eyes never left Finn's face.

"When I wanted to be a singer, it was because there was

someone really popular singing this song that spoke to my heart, to what I was feeling at the time. About being lonely and finding your way through the darkness."

Luna nodded, her grip on the mug so tight that Finn worried she might break it. She gently reached over and pushed the cup to the table, and Luna's grip loosened.

"And the psychologist?"

Finn placed the last tile, won the game, and began to mix them again. Luna glanced at the game and then continued to watch Finn.

"That's a little more complicated."

Luna huffed. "That's what adults always say when they don't want to explain things."

Finn conceded the point. "I'm happy to try to explain. I just don't know if it will make sense. And don't insult me by calling me an adult. That's just plain mean." She hadn't given it much thought in a long time. This kid was making her think of all kinds of things that should stay in the past. And now that her abuela was gone... She shoved the thought into a pocket of her brain, to be dealt with later. "I was surrounded by a lot of people I didn't understand. Situations beyond my control that I wanted to make sense of. And I wanted a job that would make my parents proud, but one that was far away from the family business. Psychology seemed like a good option."

"But it wasn't." Luna put down her tile.

"It wasn't. My heart wasn't in it, and in truth, I found that a textbook couldn't help me understand the people or situation I was in." She placed her tile and was pleased when Luna put one down that would challenge her. "So. What do you want to be?"

Luna sighed deeply. "An archaeologist."

"Cool."

Luna looked up, surprise clear in her eyes. "You think?"

"Absolutely. There's so much we don't know about our history. Archaeologists expand our knowledge of the past, and that can help us with the future."

Finn jumped like she'd been startled by a clown leaping out of a closet when Luna launched herself out of her chair and yanked Finn into the tightest hug she'd ever had. She simply gave Helen a baffled look when Helen raised her eyebrows. She lightly patted Luna's sides, certain it wasn't good form to hug someone else's kid. Mentors in movies were always standoffish. They didn't hug. They often died, too, but she was hoping to miss out on that part.

Finally, Luna let go and swiped the tears from her cheeks. She sat back down and sipped at her hot chocolate, which was likely cold by now.

They played the next two games in silence, and then Helen and the younger woman came over.

"Time to go for your lesson, Luna." Helen smiled at Finn, questions clear in her eyes. "Finn, this is Karen. She's going to be taking my place and watching out for Luna."

Karen. An unfortunate name in a decade where it had been used to designate a woman who irrationally complained about everything. "Nice to meet you."

"Likewise." Her hand lingered a fraction of a second too long. "I take it we'll be seeing more of you?"

Luna stood, taking her dwindling sack of nickels with her. "Finn is coming to dinner tomorrow night. Aren't you?"

Finn blinked. Had she missed some part of the conversation? "Um?"

Helen gently put her hand on Luna's shoulder. "Are you asking Finn? Or telling her?"

Luna rolled her eyes. "Finn, will you please come to dinner tomorrow?"

Finn looked at Helen, then at Karen, who gave her a tiny smile that made her inexplicably uncomfortable. "Don't you need to ask your mom? I'm pretty sure having random strangers come to dinner isn't her thing. Or anyone's thing, unless they're a psycho."

"That proves you don't know her at all. She's around random strangers all the time." Luna grinned. "Not as weird as you, probably, but still."

"I think it would be lovely, Finn." Helen put her arm around Luna's shoulders. "I'm sure Angie would like to get to know the woman her daughter is having so much fun with."

The sentence sounded bizarre and made Finn flinch. "I have no earthly idea where you live." That was possibly the lamest excuse not to go that she could have come up with. Playing a game in a café was one thing. Going to family dinner was another level entirely, and Finn wasn't one to get close to people.

"Write your address down, and we'll have a car pick you up." Karen took a little notepad from her bag and handed Finn a pen.

Finn held the pen like she'd never used one before. "I drive. I mean, I could drive. There's no need to send someone to get me."

Helen took the pen from Finn's hand and wrote down an address. "When you get to the gate, press the buzzer. We'll let the guard know you're coming. We eat at seven. Any food preferences? Vegetarian, lactose-free?"

Finn shook her head and Helen smiled again. With that, the three of them left Finn sitting at the table wondering what the hell had happened.

An hour later, she still hadn't figured it out and realized she didn't have a way to call to say she wasn't coming after all. She could send something to the agent, but there was no guarantee the message would get passed on in time to avoid causing an issue. Privacy mattered to Finn and hanging out at a celebrity's house was distinctly *not* in the realm of private. She thought of Luna's hopeful look and the way she'd hugged Finn, as though she felt seen. Finn had once held onto Pablo that way. Fucking hell. She couldn't cancel. Plenty of labels fit her, but kid-disappointer wasn't one of them.

She'd googled Angie Davis and her list of films was impressive. Her Wiki bio said she had extremely supportive parents, that she'd been acting since she was a child, had a period of reckless fun that resulted in a daughter, and then she continued acting once her daughter was older. It didn't give any real information, like what scent she found most appealing, or whether she preferred the greens of spring or the rusts of autumn.

Finn hadn't been able to keep herself from scrolling through photos of Angie, both in films and at events where she was camera ready. Photos dated back to when she was a child, often standing by one parent or another and posing from an early age. Now, she was truly stunning in a girl next door kind of way. Nothing vampish or dangerous, just sweet and gentle. Of course, that didn't mean she wasn't an evil energy sponge behind closed doors, but Finn had a feeling that wasn't the case.

Of course, given her own family history, she wasn't really a good judge of that kind thing.

Chapter Eight

ANGIE LEANED HER FOREHEAD against the cool windowpane and tried not to frown so she didn't give herself lines around her eyes. But if she could frown, she'd be doing so deeply and with feeling. What had Luna been thinking?

"Mom, you're overreacting." Luna's tone, as usual, implied that Angie was brainless.

"How is it overreacting when you invite some woman you've played a game with a few times over for dinner? An adult who hangs out with my daughter because apparently, she doesn't have a job to go to every day." She finally pushed away from the window and turned to Luna. "Honey, I want you to have friends. But I'd like them to be your age rather than mine."

The doorbell rang and Luna jumped up. "I'll get it!" She took off at a run.

Angie sat at the table, then stood. Then she moved to the window, just outside the lamplight so she was partly shadowed. What was wrong with her? Why did she care how she looked when Finn came into the room? She stepped into the light just as Luna dragged Finn in, holding her hand and tugging her forward as Finn leaned back, making a joke of looking around. Angie couldn't help but smile at the sound of her daughter's exasperated laughter.

"C'mon, Finn. I'm starving." Luna finally let go of Finn's hand. "This is my mom, Angie. You met when she threw money at you after she abandoned me so she could pose for the photographers."

Angie winced. "Luna. Not cool."

Finn held out her hand. "Nice to see you again. Thank you for inviting me to dinner."

Angie nearly said that she hadn't invited her, but she let it go and smiled. Finn shifted and looked around. She wore a navy blue button-down shirt under a black vest, with black jeans and scuffed black boots. Though casual, it was quite possibly the sexiest outfit Angie had ever seen on someone.

"Mom," Luna hissed. "You're totally staring. What's wrong with you? Are you having a stroke?"

Angie shook off the spell and made eye contact with Finn, which turned out to be a mistake. Her warm brown eyes were crinkled in a small, knowing smile as she met Angie's gaze.

"Something smells amazing," Finn said, her eyes never leaving Angie's.

"You're going to love it," Luna said, once again grabbing Finn's hand and leading her from the room.

Finn looked over her shoulder, one eyebrow raised at Angie.

"Right behind you," Angie said, mortified when she automatically looked at the way those black jeans hugged Finn's very nice, very firm looking ass.

Finn chuckled quietly and turned to follow Luna.

Once they were in the dining room, Luna slid into her seat and Angie took hers. Finn sat beside Luna, across from Angie, which meant she'd have plenty of time to look at her throughout the meal.

Susan, her chef, brought in the appetizers and poured wine. "Spanakopita with tzatziki for the adults," she said, setting down small plates in front of Finn and Angie, "and zucchini chips for Digger."

Luna grinned and quickly picked up a zucchini slice with her fingers, dunking it in ranch dressing and humming with satisfaction.

"Fork, Luna."

Luna rolled her eyes and picked up her fork.

Finn also dug in. She grimaced when the flaky pieces fell from the triangular pastry. "Messy, but delicious."

Angie tried to look a little more dainty, but Finn was right. The flaky pastry was so light, it fell from her fingers. Briefly, she considered the fact that spinach might not have been the best option tonight. Getting any stuck in her teeth would be even more mortifying than getting caught looking at Finn like she was going to be dessert.

"So, Finn, tell us more about you. What is it you do?" Angie asked.

Finn bit into her spanakopita and took an extraordinarily long time to chew. Angie wondered if she was trying to figure out how to explain being jobless so she could hang out in a coffee shop all day.

"She draws funny pictures," Luna said between bites.

Angie looked at Finn, who was shaking her head vehemently.

"I mean, I do draw pictures. But they're just silly stick figure things based on the people around me. They're not actually for anything. I mean, I don't do that. For a living." Finn bumped Luna with her shoulder when Luna snorted at her answer. "As to what I do, it depends on who you ask. One person would tell you I'm a retired race car driver. Another would tell you that I'm a professor of astrology on sabbatical until Mercury goes out of retrograde. And another would tell you that I work for MI5 in London, and I'm here undercover." She nodded as though that answered the question.

"Goodness. You're very versatile." Angie motioned at Finn with her fork. "And what would your parents tell me you do for a living? Because I'm willing to bet they know the truth."

Strangely, Finn frowned. The light left her eyes, and she gently set her fork down. At that moment, Susan's assistant came in, piled up their appetizer plates, and Susan brought in the main dishes.

"Greek lamb stew with orzo pasta," she said, "and vegetarian moussaka."

"You're a veggie?" Finn asked Luna.

Luna looked with distaste at the chunks of meat in Finn's bowl. "No dead animals for me, thanks."

"She's been vegetarian practically since she was born," Angie said, letting the conversation about what Finn did for a living drop. Her reaction had been anything but typical, and although Angie wasn't certain what to make of it, she wasn't about to ruin Luna's night. "She always turned away from meat, and when she could speak, she made it clear she wouldn't eat it anymore."

"A kid who knows her own mind. I like it."

Luna grinned at Finn and made a face at her mother, as though to say, "See? Finn gets me."

"Oh, she definitely knows her own mind." Angie made an appreciative sound as she tasted the stew. "But I think she's missing out. Susan, our chef, does amazing things with meat."

Finn nodded as she ate. "I agree. This is fantastic."

They ate quietly for a moment, and Angie couldn't think of a single thing to ask. Whether or not Finn was single seemed a little forward, and her line of work was clearly out of the question. "Have you lived in California long?"

Finn looked surprised. "What makes you think I'm not a native?"

"Your accent." At Finn's questioning look, Angie continued. "It's barely there, but I've caught hints of it. If you're a native, I'd guess you've got Latin blood."

Finn ate, looking at Angie contemplatively before she said, "You're good. Most people have no idea I'm not a local."

Luna speared her moussaka. "Mom is really good with accents. She has to use different ones in movies, and they always sound perfect. She can imitate anyone you can think of."

Angie's heart raced, and she blinked back tears. That was the nicest thing Luna had said to or about her in ages. "Thank you. That's really sweet."

Luna slouched a little lower. "God, Mom. Don't make a big deal of it." She turned her attention to Finn. "So where are you from?"

Angie saw the flicker of unease in Finn's eyes, and it gave her a dose of her own. Women with secrets were usually bad news. She knew that all too well. While Finn seemed fun and lighthearted, there was more beneath the surface.

"The Dominican Republic, actually."

Luna wiped at her mouth with her hand and then jumped out of her chair. She waved Angie off when she called her back.

"I'm sorry," Angie said, focusing on her meal. "I'm not much of a disciplinarian, and she runs circles around me."

"Like getting you to allow a complete stranger into your house for dinner?"

Angie looked up and caught the knowing smile. "Exactly like that."

Luna returned lugging a huge atlas. "I need to know where it is." She set it on the table between her and Finn.

Finn wiped her mouth with her napkin and moved her plate aside so she could open the book. "See here? It's a Caribbean Island, split in two. Most of it is the DR, and the rest is Haiti."

Luna's brow furrowed as she traced the outline of the island with her fingertip. "You hear people talk about going to the Caribbean all the time, but no one ever really mentions the names of the islands." It sounded like a complaint.

"That's true. The same goes for the Bahamas." Finn tapped the map. "Most people probably can't name the islands there either."

Luna closed the book and set it on the floor by her chair before she pulled her dinner back to her and dug in. "Mom did a movie in the Bahamas. What island were you on?"

Surprised that Luna remembered, given that she'd been too young to go with her, she took a sip of her wine before answering. "Crooked Island."

Finn tilted her head. "Beautiful, but small. Did you stay on the island the whole time? It must have bored you to tears."

Inexplicably, Angie's hackles rose. "I don't need constant distraction or attention. It was beautiful, and although a lot of the crew and cast stayed on Andros and boated in each day, I stayed on Crooked and got to know some of the locals."

Luna tsked in the way only a judgmental pre-teen could. "Mom spent more time in the water in that film than she did on land. She even went topless when she lost her bikini top while swimming away from a dolphin she thought was a shark."

Angie choked on her wine and very nearly spit it across the table. Finn came around and gently rubbed her back as she coughed into her napkin, her eyes watering. Finn's hand was large and gentle and didn't help at all with her breathing. When she could finally suck in some air, she nodded gratefully, and Finn returned to her chair.

Luna had the devil in her expression as she grinned at Angie, who grimaced at her.

"Anyway." She dabbed at her eyes. "Tell me about this game you two play at the café."

Finn sipped her wine, her eyes sparkling as she looked at Angie over the glass. "It's a game of numbers and letters. My grandmother used to play it with me. It's a good distraction when I'm trying to work things out. It's all about strategy."

There was no missing the shadow that passed over Finn's eyes when she mentioned her grandmother. There was another story there.

"You wouldn't get it, Mom." Luna pushed her empty dish away. "Mom isn't good with strategy. She's just good at memorizing lines and making people laugh."

Angie winced internally but didn't let it show. "Thanks, I think."

"What's your favorite movie of Mom's, Finn?" Luna asked. Her tone was only vaguely petulant, as though it was a given that Finn would have one.

Finn took another sip of wine, and this time she looked at Luna for a moment. Did she always take the time to choose her words? Was she guarded, or simply someone who considered what she said? Once again, the worry about a woman with secrets made Angie shift uncomfortably.

"Honest?" She waited for Luna's nod. "I'm afraid I don't have one. I have to admit to never having seen one of your mom's movies. Does that make me a bad person?"

Luna looked incredulous for a moment, and then her face broke into a huge smile, which quickly put another crack in Angie's heart.

"No way. Are you serious?"

Finn glanced at Angie and then back at Luna. "I'm afraid so, kid. I'm more of a book person than a movie person."

"Okay, but what kind of movies do you like?" Luna persisted, clearly not caring that Finn looked like she wanted to crawl under the table.

"Deep stuff. The equivalent of literary novels, I guess. Things that can make you cry, make you uncomfortable. Movies that make you think." She tapped the side of Luna's head, eliciting a giggle.

"That's not Mom's stuff, for sure." She put her hands over her heart. "She's all about love and things going wrong. But she always ends up with the person in the end." She rolled her eyes and made a gagging sound.

"Does she?" Finn's tone lowered just slightly, just enough to make Angie tingle.

She met Finn's gaze. "That's the nature of romantic comedies. I've been typecast to some degree, I'm aware. But for the most part, I don't mind. Laughter and love are good for the soul, and not everyone wants to leave a theater feeling like they have to change the world." It came out sharper than she meant it to, and she flushed at the twitch of Finn's eyebrow.

"That's true. There's got to be something for everyone." She laughed when Luna sighed theatrically. "The world would be a dull place if we all liked the same things. I think you'd know that better than anyone."

Conversation stopped for a moment as their plates were cleared, and Angie took the moment of silence to notice the way Finn moved. There were people who were comfortable around wealth and people who weren't. Finn was polite and clearly unfazed by the staff moving around her. Her body language was relaxed except for the slight tightness of her jaw, which suggested there was something going on beneath the surface. But Angie would bet that Finn had been raised around money.

"Churros with chocolate dip for Digger," Susan said, sliding the plate in front of Luna. "And a caramel mousse in a dark chocolate hazelnut tube for the grown-ups."

Finn smiled at Susan, who gave her a quick wink. Angie pretended not to notice, nor did she acknowledge the tiny flare of irritation. "This looks beautiful, as always."

Susan gave her shoulder a quick squeeze. "Enjoy."

Finn hooked her finger on the edge of Luna's plate and started to drag it over. "Let's trade."

Luna pulled the plate back and hovered over it protectively. "No way. Churros are the best. That'll make you going to the gym for a million hours tomorrow worth it."

Finn sighed and dug her spoon into the mousse. "Fine. But churros really are the best."

Conversation between Finn and Luna continued, and Angie was content to watch and listen. She hadn't seen Luna so animated in a long time. Was it concerning that she seemed more connected to Finn than she had to anyone her own age? Yes, unquestionably. But Finn was gentle and kind, and she didn't once talk down to her. Angie's heart ached at the easy way they chatted. She hadn't been able to talk to Luna that way in so long.

"That was stunning." Finn wiped her mouth and then tucked her napkin neatly under the side of the plate. "Thank you for having me over tonight."

Luna looked almost panicked. "You're not leaving already, are you?"

Finn tilted her head. "Isn't it a school night?"

"That doesn't matter when we have a guest." Luna turned to Angie, her expression pleading.

"You think?" Angie shook her head, knowing she was about to be the least popular person in the room. "Finn is right. It's a school night, and I have to leave early for a meeting tomorrow. It's already past time for you to be getting ready for bed."

Luna looked like she was about to protest, but Finn touched her shoulder. "I'm not leaving the country, kid. I'll be at the café as usual. You know where to find me."

Luna's shoulders dropped in defeat. "Promise?"

"Promise." Finn held up her pinky.

Luna stared at her blankly.

"It's a pinky swear. You shake my pinky with yours. It's an unbreakable promise."

Luna was quick to respond, and the grin returned. "I'll kick your butt at the tiles next time."

Finn pushed away from the table and stood, smoothing her hands down her thighs. "I shall await your hard-won victory, young gamer."

Luna shook her head and backed out of the room. "You're so weird."

Finn responded with a bow. "Always."

Laughing, Luna ran from the room and pounded up the stairs.

The silence held potential as Angie and Finn looked at one another. The spell was broken when Susan came in and cleared her throat.

"Sorry to interrupt. I just wanted to see if you needed anything else before we head out?" She looked between them, curiosity clear in her expression.

"Not for me, thank you." Finn moved toward the doorway. "It seems we all have a busy morning."

Disappointment and relief warred for Angie's attention. What was she thinking, being attracted to a total stranger? "Thank you again for coming by." She ignored Susan's smirk and turned her back on her. "I'll walk you out."

The warm air made her shiver as they stepped outside. Finn's hand brushed hers, leaving a tingly sensation behind. She pressed it to her leg, willing the feeling to sweep through the rest of her.

"So, not a race car driver then?" Angie nodded at the old truck in her driveway.

"You can't drive a race car to dinner. I have to keep it in the garage until race day." Finn played with her car keys but didn't make a move to open her door.

"Wise." Angie's stomach fluttered at the notion that Finn was reluctant for the night to end too. "What is it you do for a living? Really."

Finn shook her head ruefully and stepped into the shadows, where she opened her car door. "If I told you, I'd have to kill you."

Angie crossed her arms. "The hot mysterious stranger thing can wear out, you know."

Finn stopped halfway into the truck. "But at least I'm hot." She got in and pulled away with a wave.

Angie stared after the taillights until they were gone and then looked up at the clear night sky. She hadn't been with someone in way too long. That was the only explanation for why she hoped Finn might turn around. Shaking her head, she went back into the house.

Chapter Nine

"WHAT THE HELL WAS I thinking?" Finn missed the tennis ball she'd been throwing at the ceiling, and it bounced off the nightstand and rolled under the bed. She sighed and got up, knowing sleep was far from possible.

It was stupid. That's what it was. She hadn't wanted to let Luna down. A kid she barely knew. "I'm such a softie." She grimaced at the sound of her voice echoing off the kitchen cabinets. She rarely spoke out loud to herself, and it was an indication that she was seriously agitated. Her father had always said a closed mouth was the only good mouth.

She made herself a cup of decaf coffee and then sat in the window seat, her feet propped against the window frame. Light pollution meant there were no stars. Funny. In a city full of them, there were none where they should be.

Stars like Angie. She'd given into her curiosity and googled her movies again when she'd arrived home, looking specifically for the one where she ended up topless. Pages and pages of information filled the screen. Images of her on the red carpet at any number of awards shows made Finn salivate slightly. Her dresses were almost always low cut and figure-perfect. And yet, Finn preferred the version she'd seen tonight. Dressed down, barefoot, and smiling fondly at her daughter in a way that wasn't camera-fake. That version was even sexier, if that was possible. She marked the movie she finally thought would be the right one and ordered it for next day delivery.

"Stupid." She sipped her coffee. The last thing she needed was someone who wanted to know the truth about her. And she sure as hell didn't need to get close to someone else's kid. She'd worked hard to become a living shadow. Someone there but not there. Hanging out with a celebrity could bring her carefully constructed reality crashing down around her.

The look of hope in Luna's eyes when she'd pinky sworn that she'd still be around made her groan and bang her head against the wall. She'd been that kid. The one no one noticed until it was time to be in front of the cameras. The one left behind, the one expected to be something different than she was. If it hadn't been for Pablo and her grandmother, she wouldn't have survived to the time she could finally get away.

Like a gust of wind, a plot point she'd been struggling with solidified, which led to the next one. She practically leapt for her computer and opened to a blank page, where she began throwing down random sentences and thoughts, not caring whether or not things were spelled right or connected. It was the first breakthrough she'd had since gnomes had roamed the earth.

Two hours later, she rolled her neck and tried to blink away the grit in her eyes. Raw morning sunlight slid over the hills in the distance, a beacon for those ready to jump into a new day.

She tugged the curtains closed and stumbled into her room. As she drifted to sleep, a sweet, sultry smile and beautiful eyes wished her goodnight, and for the briefest moment, she missed having someone in her bed.

***

Finn groaned and yanked the pillow over her head. The phone stopped ringing, but then started again. Flinging the pillow aside, she reached for the phone and knocked it to the floor. It stopped ringing and she let her face fall into the thick comforter.

It began again.

"Madre de Dios." She grappled with it and rolled onto her back without looking at the screen. "If you're a telemarketer, I will find out where you live and paint the Declaration of Independence on your house."

"What a bizarre threat."

Finn nearly hung up, but she couldn't put this conversation off any longer. Her publisher and agent had both been trying to get hold of her, but she'd managed to dodge them thus far. "Did you have to call me at o'dark hundred, Paige?"

"It's one in the afternoon, although I would gladly have called you in the wee hours if it meant you'd answer." Paige, Finn's agent and continual pain in the butt, sounded unperturbed. Did a lot of her authors avoid her?

"Sorry, I got writing and—"

"You're writing again?" Paige's voice reached the level usually reserved for things flying into space. "What is it? When can I see it?"

"I'm not telling you, and I don't know." Finn swung her legs out of bed and grimaced at the cold floor under her bare feet. She needed some rugs.

"Fine. Now I know to schedule in some badgering phone calls." She laughed at her own joke, though she was probably serious. "Speaking of which. You owe a very important organization a reply, and they're freaking out because you haven't said anything. They want to announce this year's winner."

Finn looked from the coffee pot to her bedroom. Maybe she could go back to sleep and pretend this phone call hadn't happened. "I already told you, and you said you'd tell them."

"But you've had a chance to think about it, and I wanted you to ruminate on it the way you do so you'd see how ludicrous it is that you'd turn it down. It will do incredible things for your career."

She'd heard it before, and as before, it failed to make any difference. "Paige, I write under a pen name because I don't want notoriety. I like my privacy, and if I have to get up on that stage, people will start digging. I don't want them snooping around. I don't want press interviews where they ask all kinds of personal shit I'm not interested in sharing."

There was a moment of silence before Paige sighed. "Want to finally tell me why you're such a hermit? At least then I could understand."

There weren't words in any human language that could convey the real reason Finn needed to remain in the shadows. She'd changed her name for a reason, but that didn't mean someone couldn't find some kind of paper trail. And god forbid someone from her past saw her. "I don't want to tell you, no. I simply need you to accept that this is the way it is. I don't want their award. I want them to leave me alone. Thanks, but no thanks. I politely but insistently decline."

"Fine." Paige's tone suggested it was anything but. "I'll let them know. Also, your next book goes to print in two weeks. I'm having copies shipped to you so you can sign a bunch, since you're also refusing to do public signings. I don't know why you wanted an agent, Finn. You could self-publish and do everything your own way. The publisher isn't going to like it either, you know. You should just fire me, so I don't have to deal with the headache."

"And take away your commission?" Finn inhaled the freshly poured coffee. "I wouldn't dream of it. You love me. You get money and don't have to run around after me."

"My job is to build authors, to help them make their careers even more amazing. You don't let me do it, and it's giving me an ulcer." Papers rattled. "I'll be in touch soon."

She hung up, and Finn breathed a sigh of relief. The laptop was calling, but she could sense it wasn't time to get back to it just yet. The next obstacle hadn't quite presented itself, which meant it was probably a good idea for some fresh air.

After a quick shower, she jumped in the truck and headed toward hot-mom park. Popular with the local, wealthy spouses of celebrities, there were plenty of birds and people to watch. The diversion would create the space in her brain to allow subconscious thoughts to play out and give her more fodder for characters' foibles.

She pulled up, laughing at the image of her old truck stuck between a Mercedes and a Bentley. A cowboy amongst the gentry. She walked across the sweet-smelling grass and tilted her face to the sunshine. Children's laughter floated through the air, and the strangled tinkling of an ice cream truck's jingle played like a summer soundtrack. She perched on an empty tabletop, crossed her legs and let her gaze roam over the spread of nature and humanity before her.

With her notepad balanced on her knee, she flipped to an empty page and began drawing. First, the "boob joggers," as Delia called them. Four of them, two in front, two in back, wearing sports bras stretched to capacity. Tiny waists were visible above tight leggings, and the whole ensemble was so LA she couldn't help but shake her head. Those poor women probably hadn't had a carb in a decade.

Next came a drawing of a long-haired guy with a dog lying beside him on the grass. The dog, a collie of some sort if she had to guess, yawned widely and flopped onto its back. The owner yawned in turn and flopped onto his stomach. How nice to have a friendship that demanded so little. Maybe she needed a pet. Maybe that would explain why she couldn't stop thinking about Angie. Not that Angie would be a pet. She shook her head at her own insanity.

Raised voices caught her attention, and she looked toward the cement skate park. Boarders dropped in, popped up, and slid over surfaces like their boards were part of their bodies. But when one in particular caught an edge and hit the ground, Finn frowned. She'd always been good at recognizing people, probably because she studied them so often. She glanced at her watch. Surely Luna should be at school at two in the afternoon? Her skate lessons, if their games at the café were any indication, were in the late afternoon.

Finn watched for a bit longer. No one spoke to Luna, and she seemed content with that as she practiced whatever moves she was trying to perfect. She also kept checking her phone.

She rubbed her temples. Was this something she should get involved with? Should she say something? Do something? Luna was mature, yeah, but Finn would bet their bag of nickels that no one had any idea Luna was here, alone. There was no sign of bodyguards or nannies of any age.

Sighing, she strolled over to a table close to the little cement city and took up the same position she'd been in before. "Hey. Looks like you're getting that foot thing down."

Luna's head whipped up so fast, it looked painful. "Shit."

Finn nodded sagely. "Shit." She patted the table. "Should we have a conflab?"

Luna's shoulders dropped, and she slid her board under the table. "I don't know what conflab means." She straddled the bench.

"It means a private conversation." She took in Luna's hunched shoulders, the way she kept pushing her glasses up her nose, and the pinched, frustrated look in her eyes. Signs she knew well. "Spill."

Luna sat silently for a few minutes, and Finn let her figure out what she wanted to say. There was no hurry.

"There's this girl at school." Luna started picking at the split wood on the bench. "She's way bigger than me. Like, she's huge. She's thirteen, and she's almost six feet tall. Everyone's afraid of her. But she really hates me, and she keeps telling everyone she's going to beat me up so I'm even uglier."

Finn's heart ached for Luna as tears welled up and then fell like little waterfalls down her cheeks. "So you ditch school."

"Not all day. I get to my classes, but I have a free period and so does she. That's when I come here." She looked up at Finn, her gaze pleading. "I swear I go straight back for my next class. I just... I'm scared, and the jellies mean I can't concentrate. I feel like I'm going to throw up all the time. But I swear, I'm not doing anything wrong."

Finn gently thumbed away Luna's tears. "No, mija. You're not doing anything wrong, *technically*. You're protecting yourself, and I get it."

Luna blew out a breath and wiped her palms across her face. "You won't tell Mom?"

Finn opened her notebook and started sketching a wretchedly skinny kid who kept falling off his board, probably because his long hair kept obscuring his vision. "Here's the thing," she said eventually. "You slipped out of school without people knowing and came here. You have a bodyguard and a driver at school, right?" She glanced at Luna, who nodded without looking up from the piece of wood she was peeling off. "But no one on earth knows you're here. If I'd been some kind of psycho kidnapper, it would be hours before anyone even knew you were missing. That's dangerous stuff."

Luna rolled her eyes and flung away the splinter of wood. "I'm not stupid. I come to this park because a lot of rich people hang out here. I know at least three of the women over there. They're the moms of girls in my class. If I got into trouble, I'd yell."

Finn tilted her head to concede the point. "That's smart thinking. But what if they didn't hear you? What if you couldn't yell?"

"It's not like Mom would care. Then she could go off and do movies all over the world and never worry about me getting in the way. Maybe life would be better somewhere else."

"Hey!" Finn tapped her shoulder, a little harder than necessary. "Don't say that. Your mom loves you, and life here is pretty sweet. People who take kids—" She shook her head. "They're evil, and you don't ever want to get near them. Not just for your mom's sake, but for your own. Trust me."

Luna's eyes were wide, her gaze searching as she stared at Finn.

"Anyway." Finn started sketching again. "Running from shithead bullies who make life miserable is a rite of passage for people like us. But you have to make it stop eventually, or they never back down."

"Is this where you tell me to stand up to her?"

"God no. You'd get creamed." She laughed at Luna's look of disbelief. "But we have to do something. And you shouldn't be doing it alone." She showed Luna the picture of the skateboarder, and she grinned half-heartedly.

"But what do I do? If I go to a teacher, then everyone at school will make fun of me or call me a snitch. If I tell Mom, she'll go all nutty protective and call the girl's parents, and then it will be even worse. I'll just keep hiding in the library or coming here."

The stubborn tone let Finn know where this was headed. "Come on. Let me take you back to school, and we'll both think about it, okay? I won't tell your mom *yet*, but you have to promise me that you'll send me a message if you're heading out on your own. Then at least one person will know where you are." Even as she said it, she had a feeling it was the wrong thing to say. Angie had a right to know that her kid was in trouble and not where she said she'd be. But Luna needed someone on her side too. She punched her number into Luna's phone, saving it under Weird Finn, Game Nerd.

Luna picked up her board and ran and got her backpack before meeting Finn back at the truck. "This is what you drive? Do you have to power it with your feet?"

"Why do you think I wear such big boots?" She set off and took directions from Luna. It wasn't that far to the school, which was something. The promise she made was niggling at her though. "Look, Luna. We need to figure out something quick, because if anything happens to you, I'd never forgive myself and your mom would probably put out a hit on me, if she didn't kill me herself. And I don't want anything to happen to you. You're pretty cool."

Luna sat still, holding the door handle. "I don't know what to do," she whispered.

"Write down your schedule for me." She passed Luna her notepad and took it back after. "We'll figure this out, okay, kid? You're not alone."

Once again, she was startled when Luna threw herself across

the seat and pulled Finn into a tight hug. Her tears left a wet patch on Finn's shirt, and then she darted from the truck and around the side of the school.

Finn rested her head against the window. "What the fuck am I going to do now?"

Chapter Ten

ANGIE SAT IN THE shade by the pool, reading over the new script and making notes. Lunch, a long-forgotten quinoa salad, sat neglected on the table beside her. The sound of the sliding door made her look up, and Karen came out.

If it weren't for Luna's quick approval, Angie might have had second thoughts. She was polite and Luna seemed fine with her, but there was something about her, about the look in her eyes that made Angie wary of showing any tender underbelly around her. And that didn't sit well in her own home.

"Hey. Everything okay with Luna?" she asked.

"Totally. She's a gem. So much easier than the other kids I've worked with. It's like she's hardly there."

Not exactly what Angie wanted to hear, but she couldn't put her finger on why. "If you have any luck convincing her to go to some of the parties the other kids have, I'd be grateful." Despite Luna's protestation that she didn't have anything in common with other kids, Angie couldn't let her sit around by herself all the time. Surely she was supposed to encourage social engagement, whether Luna really wanted it or not. Right?

Karen sat down at the table, and Angie gently closed the script when she noticed Karen's gaze settle on it. Again, that feeling of mistrust reared its head.

"The thing is," Karen said, plucking an orange from the basket in the middle, "she really isn't like other kids. She's way smarter and clearly doesn't care about fashion or pop stars." She shrugged. "I don't understand what she's talking about half the time."

A nanny Luna couldn't talk to wasn't a good thing. Maybe she needed to ask her if she wanted to look for someone else. She searched for a response but couldn't find one that didn't have to do with Karen not being as intelligent as her twelve-year-old. They sat in awkward silence for a moment, the only sound that of Karen ripping the peel from the orange.

Thankfully, Luna came in. "Mom, can I go meet Finn at the café?" She glanced between Angie and Karen as though she sensed tension.

"I'd say you shouldn't bother her, but if she's just sitting around drinking coffee, then I can't see the harm." Angie stacked her materials and thought of Finn's sultry smile. "Although, you could just invite her here. We'll get coffee and cake delivered, and you can play your game in peace."

Luna bit her lip, her eyes narrowed. "You're always telling me to get out of the house. Now you're telling me to stay here. What's your game?"

Angie's eyebrow quirked. "My game?"

Luna folded her arms. "That's right."

"No game. If you want to go to the café instead, you can. I just thought it might be nice for you since your skate lesson has been cancelled." A rare storm was passing through, which meant California came to a standstill until the pavement was dry once more.

Luna stared out the window, clearly mulling it over. Finally, she nodded decisively. "I'll call her."

"*Ask* her, Luna. Don't tell her. Remember your manners." Part of her wanted to ask Luna for Finn's number, but she couldn't think of a reason why.

Luna ran off up the stairs and Karen wandered out of the kitchen, much to Angie's relief. She missed Helen's easy company and the way she and Luna could always talk to her. She wasn't ever going to have that with Karen, but so be it.

Luna's footsteps pounded down the stairs. "She's coming when she's done at the gym!"

Angie told herself that the excitement she felt at the announcement had everything to do with Luna's happiness and nothing to do with the prospect of spending time with Finn again. The feeling clashed with the knowledge that her kid's only friend was an adult. It wasn't normal. But then, Luna wasn't a normal kid. At least this way she could keep an eye on things.

Luna lifted herself onto the kitchen counter. "Who should we call for coffee and cake?"

"How about JamBean? I could go for one of their Matcha Latta Lattes."

"Ooh, and I want one of their Wacka Wacka Waffles with bananas and chocolate sauce." Luna started typing into her phone. "I'll see what Finn wants."

Angie wished more than anything that Luna was this excited about someone her own age coming over. Was she being a bad parent by allowing this odd friendship to continue? She thought of one of Luna's favorite animated movies, where a kid befriended an old man. If Disney said it was okay, that should be enough.

"She said she trusts me to choose something awesome for her." Luna worried at the seam of her sweatshirt. "What if I choose wrong?"

Angie leaned on the countertop next to her and scrolled through the menu on her own phone. "Well, she wanted your churros the other day. Maybe something with cinnamon?"

Luna's eyes lit up. "The Cinnamon Stack with a cinnamon latte!"

Angie added it to the order. "And if she stays for dinner, what do you want for dessert? Or do you want Susan to come up with something?"

"Do you think Susan could make something from the Dominican Republic? I read that tres leches cake is popular."

Angie smiled at her thoughtfulness. "I think that's an awesome idea. And if she can't make it, maybe we can find a place who does. Why don't you text Susan and ask?"

Luna's thumbs were a blur as she sent the message. Some

days, Susan was around the house all day, others she popped in just to make dinner. It usually depended on Angie's work schedule, and Angie knew full well that Susan spent more time at the house when Angie was gone, just so Luna would have more company.

"She says she can try but not to expect miracles, and she wants to know if you want something special for dinner." Luna set the phone down and swung her legs.

They hadn't talked this way in years, and it hurt Angie's heart, but she'd revel in it while she had it. "Do you feel like anything specific?"

"Enchiladas?"

Susan made amazing enchiladas, but they weren't good for Angie's waistline. As she got older, it was harder to keep the weight off. She'd just have to spend more time in the gym next week. "Perfect. Spinach and onion for you, and chicken for us."

Luna sent the message and then fiddled with the phone. "Mom, have you thought any more about my trip to Turkey?"

Just like that, Angie felt the special moment slip away. "I'm still thinking about it." When Luna's expression fell, she took her hand. "I'm not saying no, sweetheart. I just need to give it some real thought, okay?"

Luna's gaze was searching as she looked at her. "You mean it? You're really considering it?"

"I am."

Luna's smile could have made the sun look dim. "Yes!" She raised her arms in victory.

"Hey now, I haven't made a decision yet."

"Yeah, but before you wouldn't even listen to me about it. Progress for the people!" Luna jumped from the countertop. "I'm going to go see what the dig's webpage says." She took off, thumping up the stairs.

Angie shook her head. Seeing Luna so happy made her think she really should let her go on the dig. And if she could go with her, that would be fine. But she'd be working over Luna's birthday, and that would mean she wouldn't get to spend it with her. If she were working though, wouldn't it be better for Luna to be doing something she had her heart set on? She wouldn't even notice Angie wasn't there. And Karen would be with her. That should make her feel better, but it didn't.

She went back to her script but found she couldn't concentrate. Instead, she opened her laptop and pulled up the archaeological site Luna was so crazy about. Research had been extensive, and she had to admit that it looked impressive. The small city nearby clearly catered to tourists, though hotels were sparse.

Snapping the laptop closed, she sighed. Should she really let her twelve-year-old go to another country without her? Plenty of celebrities did. They had the staff to accompany their kids anywhere on earth. She could hire a full team to go with Luna, if only to make herself feel better.

The doorbell rang, pulling her from her circular thought pattern.

Luna came flying down the stairs. "Finn's here!"

Susan came in carrying a massive bag, followed by Finn and Luna, who both carried more bags.

"Susan, you're a godsend." Angie took the bag from Finn and hefted it onto the counter.

"You should tell me that more often." Susan set her bag down and rolled her shoulders. "Now get out of my kitchen."

Angie shooed Luna and Finn outside and tried very hard not to notice the way Finn's faded, well-worn jeans hung loosely from her hips, while the simple grey V-neck hugged her slim waist. Her short, thick hair looked soft as Finn ran her fingers through it.

Caught staring once again, Angie flushed and looked at the pool instead after they'd sat around the table. "Once Susan's assistant gets here, I'm sure they'll ask if we want something to drink. But I know better than to get in her way when she's setting up."

"She's mean when you get in her way." Luna nodded and pushed her glasses up. "But if you stay out of her way, she'll let you lick the spoon she uses for dessert."

"Nothing better than licking the spoon."

Finn's first words since she arrived made Angie's mouth go dry. And when she added a tiny, knowing grin, Angie had to cross her legs against the thrum that started.

"Thanks for coming over. Luna asked if she could meet you at the café, but I was enjoying my time with her."

"Understandable. I wasn't up to much anyway." A brief frown crossed her handsome face but was quickly replaced with a smile. "I brought our game. Luna's getting good."

Luna tapped the table. "Let's do it."

Finn glanced at Angie as though for permission, and Angie nodded. "I'm looking forward to seeing this in action."

Angie watched as they spread out the tiles and then began to move them strategically. While it appeared simple once she understood the rules, it quickly became clear you had to think five steps ahead in order to win. Luna was down another three nickels before Susan's assistant came out with the order from JamBean.

"Thank you," Angie said.

"Anytime. Really," the assistant said, her gaze lingering a moment too long before she headed back inside.

"Subtle." Finn dug into her cinnamon bread and sniffed the cinnamon latte appreciatively. "But I guess you're used to it."

"Not in my own home." Angie took a sip of the matcha latte. "Susan uses assistants from the local cooking school. She says it's her way of giving back, and she checks them out to make sure they're okay to bring over."

"But you can't keep someone from trying their luck, can you?" Finn's smile was devious. "Because you never know when lightning will strike. One minute they're serving you drinks, the next, you're married and living a domestic life of bliss."

Luna made gagging sounds. "Not me. I'm never getting married. And Mom doesn't date anymore, so she'll never get married either."

"Anyway." Angie shifted uncomfortably, not wanting to discuss the reasons she no longer dated. Especially not with Finn, who clearly had her own secrets. "Can three play this game?"

Finn gave an almost imperceptible nod, as though acknowledging Angie's desire to change the subject. "You can have up to four players, and it makes it a lot harder. Let's see if you have what it takes."

Angie was quickly immersed in the game and banter flowed easily as they tried to outwit each other. It was obvious that neither she nor Luna could compete though. Luna lost four more nickels and Angie was in debt, since Luna refused to give her a nickel loan. They made easy work of the snack from JamBean, and Luna's smile when Finn told her she'd chosen perfectly made Angie smile in turn. And when Finn made an offhanded comment about having watched a certain movie where the actress could never seem to find her top when she was in the ocean right as Angie was about to make her move, Luna giggled herself into a coughing fit.

Susan came out, a dishtowel thrown over her shoulder. She stood beside Angie, her hand resting lightly on her shoulder as she stared at the game on the table. "Poker is about all I can handle. Come on in. Food's hot."

Angie didn't miss the way Finn's head tilted slightly as she watched Susan's hand slide from Angie's shoulder. There was no need to read into it though. Her relationship with Susan had never been anything more than platonic. Not that it was any of Finn's business. She met Finn's amused gaze with one of her own, and Finn's eyebrow twitched.

"I'm starving," Luna said, oblivious to the unspoken conversation happening around her. "And we asked for something special for dessert too. It's a surprise." Luna darted inside ahead of them.

"Thank you for inviting me over," Finn said as she slid the tiles back into their bag. "It's a nice break."

"From?" Angie asked.

Finn grinned. "From the reconnaissance mission I'm running

from the café, of course."

"Of course." Angie crossed her arms. "You know, having someone in my house and in my daughter's life that I know literally nothing about isn't smart. I might have to rethink it."

Finn moved closer, her height forcing Angie to look up at her. "Every woman likes a bit of mystery, don't you think?" Her gaze caressed Angie's face like a physical touch, her eyes dark with promise.

"Oh my god, I'm going to starve to death!" Luna's voice splintered the tension between them.

Finn stepped back and smiled. "We can't let your child waste away." Her smile faded slightly. "But I promise you, Angie, I'm one of the good guys. If I make you uncomfortable, say the word and I'm gone."

Finn's tone was so gentle, so sincere, that Angie relented on the teasing, although she'd been serious too. "Maybe one day you'll open up to us. For now," she said and motioned toward the house.

Unsurprisingly, the meal was exquisite. Finn said the enchiladas were the best she'd ever had, and Luna regaled them with facts about the history of Troy. When they were finished and the assistant had cleared their plates, with more than one *accidental* touch of Angie's hand or arm, they made their way poolside once again.

"I'm stuffed. I don't think I'll eat another thing for a week." Finn closed her eyes and raised her face to the setting sun.

"You have to!" Luna sounded almost panicked. "It's special."

Finn cracked one eye open and looked at Luna sideways. "Are you trying to get me fat so you can cook me later?"

Luna's expression made Angie laugh. "Gross. I'm not a cannibal. You're so weird."

"You don't know the story of the Ciguapas, I take it." She tilted her face back to the sun as though she was done speaking.

"Well?" Luna tapped the table impatiently. "You have to tell us now. It's a rule."

"Well, if it's a rule." Finn moved to face them, her expression serious. "Ciguapas are beautiful mythical creatures. Women with hair so thick and long you can't see the blue skin of their bodies. They live in the forests, but if you see one, it's probably the last thing you'll ever see."

Angie hung on Finn's words. The tone of her voice, the intensity of her gaze, the way her lips moved. She was a natural storyteller. Luna looked equally rapt.

"People disappear on nights of the full moon, and everyone knows it was a ciguapa who lured them into the forest with their beauty. Once there, the ciguapa kills them and drinks their soul. No one can track them, though."

"Why not?" Luna breathed out, her eyes wide.

"Because their feet can turn backwards. There's no telling which direction they've actually gone. And if you do manage to find one...well." Finn sat back and shrugged.

Angie could almost picture the creatures Finn was describing, and she took a breath as she chuckled. "Wow. That's some tale."

Luna was frowning. "But you asked if I was overfeeding you, so I could cook and eat you. The Ciguapas drink souls, they don't eat bodies. So that doesn't make sense."

Finn began to laugh, a deep, open-hearted sound that made Angie and Luna begin to laugh in response.

"You're right. But I've always thought that a cooked soul would taste better than a raw soul. I guess I just prefer cooked food."

Luna giggled and pressed her shoulder to Angie's. It was the first time she'd gotten close in a long time, and Angie pressed back.

"It's kind of like Medusa," Luna said. "She killed people who found her too."

"Ah, but the Ciguapas were born to be the creatures they are. They can't help doing what they do. Medusa was turned into a creature of death by a jealous goddess. She was a victim before she was a bad guy."

A look of sadness crossed Finn's features, barely long enough for Angie to wonder if it had actually been there.

"Those are the stories that are most interesting, in my opinion." Finn drew concentric circles in the condensation from the glass on the table. "Like your Troy. Helen fell in love and left her aged, fat husband that she didn't want to marry in the first place for a guy she really did love. History paints her as a temptress, as a cheater. But really, she took control of her own destiny and made a choice about who she wanted to love. She was both hero and bad guy, and that's part of why her story has come down to us through the generations."

Angie had never seen Luna look so reverently at someone as she did at Finn in that moment. Had she ever had a conversation with her daughter about the history she was so passionate about? She couldn't think of one. And yet a total stranger could come in and share that passion with ease. Tears sprang to her eyes, and she dashed them away.

"Angie? Have I said something wrong?" Finn reached across and touched Angie's hand.

"Mom's a sucker for a good love story, that's all. She cries at them all the time." Luna bumped Angie with her shoulder. "It's just a myth, Mom."

Finn raised her finger. "Ah, but is it? You've seen the dig. Once upon a time, scholars thought Troy itself was a myth until they found it. Like the site at Corinth, where Medea was said to have killed her rival and her own children. Archaeologists just like you uncovered the well and the nearby graves of two children and they think she may have been a real person." She smiled gently at Luna. "You may uncover evidence that Helen of Troy was a real person too."

Luna practically vibrated with excitement, and her smile could have lit up the Hollywood sign. "You really think so?"

"I think we never know what we'll find of lost history until people like you go hunting for it." Finn gave a lopsided grin as she stared into Angie's eyes. "And then people like your mom can make movies about it to share those stories with the world."

Luna looked at Angie. "I never thought of what you do that way."

Angie's heart ached at the thoughtful respect in Luna's expression. For this moment, she'd happily owe Finn for the rest of her life.

Susan came out carrying a metal cake stand with a cover over it. "Dessert is ready." She gave Finn a nod. "You'll have to let me know if I've done it right."

The assistant followed carrying plates and forks and gave Angie a lingering look of longing before Susan said, "Off you go."

The assistant blanched and retreated into the house, and Susan shook her head. "Sorry, Angie. I thought this one would be okay, given that she's married to a guy who looks like he swallows weights for dinner."

"Don't worry about it. Thanks for making something special today." She had no intention of discussing the issues surrounding women throwing themselves at her in front of Luna. She'd been through enough because of Angie's bad choices.

"My pleasure." She took the lid from the cake tray with a flourish.

"Is that it?" Luna inspected it, her eyes narrowed. "It doesn't look like the pictures."

Finn inhaled deeply and made a sound of appreciation. "It looks like the dessert of angels and smells like it came out of heaven's oven." She smiled at Susan. "Thank you. It's not an easy thing to get right."

Susan tugged the dishtowel from her shoulder and twisted it between her hands. "Well, be sure to let Luna know if I did her proud. Unless you need anything more tonight, I've got a date."

"You've done more than enough, and if we do need anything, we've already got a delivery place lined up, don't we, Luna?" Angie smiled as Luna stopped midway from sticking her finger in the icing.

"Can we try it now?"

Susan handed Finn the cake knife and then gave a salute. "Have a good night."

Finn sliced a big piece and handed the plate to Luna. "Your first one shouldn't be something a mouse could eat."

Luna dug straight in.

"Angie?" Finn held the cake knife up. "What size would you like?"

A slice as big as the one she'd given Luna would be perfect. "Half the size of Luna's, thank you." With a new movie role coming up, she couldn't afford to ignore calories, and the enchiladas were going to be hard to work off next week.

Finn handed over the slice, and then took one the same size as the one she'd given Luna. She moaned as she took the first bite, and the sound went straight to Angie's clit. She tried to focus on the cake instead, but it was going to be a losing battle, given the subsequent sounds issuing from Finn's mouth.

"This is really good," Luna said. "Not as good as churros, but good."

Finn sighed happily and licked a bit of cream from her lip. Angie swallowed hard.

"Your chef must have ripped the family recipe from some grandmother's cold, dead hands, because this isn't one you'd find on Google." She dipped her finger in the cream and raised it to her lips. She caught Angie's eye as she put her fingertip to her lips and sucked the cream off.

Fortunately, Luna was engrossed in eating and didn't notice Angie nearly faint. Could you swoon in real life? If so, she was swooning.

Finn grinned and sat back. "Thank you for this surprise. I haven't had a taste of home like that in a very long time. My abuela used to make it very much the same way."

Luna finally looked up. "Abuela?" She pronounced it slowly.

"Grandmother." Once again, sorrow flashed across Finn's eyes, and this time it didn't fade as quickly.

"Were you close?" Angie asked.

It took a moment for Finn to respond. A light frown creased her forehead as she toyed with her fork. "Yes. We were very close.

She passed away last week actually. I'm going to the funeral in a few days."

The pain in her words underscored their closeness, and Angie reached for her hand. "I'm sorry. Losing someone you love is hard."

"Did she just die of being old?" Luna asked. "That's how I want to go."

Finn gave Luna a sad smile. "It's a good way to go, isn't it? Lay down and go to sleep after a long, full life."

Luna nodded, pushing her glasses up her nose. "I don't know my grandparents."

Angie stood, bumping the table and making everything rattle. "What's next on the agenda, Luna? This is your party." Her hands shook as she began to pile up the plates. She had no desire to talk about her parents.

Finn's hands covered hers. "Let me."

When she met Finn's gaze, understanding was clear.

"I should probably get going. Overstaying one's welcome is a sure way not to get invited back."

Luna looked stricken. "But you were supposed to stay all night!"

"Was I?" Finn looked genuinely surprised. "I'm pretty sure we haven't reached the level of slumber parties. And I have to work tomorrow, hija." She flinched like she'd said something wrong but moved on quickly. "You made today really special, thank you. It's been a long time since I had a family dinner like this."

"What does hija mean?" Luna asked.

Again, Finn looked vaguely uncomfortable. "It's a contraction of sorts. My and daughter put together." At Angie's look of surprise, she said quickly, "In the DR, it's a familiar form of address when we're talking to kids."

"That's cool. You have to stay longer!" Luna looked at Angie as though for help.

"It's early yet, and I bet we've got a film you and Luna would agree on."

"Yes!" Luna leapt from her seat and ran toward the house. "I'll find one!" she shouted over her shoulder.

Finn continued stacking plates. "Angie, I really appreciate the invitation, but—"

"I'm enjoying your company, Finn. I don't get to talk to normal people very often, and clearly Luna has some serious hero worship going on." She opened the sliding door. "If it isn't too much of an imposition, I'd like you to stay."

Finn set the plates on the counter but didn't turn around right away. When she did, the look in her eyes made Angie's breath catch.

"Angie, you're a stunningly beautiful woman, and I like your company too." She moved closer and brushed a stray hair from Angie's cheek. "But I don't want Luna to get used to having me around. I move a lot, and I don't have a lot of connections that aren't brief." Her meaning was clear as she slid her fingertip over Angie's lower lip.

Angie's breath trembled in her chest, and a wave of desire crested over her. "That makes sense," she whispered. She took a step back and put her hand on her chest as though it could slow her racing heart. "But maybe you could finish out the day with us? If you leave now..." She couldn't finish the sentence with anything that would make the least bit of sense. She simply didn't want Finn to go.

Finn leaned against the countertop, putting more distance between them. "Tonight it is."

Angie led the way downstairs to the cinema room, where Luna already had a movie ready to go. She didn't care what they were watching. Finn was sexy, intelligent, mysterious, and kind. She was also unavailable. Which was fine, of course, since Angie wasn't looking for something of substance. But damn, what a woman.

Chapter Eleven

FINN GOT OFF THE plane and took in a long, deep lungful of hot, humid air. It had been nearly two decades since she'd last breathed in her home, and she couldn't deny it felt good.

Once she had her baggage, she headed to the main lobby and instantly saw Pablo watching for her. He leapt forward, hugged her hard, and then grabbed her case.

"I can't believe you really came." He led the way to the parking lot.

"Cumplir, primo."

"I know we have an obligation, but your abuela would have understood if you didn't come for the funeral. Have you been keeping the nine?"

The nine days of mourning. Finn had felt each one in her soul. "I missed a day of silence, but I kept the grieving. There are two more days of release. I figure I might as well do them here."

He tossed her bag in the trunk and waved her into the car. "We'll do them together at my place." After pulling into traffic, he glanced at her. "Anyone else know you're here?"

She shook her head and didn't say anything, and he simply nodded. He knew her history all too well, and he'd never judge the decisions she made because of it.

He chatted all the way to his house, pointing out things that had changed, talking about people who hadn't, and basically making her feel like this trip wasn't a terrible idea. He was right, her abuela would have understood. But she owed it to her memory. The moment the funeral was over, she'd be back on a plane to California.

Once they were at Pablo's, a large home with a view of the ocean in the distance, she took her bag upstairs and collapsed on the bed, exhausted from a combination of the nine-hour flight and her rollercoaster emotions.

When she woke it was dark, and the smell coming from downstairs brought back a flood of memories. As she went down, she noticed the photos on the wall. Many were of her and Pablo together, and there were even a few of them with her abuela. Tears blurred her vision, and her chest ached.

"Come on," Pablo said from where he was looking at her. "Food."

She joined him in the kitchen and breathed in over the pot. "Abuela's stew."

He nodded and held up a spoon for her to taste it.

"Just like her. Salty, hearty, and warm." She brushed tears away. "She gave you her recipe?"

He lifted an old recipe card off the counter. "She said you wouldn't have the patience, and no one else deserved it." He placed it reverently into a recipe box.

"She was right." Finn settled at the table and rested her chin in her hands. "Thanks for making it tonight."

He dished the seven-meat stew into bowls and placed them on the table, along with thick slices of bread. "Two more days of letting go. No one needs to do that more than you."

She raised an eyebrow. "Something to say?"

"Nah. I'm just saying she was your only tie to this place. Now she's gone, maybe you can let go of some of the baggage your parents gave you."

"Losing her has nothing to do with what they *gave* me." She tore at a chunk of bread. "This is nearly as good as hers."

"It'll never be the same."

They spent the next few hours reminiscing about their childhood. Days spent playing in the sea, trying to find the best seashells, running through the fragrant outdoor markets, and telling ghost stories with friends in the old, abandoned cemetery. Her abuela was the lynchpin to every story, always there with a hug, a cuff upside the head when they did something dumb, or a shoulder when they were feeling lost.

"Did you read her letter?" Pablo asked, passing her another beer.

"I can't. Not yet. Maybe after the funeral." It was sitting alone in the middle of her coffee table, a harbinger of goodbyes and loss. Her abuela's final words, the only ones she'd ever get. Once she read them, it was real.

"Okay. Tell me how things are going in the land of stars."

It was on the tip of her tongue to give a glib answer, to say everything was the same as always. But it wasn't. "I've met someone. Kind of."

It was amazing his neck didn't snap, he looked up so fast. "You meet a lot of people. You mean, met-met? Like, someone you want more than ten minutes of bliss with?"

"Ten minutes? You're such a guy. I take far more time than that, primo." She grinned as he rolled his eyes. "And I don't know. I like her a lot, which means I've avoided seeing her for the last few days. Plus, she has a kid, a really great kid."

"And that complicates things even more." He tapped his beer bottle to hers. "It's good you're opening yourself to more. You deserve that."

"You know I don't settle in one place for long. And I wouldn't want to drag her into my history."

"Yeah, I get that. But you've put all that behind you. Changed your name, moved far away, cut ties. That life wouldn't touch your new one unless you allowed it." He tilted his head to look at the blanket of stars above them.

"But what if it did? What if he found me? Came around and messed things up again?" She shuddered at the thought.

"Then you'd deal with it."

"She's a celebrity. Bodyguards, paparazzi, media. The whole

thing. It could blow my life to pieces."

He whistled softly. "When you put it that way, yeah, you should find someone else. Some hermit who likes dark rooms and shuns people. Like you."

She tossed a beer cap at him. "I'm not a hermit. I go out all the time."

"Going to a coffee shop and hanging out watching birds you don't care about isn't going out." He stood and stretched. "Are you going to the mass tomorrow?"

"Nah. I thought I'd go down to the beach and have a mass of my own." Walking down memory lane had made her realize how much time they'd spent there. Not to mention, she didn't want to chance being recognized. Granted, she looked completely different than when she'd left, but still. The old fear was unshakable, having become a permanent part of her soul.

"Want company? I've done the others. No one will notice I'm not there for this one."

"I think I'd rather go alone, if that's okay." She hesitated and then looked up at him. "Has he been to all the masses?"

"All of them. He's making a big show of observing the nine, and he's dragging your sisters along too. The newspaper mentions what he's doing each day, and who's invited to the house every night." He nudged her leg with his bare foot. "You sure you want to know?"

"No." She tugged on his big toe. "But if he's in your life, even in a small way, I need to know. I want to know you're safe."

"No one can hurt me." He flexed his biceps and made her laugh. "The funeral is at two in the afternoon day after tomorrow. What's your plan?"

"Do you remember the crypt with the weird angel on it? The one holding a knife in one hand?"

He nodded, looking into the distance as though to picture it.

"I'm pretty sure it has a view of the family crypt. I can stay behind it and watch from there. No one should see me." She'd already planned it out, along with what route she'd take if anyone approached. "After, I'll take a taxi straight to the airport."

"That's dumb."

She blinked. "What?"

"You'll have your luggage with you, estúpida. You think no one will notice someone with a suitcase in a cemetery? You'll draw attention. At least take a taxi back to my place and then to the airport."

She laughed. "I hadn't thought of that. Not like you vacation at the cemetery, is it?" She stood and hugged him. "What would I do without you?"

"You'd live in Hollywood and date celebrities you shouldn't date while watching fucking birds." He squeezed her tight. "I'm going to bed. See you whenever tomorrow."

Left alone on the porch, she listened to the sound of Latin music drifting on the night air along with the hot sea breeze. The DR wasn't so different from California in a lot of ways. And yet, there was always the pull of where she'd come from, the desire to see the land and cities that had formed her.

But it wasn't worth it. This would be the last time she set foot in this country if she had any say in the matter.

***

The day of the funeral Finn lay in bed staring at the ceiling until Pablo knocked and came in.

"This fucking tie. Help."

She rolled out of bed and straightened out the mess he'd made of the silk tie she'd bought him years ago, after she'd sold her first book. "You look nice."

"I look like the Hulk dressed as a penguin." He tugged at the tie, and she slapped his hand away.

"Tell her goodbye for me, would you?" Tears slid down her cheeks as they'd been doing all day, and she didn't bother to wipe them away. She didn't need to be tough here. She didn't need to be anything or anyone other than who she was right in this moment.

"Tell her yourself. I love you, prima. Let me know you're back safe in LA." He hugged her for a long moment. "Stop getting snot on my suit." He kissed her forehead and left.

She showered and felt marginally better, then dressed in a simple black suit. She gathered a candle, a blanket, and a bottle of rum, and then took a taxi to the rear gates of the cemetery. Hundreds of people were gathered along the pathway to the family crypt. A line of cars made its way slowly toward the final destination, and she pressed hard against the crypt she was hiding behind as she recognized him in the lead car.

Her father. Evil personified, playing a grieving son to a woman who'd been cherished and revered for nearly a hundred years. Most people knew she wanted nothing to do with him and hadn't for a long time.

Tears dropped onto dusty marble as she watched him get out of the car and stand beside the open crypt, a dark passageway that would take her abuela away from her forever. From the car behind his, her three sisters emerged. All dressed in their best, they were so much older than she remembered. She'd missed so much of their lives, but she made a point of never asking Pablo about them. They were part of her past. The moment she'd left, Finn had cut those familial strings like silk webbing.

Her sisters followed their father, and the crowd surged around them, cutting them from view. Finn knelt on the blanket and lit the candle as the prayers began to filter above the sound of the singing and wailing. She poured some rum into the dirt for her abuela, and then took a long drink herself, liking the way it burned a line of fire through her.

Singing rose and fell, crying filled the air, and then they slid the shiny white coffin into place. As it disappeared, Finn felt a piece of herself slide in with it. She spotted Pablo close to the crypt, and he turned and looked at her, tilting his head to show his sorrow, before turning away again so he didn't draw attention to her.

She rested her head against the strange angel's marble feet, letting her tears wash away the dirt. It was over, and it was time to go back to the life she'd built. She gathered her things and took a quiet route back toward the rear gate. A sound made her turn, and she froze.

Watching from behind another crypt were two women, one tall, one short. The short one had graying hair, but Finn would recognize the shawl she wore anywhere. A shawl her grandmother had made.

For her mother.

She made a strangled sound, unable to form a coherent word, and the women turned toward her. There was a moment, a single breath, where the short one's eyes grew wide, and then the other one yanked at her and pulled her away around the crypt.

Finn stumbled forward, dodged around crypt after crypt, but they were gone as if they'd never been. She leaned against the wall of an ancient tomb, long forgotten.

Could it be true? Could her mother be alive?

***

Surreal. It was the only word she could think of to describe how she was feeling. The way everything was moving slower. The way sounds were muted like her ears were stuffed full of wilting flower petals.

In an effort to get some sense of normal, she opened her laptop. There were two emails that eased the tightness in her chest. One was from Luna, and one was from Angie. She opened Luna's first.

"You haven't been at the coffee shop. Mom says you're probably at your abuela's funeral and I shouldn't bother you. She also says I should find friends my own age, which is dumb. Anyway. Bye, I guess."

Finn had been keeping her distance, but it wasn't just because she couldn't get attached. She'd been concentrating on this trip and getting some work done before she left, so she hadn't been in touch. Checking in with anyone hadn't been on her to-do list in years. But damn it, she didn't want to hurt a kid who simply wanted someone around who understood her.

"Sorry, young diviner of historical mysteries. Your maternal parent is correct. I've been on a sojourn to my homeland to see someone I love taken to the realms of forever dreams. Upon my return, I expect caffeination to resume, along with our now formidable battles of the tiles. I shall make contact whence I land. Forget not your strength and ambitions. Your servant, Finn McGilliCuddy of the Highland Muses."

She hoped that would suffice to let Luna know she wasn't alone. Her finger hovered over Angie's email. That situation had potential, and potential meant complications, and complications could mean loss.

Still, she opened it.

"Dear Finn, I know things got a little heated the other night, and I have to say, I really enjoyed it. I know you said you're not available for anything serious, and honestly, neither am I. I'll be shooting again soon, and my time won't be my own. But I could really use a friend, and I think maybe you could too. What would you say to spending more time together? No strings attached. Just food and conversation with a bit of attraction thrown in. I hope you'll consider it. And I hope your trip allowed you to say the goodbyes you needed to. I'm a good listener, if you need one. Love, Angie."

Finn blew out a breath. Damn. Food, conversation, and attraction were usually exactly how she spent her brief encounters with women. The fun, sexy banter with Angie had made her crazy in a good way, but it wasn't a good idea to take it any further. And with everything going on with her abuela, she'd forgotten to figure out the situation with Luna's bullying. Some mentor figure she made.

She closed the laptop without answering Angie's email. Luna

would tell her she'd emailed back and for now, that needed to be enough. There was something about the pair that brought up old memories of family, of love and laughter.

Family.

Her hands shook as she lifted her bag to her shoulder and boarded the plane. She'd meant to leave all the complications in her life behind. But trust life to throw everything in a blender just when you thought the drink was finished.

Chapter Twelve

Angie was glad for Luna's sake that Finn had responded. She'd been despondent when Finn hadn't been at the coffee shop for several days. Motherly instinct kicked in, and she wanted to tell Finn off, but how could she? Finn didn't owe them anything, and she'd made it clear that connections weren't her thing. That meant she needed to put a stop to their friendship in order to protect Luna.

But at the simple happiness in Luna's expression, she knew she couldn't do it. The fact that Finn hadn't responded to Angie's email spoke volumes though. Whatever attraction was between them would remain buried, and that was for the best. Disappointment wrapped itself around her ribs and made it hard to breathe whenever she thought of the way Finn's eyes darkened with desire and the way she ran her hand through her hair like some kind of sexy model for the next hot Latin lesbian calendar.

She set aside the script she'd been studying and went outside for some fresh air. Or as fresh as it could be in southern California. The palm trees swayed and wispy white clouds slid slowly across the azure sky. She breathed deeply and flexed her toes in the grass. How long had it been since she'd spent time with someone who wasn't in the business in some way? Even the few people she counted as friends were other actors.

Music filtered down from Luna's room, making Angie smile. She'd loved that Joan Jett song once upon a time. The rebellious, intense singer had made Angie think she could be a rebel too.

Some rebel. Not only had she become the actress her parents had insisted she be, she'd become a typecast good girl. This new role could change all that. She headed back inside and curled up on the sofa again.

"Finn's back!" Luna shot past, her backpack jingling with the sack of nickels inside. "See you later."

Karen gave a little wave as she followed Luna out, car doors slammed, and then Angie was alone. How was it that a house could feel so utterly empty? She rested her head on a throw pillow and then jumped up and grabbed her phone.

"Hey. Is it wine time?"

"It was wine time two years ago, but I guess that's given it time to breathe," Barb said. "Time?"

Angie gave a quiet sigh of relief. Barb Berridge had been her closest friend for years, but they'd both been too busy lately for any kind of hanging out. "Now?"

"Consider it uncorked and waiting. See you soon." Barb hung up without another word.

Angie didn't bother with her hat or sunglasses since Barb's house was even more well-guarded than her own, and Barb almost never went out in public. Within twenty minutes, Angie pulled up to the security box and pressed the buzzer, and the gate swung open.

Barb's doorman waved her in and directed her toward the smaller of the living rooms, and when she entered, Barb jumped up and pulled her into a tight hug.

"Your hair smells amazing," she said, taking a long, loud sniff.

"Some kind of honey shampoo my daughter's new nanny ordered for us. She says it's all the rage."

"Probably made from the hair of baby monkeys dipped in candlewax," Barb said, leading her to the thick, comfy sofas. "Or, alternatively, it's nicely scented dish soap with an elegant label. Horseshit, either way."

"Nice smelling horseshit." Angie accepted the glass of wine and murmured her approval. "Tell me about Norway."

Conversation flowed as if it hadn't been interrupted by two

years and multiple continents. Angie's shoulders dropped, and she laughed at the tales Barb shared about her co-stars.

"He then proceeded to tell everyone they needed to look away whenever he was around. They weren't allowed to make eye contact because it would wreck his flow." Barb snorted. "His flow of self-important megalomania, maybe."

Angie shook her head. "Some of these people are really out of touch, aren't they? Chrissie Kicks made them deck out her trailer in diamond-studded leather. I heard someone say the so-called diamonds were plastic from the local craft store, but she was too dim to know the difference."

"We're insane for staying in this business." Barb topped up her wine. "Any news in the getting laid department?"

Angie groaned and let her head fall back onto the couch. "I wish. I thought there might be a chance with someone, but it isn't going anywhere."

"Do tell. Who is the foolish woman not in your bed yet?"

"Her name is Finn Montoya." Angie opened her eyes because picturing Finn made her twitchy. "She's a friend of Luna's."

"Gross." Barb frowned at her. "Explain, please?"

Angie told her the whole strange tale, and then laughed at Barb's expression of bemusement. "Weird, I know. But Luna—"

"Is amazing and her own soul." Barb nodded. "I'm ordering Indian food before we get sloshed and forget we're just friends."

Angie held up her glass in acknowledgement. Barb had often joked about them becoming an item, but she knew full well that Angie's taste lay in butch women. Barb was classic Hollywood. Painfully thin, she also had long hair and was as feminine as Angie. Granted, Hollywood would find them socially acceptable, but Angie wanted someone who balanced her, not someone who was like her.

Someone like Finn.

"So, let me get this straight," Barb said, sliding back into her position on the couch. "This insanely sexy Latin woman tells you she thinks you're hot, but then disappears on you. You know nothing about her. Not what she does for a living, not anything about her family."

"Zero. She has no online presence that I can find. No social media accounts of any kind."

"Dude." Barb took a sip of wine and looked at Angie seriously over the rim. "You've let her into your house? She could be a serial killer. Or worse, an undercover pap."

Angie laughed. "It's not good that I get why one is worse than the other." She bit her lip as she pictured Finn laughing with Luna. "If you spent time with her, you'd understand. There's something about her."

Barb's eyebrows raised. "You sound genuinely interested."

Angie sighed. "I was. But she shot me down, and it's clear she's not interested. I'm just glad she hasn't let Luna down the same way."

Barb nodded at the staff member who brought in their food and set it on the table. "I can't say I get it, but at least Luna is happy." She handed Angie her carton of dahl. "But I still think you should get back on the horse."

"Because there are so many eligible and out lesbians in our world?"

"Your Finn proves that you don't need to date within our world."

Your Finn. Why did that sound so good? "I think she's a one-off. It's not like I can just go ask someone out."

Barb inclined her head. They both knew how hard it was to find real friendship, let alone an actual romantic attachment, as movie stars.

"What about you? Who's your newest playmate?" Angie asked as she calculated the calories in her dahl.

"I had a fling with Robyn Keegan during our last shoot. We both knew it was temporary and that made it fun." Barb shrugged. "I don't miss her."

"A good indication of a fling." Briefly, Angie wondered what a fling with Finn would feel like. Would she miss her after? Hell, she missed her now and nothing had happened between them.

They moved off the topic and on to others, catching up as only good friends can, with plenty of tangents, sarcasm, shared frustrations, and talk of aging in an unforgiving career. By the time Angie got up to leave, she felt a million times better.

She hugged Barb to her. "Thank you. It can be really easy to forget you're not alone out there."

Barb held her at arm's length. "Never. We need to make more time to see each other." She hesitated. "And you know, maybe you should give this Finn a little nudge. Sometimes that's all it takes for someone to know they're really wanted."

The swift but unmistakable sadness flitted through her eyes, and Angie ached for her. But not enough to pretend to feel something she didn't. She kissed Barb's cheek. "Let's get together again before I start filming."

Barb nodded and stepped back into the house, the light making it hard to see her expression. "I'm around whenever you want me."

The drive home was accompanied by soft, whirling thoughts that bounced off one another. Should she invite Finn over again? Ask her to dinner? Just one more try, and if Finn wasn't interested, then she'd move on. Was it unfair to Barb to keep their friendship going, knowing that she had more than platonic feelings for Angie?

When she got home, it was silent but this time it was the silence of other people being in the house. It was hard to describe, that sense that other people were breathing, dreaming, being, even though they were nowhere to be seen. It was comforting.

She cracked open Luna's door and smiled. Luna had fallen asleep with her small lamp on, a thick atlas askew on the comforter beside her. Angie closed the book, set it on the desk, and took the moment to really look at her. She was so small, so fragile-looking when she was asleep and unguarded. Without the preteen attitude, she looked like the vulnerable child Angie still thought of her as. A poster of some Greek goddess caught her eye, and she looked around. She hadn't been in Luna's room recently, wanting to respect her privacy.

Copies of *Archaeology Today* magazine were piled on her desk. Picture frames held photos of the seven ancient wonders of the world. Some of the T-shirts she'd created were pinned to the wall with thumbtacks. A quote about archaeology being the key to understanding all of humanity was stenciled around the window.

There were no posters of boy bands, or girl bands, or pop stars. This room was uniquely Luna, and she needed to let her child be exactly who she was. As Angie softly closed the door to Luna's room, she wondered if she'd ever know who she was the way her daughter knew herself. It was an uncomfortable thought, one she pushed away. Tonight, she'd dream of Finn. Tomorrow, she'd deal with reality.

Chapter Thirteen

THE WHITE ENVELOPE SAT stark against the wood coffee table. Finn had moved everything else off it so only the letter from her abuela held court. It seemed almost offensive to have anything else near it. The last words she'd ever get.

Her phone buzzed with a text, and she scrambled for it, desperate for anything to pull her attention from haunted memories and questions she wasn't sure she wanted answers to.

I'll be at Urth at 2 to kick your butt.

A small smile tugged at her lips, the first for days. She'd let Luna know she was back, but she had yet to contact Angie. Everything felt like too much right now, but Luna's innocent presence was a balm to soothe her weary soul.

I wish you Godspeed in your quest, young warrior. But I shall pull no punches.

Leaving the letter right where it was, she gathered her things and left the house. It had waited this long; it could wait a little longer. Maybe forever.

Luna was already sitting at Finn's usual table when she arrived, and Delia nodded toward her as she made Finn's drink.

"It's good to see Luna talking to someone other than her nanny." She grimaced as she looked toward Karen, seated far closer than Helen used to sit. "There's something about that one. I don't like her."

"Are you going to spike her drink with some herbal flower thing that wouldn't leave a trace?" Finn opened a bag of absurdly expensive chocolate almonds and popped one in her mouth.

"If I told you, I'd have to put it in your drink too." Delia winked and handed over her drink, complete with an ornate mandala in the foam.

"I'd like to live through today, so mum's the word. If she goes down, I know nothing." She took her large mug over to the table and gave Karen a quick smile, making sure not to maintain eye contact for more than a second or two.

"You're late." Luna didn't look up from the notebook she was scribbling in.

"LA traffic is a force unto itself. I'll never really understand how it creates a cosmic void of time while standing still." Finn relaxed into the seat and sipped her drink. "How's school?"

Luna flinched and her gaze darted to Karen, who could probably hear them from where she sat scrolling through her phone. "Fine."

"Fine as in, I love being there and never want to go home, or fine as in, I wish they'd all get sucked into a fairytale, never to be seen again."

"Option two." Luna tapped on Finn's notebook. "Can I draw something?"

Finn raised her eyebrows but opened the book to a fresh page before pushing it in front of her. She watched as Luna flipped back a few pages, looked at Finn's doodles, then proceeded to make her own, very much in the style of Finn's creations.

One tall stick figure had a deep frown and fists raised to fight. The other, a much smaller figure, cowered away from her, skateboard in one hand, the other raised to ward off a strike. Finn watched silently as Luna drew, occasionally wiping away tear drops on the paper.

She finished, slammed it shut, and shoved it back to Finn. "Thanks."

"Mmm." What could she say with Karen sitting there? What could she say at all? She needed to tell Angie, as things were clearly out of control. She caught Delia's eye and tilted her head toward Karen. "How's your mom?"

"Why did you disappear for so long?" Luna countered. "You didn't say last time, and I didn't want to force it out of you."

Before Finn could answer, Delia walked past them to Karen. "Hey, sweetie. I'm really sorry, but I've got a customer coming in soon who absolutely insists this is his table. He won't sit anywhere else. Would you mind taking that one instead? Thanks." Her tone brooked no argument, and she picked up Karen's mug and muffin, already taking them to a table where Finn and Luna couldn't be overheard. Karen looked suitably bemused but did as she was asked. Delia gave Finn a wink and squeezed Luna's shoulder on her way back behind the counter.

"I had to go to a funeral." Finn's chest ached at the admission.

"Your abuela's." Luna nodded, looking thoughtful. "Was it hard? Did you cry? You look too tough to cry."

"I look tough?" Finn flexed her biceps and then sighed as she dropped her arms. "Yes, I cried, and yeah, it was really hard. But tough people can cry too, you know? Being sad doesn't make you less tough."

Luna's gaze was sharp as she stared at Finn. "Did you see your family?"

An image of her father flashed in front of her, and she shut her eyes. "I'm not close to my family." She opened her eyes and tapped the notebook. "What are we going to do about this?"

"Move to another school. Drop out and home school." Luna shrugged. "I have options."

Finn nodded slowly and sipped her coffee. "Options are good. But not running is better." She'd never felt like such an enormous hypocrite in her life. Who was she to tell someone not to run? A bully was a bully, after all.

"Why is not running better?" Luna glared at her.

"Because it sets a bad precedent. You run from this, take the easier road, and the next time you face a bully, and you will because the world is full of them, you'll search for an easier road again. But what if there isn't one? What if it means leaving your job, your wife, your country?"

Luna leaned forward. "Is that why you left the DR?"

Finn shook her head. "Nope. Not getting sidetracked. Nice try."

Luna huffed and sat back, her arms crossed. "So what do I do?"

"You're not going to like it." Finn waited until Luna gave her an impatient look. "You need to tell your mom and get some adults involved. The movies will show you standing up to bullies and taking a beatdown, and then everything is great, and everyone is friends. But that doesn't always happen. Sometimes it means that other bullies join in the fun. So, we get the adults involved and put a stop to it."

"I told you, the other kids will call me a snitch." Luna's eyes had welled with tears, and she brushed them away.

"I'm going to ask you a harsh question." Finn took a deep breath. They'd established a certain level of trust and bluntness. She couldn't back down from it now. "Do you have a lot of friends among the ones who'd call you a snitch? Do you have friends who would dump you for it?"

Luna's tears ran freely now, and she tucked her chin against her chest. "No," she said so softly Finn barely heard it.

"Then fuck them."

Luna's head shot up, her eyes wide. "What?"

"You heard me. Fuck what they think and how they'd respond. If they were your *actual* friends, maybe it would be different. But they aren't, so who cares what they think? You do what you need to do to get through school so you can go out and be the best damn version of yourself you can be. You'll leave them in the dust you'll send flying as you dig for the answers of the centuries."

Luna began to giggle, and then she began to laugh. "You're totally not supposed to talk to kids that way, Finn."

Finn winced and leaned forward. "Maybe let's not tell your mom the *exact* words I used."

Luna dried her eyes on her Iggy Pop T-shirt. "On one condition."

"Oh, you're bargaining now, eh?" Finn could breathe again now that Luna's tears had stopped. Seeing kids cry was like wounding a puppy.

"You have to come over and be with me when I tell her." Luna gave Delia a quick smile when she set down a fresh hot chocolate.

"Nooo. No way. I'm not facing your mom's wrath when she finds out that I knew and she didn't. I like my arms and legs right where they are."

Luna's expression fell, and she pushed up her glasses. "I don't think I'm brave enough to tell her, Finn. She gets all protective and crazy. You can keep her calm."

"Why on earth would you think that?" She hadn't even responded to Angie's email. Now she was going to sit with Luna while her kid told her she was being bullied. How would that make a parent feel? Not great, probably.

"Please? She really likes you, and she's missed you too. I know it. Please?" Luna held her hands in a prayer position.

It was a bad idea. Unquestionably. "Okay. Fine. But you owe me one."

Luna jumped up from the table. "Let's do it now before I freak out and run away from home instead."

Finn slid slowly from her seat and gathered her things. "If she dismembers me, promise you'll bury my pieces somewhere nice. Don't just throw them in a river or something."

Luna took her hand and waved at Karen, who followed quickly. "I promise. And when the rosebushes grow over you, I'll be sure to talk to them."

***

By the time they pulled up in front of Angie's house, Finn was certain her heart was going to give out. This was why she didn't get involved with people. They had *things*. They had dramas, and needs, and messy emotions that she didn't have time for. Why hadn't she said no to Luna? Told her she was strong enough to handle it herself? Or, worse yet, simply sent Angie a text letting her know what was going on? Wasn't that what other responsible adults would do?

Luna waited on the front steps, her hands on her hips. Karen waited beside her, looking confused and a little irritated. Messy. Complicated. Emotional.

Finn sighed down to her toes and got out of the truck. "I'm coming."

She followed Luna and Karen through to the living room, where Angie sat curled up on the sofa, a massive chunk of paper on her lap. She looked up in surprise when they entered.

"Hey. I thought you had skate practice today. And I didn't expect to see you again." There was no mistaking the tinge of hurt in Angie's tone as she looked at Finn.

Karen settled herself on a barstool, clearly not about to be left out of whatever was happening. Luna sat on the coffee table opposite Angie, leaving Finn to stand there awkwardly, her hands shoved in her pockets.

"Mom, I have something to tell you, but you *can't* freak out."

Angie looked from Luna to Finn. "What's going on?" She pushed the mountain of papers away and moved to face Luna. "Are you okay? Has something happened?"

Luna looked over her shoulder at Finn, who gave her a nod of encouragement. She turned back to Angie. "You have to promise not to freak out. Promise, or I won't tell you."

Finn winced and looked down at her shoes. That kind of bargain didn't go over well with parents, generally. She didn't need to have shoved a kid out of her hoo-ha to know that.

"Luna, you're scaring me. What's going on? And why is Finn here?" Angie started to get up, but Luna grabbed her hand and tugged her back down.

"She's here for moral support and to make sure you don't get nutty." Luna bit her lip, pushed up her glasses, and took a shaky breath. "There's a bully at school. She keeps threatening to beat me up, and I've been leaving school to get away from her, and Finn saw me and told me I had to tell you and that I can't run from the bullies and fuck the people who think I'd be a snitch and that sometimes adults have to get involved and the stupid kids don't matter anyway, and I don't want to get beat up."

Luna finally took a breath, and the tears dripped from her chin.

Angie blinked rapidly as though taking it all in, then she pulled Luna into a fierce hug. They stayed that way for a long time, and then Angie pulled back and wiped Luna's tears away. "Honey, if I go crazy, if I freak out, if I go nutty, it's because I love you and no one, not a single being on this planet, has the right to make you feel this way." She looked over Luna's shoulder at Finn. "And I think we need to discuss appropriate language when talking to a twelve-year-old."

"It isn't Finn's fault." Luna sniffled and wiped her nose on her sleeve. "She told me I needed to tell you, but I didn't want to."

Angie brushed the hair from Luna's eyes. "I understand. I really do. But I'm glad you've told me now so we can deal with it together, okay?"

Luna nodded. "Can I go now?"

"Sure."

Finn gently returned Luna's hug before Luna headed upstairs. Only when they heard her door shut did Angie stand and round on Karen. "Did you know about this?"

Finn took a step back, knowing full well she was next. To her credit, Karen didn't look intimidated.

"I had no idea, Angie. She doesn't talk to me a lot yet. We're still getting to know each other. I know she doesn't really hang out with other kids, but it doesn't seem to bother her." She glanced toward Finn. "She's always more interested in what Finn says and does than she is any kids from school."

Fantastic. Finn got ready to run for the door. Hopefully she wouldn't have to dodge anything being thrown at her head.

"How long have you known about this, Finn?" Angie's direct

gaze was concerned but didn't look overtly hostile yet.

"A week or so." When it looked like the hostility was about to rise, Finn held up her hands. "I told her if she was leaving school, she needed to text me to tell me where she was so someone knew, and I told her she was going to have to tell you—"

"*Leaving school*? Karen, how did you not know? How did she slip past everyone? And *she* was going to have to tell me?" Angie stepped closer. "She told you, an adult, and you made a conscious decision *not* to share the information with me? That my daughter was in trouble, and that she wasn't where she could be watched over?"

Finn could hear the voiceover of the documentary narrator, describing the way a mother lion was about to close in on its kill. "You're right. I'm sorry. She begged me not to tell you, and I didn't want to betray her trust—"

"So you let her go around being bullied and wandering the streets alone?" Angie hissed the words at her, clearly making an effort not to allow Luna to hear her. "You don't think betraying her trust was worth making sure she was safe and could go to school without being threatened?"

Finn bumped up against a wall, and there was nowhere else to go. "Angie, I'm sorry. You're right. It's just that I've been that kid who didn't have anyone to turn to, and I figured it was better that she had at least one grown up she felt she could talk to."

At the strange combination of rage and defeat in Angie's eyes, Finn stopped talking.

Angie stepped back. "I think you should go."

Finn nodded so quickly it hurt her neck. "Agreed." Before she stepped out of the room, she glanced back. "I'm really sorry, Angie. Luna's an amazing kid." She couldn't think of anything more to say, so she gave a small shrug and left.

Once she was back in her truck, she rested her head on the steering wheel. For a moment, it looked like Angie might actually whack her upside the head. As uncomfortable as the situation had been, at least now Luna would get some help. Finn began to grin, and as she threw the truck in drive, she pictured Angie angry. She was so damn sexy. That kind of passion made parts of Finn come alive that had no right making themselves known. Fierce, funny, protective, and insanely hot. Angie had it all.

Finn shook her head. Her dreams were going to be busy tonight, that was for damn sure.

Chapter Fourteen

ANGIE TOOK A DEEP breath as she opened the door to Luna's school. Enough kids from rich families attended the institution that there were double doors with locked entries, and the student gates were locked throughout the day. She couldn't imagine how Luna had found an escape route but wasn't surprised that she had. She'd always been ingenious, even managing to crawl out of her crib as an infant. Angie would find her asleep in a pile of teddy bears.

She smiled at the principal, whose hair was too slick and smile too smug. "Nice to see you, Principal Lowry."

He waved her into a chair and sat in the one beside it, his knees nearly touching hers. "It's been too long, Angie. I'm surprised to see you, though. Luna's grades are exceptional as always."

His cloying aftershave made her want to blow her nose. "I'm afraid I need your assistance. Luna is being bullied."

He tilted his head, the fake shock obvious. "That's terrible. I had no idea."

"It's a girl named Heather."

"Ah." He sat back and nodded. "Heather has been brought to my attention more than once, I'm afraid. But her father is a politician who provides a uniquely large sum of money to this school, so there's isn't much I can do."

Angie stared at him. "You're going to let students get bullied because their father gives you money? Forgive me, but I'm sure that your job is to protect the students, not throw them under the bus because you get paid well."

He held up his hands. "Angie, you have to understand what it costs to run a school like this—"

"I pay Luna's tuition. I fully understand how much is coming in." She leaned forward, forcing him to meet her gaze. "And I fully understand that anything at all leaked to the press about students not feeling safe enough to go to school here would rather diminish the amount coming in." She stood, smoothing down her skirt. "I suggest you take care of this, or I promise I will make a scene."

He was sputtering apologies and assurances at her back as she left his office and walked down the hall. Poor Luna, who had felt the need to escape school because the school wouldn't protect her from a known bully. It hurt that she'd felt the need to bring Finn as backup, and as furious at Finn as she'd been, eventually she'd done the right thing and gotten Luna to turn to her mother for help.

She sighed, her hands tight on the steering wheel as she navigated the streets to the studio. What would she do if the principal didn't follow through? Home school seemed like an option, but Luna was already so isolated from her peers. Taking her out of school would make that even worse.

She entered the dimly lit studio and headed toward the dressing room. She was greeted with plenty of kindly hellos and someone slid a matcha tea into her hand. They were doing table reads today, and she remembered that it would be the day she'd meet Elodie Fontaine. It was unusual that the director wanted them in real makeup for just a table read, but he said it would provide authenticity right from the start. The real-world problems faded as she moved into work mode. More than anything, she needed to make a good first impression. Elodie was well-known for being a perfectionist, and this role would be different for her too. She liked action films where she got to do her own stunts, and this movie was definitely far from that.

The door opened and she walked in, and the fan girl in Angie almost squealed. She stood and held out her hand. "Hi, I'm Angie. It's so great to finally meet you."

Elodie's hand was warm and firm in hers. "I loved *Secret Passions*. It was brave of you to take on the topic. I know it was a rom-com, but anything dealing with addiction is still a big deal. You handled it really well."

Angie almost couldn't think of a response. "Wow. To get a compliment like that from you is incredible. Thank you."

Elodie nodded and took the chair near Angie's as they both surrendered to hair and makeup. "I think we're going to rock this film together, Angie."

Angie had to stay silent as the makeup artist moved around her mouth, but then she said, "I'm so glad you're doing this film, but I have to admit, I don't fully understand it. You're not old enough to be my mother. You could barely be my older sister."

Elodie laughed, low and husky. "I read the role and had to have it. The makeup folks will make sure I age prematurely."

Angie concentrated on the makeup and wardrobe, although Elodie was the kind of eye candy that made it hard to think past her libido. Tall, butch, muscular, confident... If she weren't already happily married, Angie might have considered making a play for her. An image of Finn's dark eyes and smooth brown skin played out behind her eyelids as she closed her eyes for the makeup artist, and not having a chance with Elodie didn't seem nearly as disappointing anymore.

The rest of the day flew past. The table reading went beautifully, and all the comments were constructive, with the cast falling into a flow that was unusual with people who hadn't worked together before. Angie pulled out of the parking lot riding the buzz she so often got from starting a new project. This one was going to signal a new stage of her career, and the notion was exhilarating. Finn's assertion that she preferred movies that made her think had hit a sore spot.

And just like that, the buzz faded into a dull thrum as her daily life came rushing back. At a stoplight she dug her phone out of her bag, which she'd put in and not touched all day so she wasn't pulled from her flow. There were three voice messages.

The first was from Luna's principal, who wanted to let her know that he'd been in touch with Heather's family and would let her know the outcome of their meeting. The second was from Karen to tell her that Luna was spending extra time with her skateboarding instructor.

The third made her pull into a parking lot so she could pay closer attention.

"Hey, Angie. It's Finn. I hope it's okay that I asked Luna for your number. I wanted to apologize. I overstepped, and I should have told you right away. It's a good thing I'm not an actual parent, huh?" There was a pause. "Anyway, I'm sorry, and I hope we're good. Bye."

Angie played it again, just to listen to the sexy tone of Finn's voice. It was nice that it wasn't a text message. This way she could listen to it whenever she wanted to. She laughed at herself as she pulled back onto the road. How pathetic, to listen to the voicemail of someone apologizing. Their last conversation had been anything but friendly, and she was reminded of something Finn had let slip. What had she meant when she'd said she'd been the kid who had no one to turn to? Was that why she had an affinity with Luna?

There were so many questions and not nearly enough answers. It was time to change that.

***

Angie opened the door to Urth Café and the cool air made her shiver. Autumn was closing in, and although that didn't mean a whole lot in LA, it did mean the difference between the outdoor heat wasn't as marked as the indoor cool.

There was a line, and that gave her time to watch Finn, whose head was bent as she wrote furiously in a large notebook. A lock of hair kept falling over her eye and she kept shoving it back, but her pen never stopped moving. Now Angie felt bad. Should she leave her alone since she was so clearly in a zone?

Finn set the pen down and flexed her hand before she glanced up and met Angie's gaze. Her eyebrows rose and she gave a tentative smile, and Angie gave her a genuine one in return.

"Hey, Angie. I was surprised Luna wasn't here playing that weird game with Finn," Delia said as she punched in Angie's drink, along with one she'd ordered for Finn.

"Karen called to say Luna was spending extra time with her skate instructor today." She hadn't thought it strange, but now, she did. It wasn't like Luna to give up her time with Finn. "So I thought I'd come play the weird game with her instead." There was truth to that. Weren't all relationships some kind of game or another?

"Well, good luck. She's barely had her head out of that notebook today." Delia placed the lattes on the counter, both with tree patterns in the foam.

"Do you know what she does for a living?" Angie asked, analyzing the foam and trying not to look interested in the answer. "We haven't gotten around to that yet."

Delia laughed and shook her head. "Nice try. You know as well as I do that she's a spy who likes dressing as a clown for the circus on weekends." She winked and went to help another customer.

Angie shook her head and took the drinks to Finn's table. "I feel like it's bad form to not even tell your barista what you do for a living. That's just plain rude."

"How do you know she doesn't know? Maybe she's in on it. Maybe she's my handler." Finn took a sip of her drink and nodded in thanks.

The notion of handling Finn made Angie twitchy, and she picked up her drink to distract herself from the image.

Neither of them said anything, but Angie felt Finn's gaze like a physical caress, like a kind of fraught foreplay.

Finally, Angie said, "You don't mind silence."

"I don't. I find that truer things are often released into the air after a bit of silence."

"What an interesting idea." Angie tapped the notebook. "Can I see?"

Finn slid it from the table and onto the seat beside her. "Sorry. State secrets."

Angie sighed and rested her chin on her hands. "More secrets. Seems like you're full of them."

Finn flinched. "Angie, I really am sorry about Luna—"

"Not what I meant. I mean, you seem to have plenty of your own. We know nothing about you, Finn. Speaking of, why isn't Luna here with you? Did something else happen?"

Finn toyed with her expensive-looking pen. "I texted her and let her know that maybe she should do some stuff other than hang out with me, since you were pretty rightfully pissed at me right now." She glanced at Angie and then back at the pen. "I'm a novelty, and I'm sure it will wear off if she spends time doing other things."

There it was again. That subtle pain that curled under and around Finn's words like a vine. "First of all, you and I both know Luna isn't that type of kid. Second, what did you mean when you said you'd been like her once?" When it looked like Finn was going to blow off the question, Angie took her hand and thrilled a little when Finn interlaced their fingers. "Finn, I'd like to get to know you. Yeah, you made a big mistake by not telling me about Luna's bully. But you also made her come home and tell me about it so I could put a stop to it. And that means something." She squeezed Finn's hand a little tighter, liking the way it felt wrapped around hers. "And yeah, the way you've come into our lives is odd, but this is LA, and that's the way things work here. I like you, and I think under all that mystery is someone I'd like to have around."

Finn's expression was thoughtful, and she didn't let go of Angie's hand. Instead, her thumb ran over Angie's knuckles, making her tingle. Too soon, she gently pulled her hand away.

"I like you too. You're more down to earth than anyone else I've met in this city, and you've got a great kid." She sipped her drink and didn't make eye contact. "But I have my reasons for not talking about myself, Angie. I left behind a life, and people, that needed to be left behind. I don't like bringing them up outside of medical history."

Angie missed holding Finn's hand. "I can respect that."

"Luna said she'd never met her grandparents?" Finn nodded. "Sounds like you understand."

Angie tilted her head. "I have a feeling my story isn't nearly as dramatic as yours. My parents were all about making me a star the moment they thought I was pretty enough. I was doing commercials from the age of four, and they took me to every audition they could walk or talk me into. They became my managers instead of my parents, and any money I made went straight into their bank account." How Angie hated the way thinking of them could still make her shake inside. "When I told them I didn't want to act anymore, that I wanted to be a normal teenager, they managed to get me a movie role in Thailand without even telling me first. The contract had been signed, and I was on a plane."

"That's awful. I'm really sorry. But you kept acting anyway?" Finn sipped her drink, looking over the brim at Angie, her eyes full of empathy.

"That movie in Thailand made my name, and work flooded in. I dealt with my parents and their greed for a few more years, and then I had Luna. Their first reaction was to take photos of her to send to agents." Angie smiled sadly, remembering holding Luna, who was quiet and thoughtful even as a baby. "I told them I was done with them. That Luna and I weren't going to be in their lives any longer. They hassled me, but I put my foot down. I wasn't about to let them do to Luna what they'd done to me."

Finn tilted her head. "But you kept acting," she said again.

Angie shrugged. "I'm good at it. And the truth is, without the pressure they put me under, and with the ability to choose my roles, I really like what I do now. I had a table read today that went amazingly well. Elodie was full of great adv–"

"Elodie Fontaine?" Finn's eyebrows wiggled, and she gave a side grin. "Now that's a woman after my own heart."

What the hell was it with Angie's shots of jealousy when it came to Finn? First her chef, now a co-worker. "I thought you didn't like movies?"

Finn laughed. "I said I like movies that make me think, and she's done a couple that sank in the theater because they were heavy, but they gained a place in my movie library. And I don't think you can be a lesbian and not know who she is. That's simply not allowed."

"Oh, but you can be a lesbian and not know who I am?" Angie giggled at Finn's sheepish expression. "Teasing. You're right, she's a super-high-profile, short-hair gay. I'm a low-profile, femme gay, which is a different beast."

"Hardly a beast." Finn's eyes sparkled, and the sexy turn to her lips was back. "So you're out, but there isn't a lot of press about you and the women you've been with. Why is that? Celebrities aren't usually good at keeping their private lives private."

"Ugh." Angie winced at the taste of her cold latte. "Hold that thought. I need another."

Finn moved so fast she upset the table and had to steady the mugs. "Let me."

She took the half-empty mugs to the counter, and Angie had to fight not to turn to watch her walk. So far they'd had a beautifully uninterrupted chat, and the longer she could keep from being recognized, the better. She kept her eyes on the table and read the brand name on the pen. Visconti. She frowned, trying to remember where she'd seen that brand before. It looked expensive and classy. She'd been writing in a notebook with it.

"Here we go." Finn set the mugs down on the table. "Now, back to your shadowy dating life."

"Nope." Angie tapped the pen. "Normal people don't write in leather embossed notebooks with expensive fountain pens. I read that Elodie gave one of those to her wife as an anniversary gift. I can respect that you don't want to talk about your past. But this is your present. You're a writer, aren't you?"

Finn groaned, but a smile played on her lips. "How do you know I'm not someone who writes classical concertos for the piano and feels most inspired when I do it in a classical way?"

"You also spin words beautifully and artfully." Angie crossed her arms, waiting. "I can hold out for the truth to pop up in silence too."

"Not exactly my words, but close enough." Finn's gaze was searching as she clearly considered what she was going to say. "Yes, I'm a writer. That's how I make my living." She held up her hand when Angie started to speak. "No, I won't tell you what I write. No, you can't read it, and no, I won't tell you what name I write under."

"Why no to all those questions?" Angie asked, the warmth of the coffee nothing compared to the warmth she felt under Finn's gaze.

"Because I'm a hermit writer. I've made an art of it. My agent and my publisher are the only people in the world who know my real identity, and that keeps me safe."

Angie's heart skipped a little at the use of the word *safe*. Finn knew words, and she didn't throw them around with abandon. "Why wouldn't you be safe?"

Finn sighed and pinched the bridge of her nose, her eyes closed tight. "Because of the past I won't talk about."

"Okay. Fine. But why couldn't I read it? Would I think you were a deranged maniac?"

Finn laughed and her shoulders dropped. "Definitely. And that's date four material, at least."

"Ah, so I have to date you to get the goods." Angie grinned when Finn spluttered in her foam.

"Which leads us back to why there's so little about you in the press." Finn raised her eyebrows and nodded affirmatively at her win.

"That's date two material, at least." Angie stood, picked up her handbag, and leaned over to kiss Finn on the cheek. "So you'd better get around to date one."

She walked out, swinging her hips just a little more than usual, knowing full well that Finn was watching. She could see her doing so in the reflection of the glass door, and she turned and winked at her before she opened it. Finn gave her a sexy, crooked grin and ran her hand through her hair.

Trust Finn to get the last word, even when they weren't talking.

Chapter Fifteen

A STARING CONTEST WITH a crow wasn't what Finn thought she'd be doing when she woke up that morning. And yet, here she was, squinting against the sunlight as she fought not to look away. The crow rustled its feathers and chirped out a disgruntled sound that was most likely an insult to do with her tired eyes or rumpled shirt. She was sorely tempted to respond, but a squirrel bounded up the tree, a huge nut in its mouth, and the crow turned its vocal ire on the furry-tailed intruder instead. It hopped to a higher branch and glared down at Finn.

"I win," Finn said. "Ha!"

Gertrude sat heavily on the log beside her, the purple tint in her gray hair reflecting the sun. "Bit of a bust today for the Wingers. Hardly a white-crowned sparrow to be seen, let alone any birds of prey or special tits."

The twelve-year-old alive and well in Finn snorted internally at the idea of special tits. Weren't they all special in their own way? Though Gertrude probably would have found it funny, Finn's humor was out of sorts today. "There's a crow. He's an arrogant cur, though. Thinks he knows it all."

"He probably does. Crows are smart. They know things." Gertrude nodded up at the bird watching them. "He probably knows why you're looking as glum as a piece of chewed-up gum stuck to a horse's hoof."

"I bet he doesn't know that at all. I bet he thinks we're all gangly string beans slowly growing older until we finally end up in the dirt he pulls worms from." That image combined with Gertrude's to create an odd visual image, like a Salvador Dali painting done by a toddler.

"You want to talk about it?" Gertrude's wrinkled hand was light on Finn's leg.

"Nope. I do not. But thank you." She gave Gertrude a quick smile, sure not to maintain eye contact too long. The bird watcher had a way about her, much like the crow. She could see into your soul if you let her look long enough.

They sat together for a while, and Finn found the silent company comforting. Did she want to talk to someone about her messed-up childhood, about her pathological father, about her missing mother, whom she might have seen in a graveyard recently? She did. But talking about things could be dangerous.

"My husband snored like an elephant."

Finn looked over at Gertrude. "Must have made it hard to sleep."

"Forty-six years, he snored so loud they could hear him on the space station." Gertrude pointed at a small bird that shot past. "After I got used to it, I found that it only bothered me if I had other things on my mind. For the most part, I would sleep through it."

Finn wasn't sure how to respond, so she didn't. Sometimes people just wanted someone who would listen.

"It was August, six years ago, when I woke up because it was too quiet. He wasn't snoring." Her gaze stayed on a robin that was hopping around in a pile of leaves. "I've missed that elephant's snoring every day since."

The heartache in Gertrude's tone made Finn's hurt in response. "Seems like we're doomed to have our hearts broken no matter which way we turn. Love someone with your whole heart and feel like a part of you has been ripped away when you lose them. Choose not to love and spend the rest of your life wondering what it would feel like to be someone's moon and stars."

"I'd take losing a limb any day. All those beautiful memories are worth the pain of not having him now. My life with him was like the *Wizard of Oz*. Dull and gray before, a world of color and adventure after." Gertrude stood and brushed off the jeans that hung loose on her thin frame. "Seems to me you need to find your color, Dorothy."

She sauntered off, whistling, and then called to the other bird watchers to head farther up the path, deeper into the woods, in the hopes of seeing something winged and wonderful.

Find my color. Finn thought of the colors surrounding her grandmother's funeral. The color of the shawl the woman in the cemetery had been wearing. The black of her father's eyes. Finn had been trying to get hold of Pablo for the last several days, but he hadn't answered his phone. That wasn't terribly unusual. He was busy and it was often hard to get hold of him. But she needed to ask him about the woman in the cemetery. She needed to read her abuela's letter, but she needed Pablo on the line while she did it. Somehow, she couldn't find the courage to do it alone.

Find my color. The thought brought with it an image of Angie's smile. The way she lit up a room, the way her laugh made rainbows dance across the air. She thought of the way Luna looked at her, head cocked like a curious, wary animal. They were color personified, shifting and moving in the light to display the deeper shades of what it was to be human.

The flirtation with Angie at the coffee shop had been electrifying. Holding her delicate hand, feeling the genuine desire from Angie to know more about her. It had been a long time since someone had wanted to really know Finn. The occasional hook-ups meant only to scratch a sexual itch were never about getting to know one another beyond the biblical sense. Friendships that moved beyond the topics of birds or books were taboo and had been since the moment she'd left her childhood home behind. But Angie and Luna had slipped past her defenses, and it was becoming difficult to want to keep them at arm's length. Hell, she didn't want any length at all coming between her and Angie. But damn the complications of it all.

The temptation to take Angie out on date one was consuming.

Tossing and turning at night, she'd imagined what a date would consist of. What it would mean. But why did it have to mean anything?

Because of Luna. Because Angie wasn't looking for a bit of itch-scratching. Because they were special.

She sighed and tilted her face to the sun. Her phone buzzed in her pocket, and she pulled it out.

Do I constantly have to make the first move? I'm going to get a complex. Most people can't wait to ask me out. A.

Finn grinned, her heart thumping a little harder in response to Angie's text. *You'll find, I think, that I'm not like most people. And now that you've made the first move, I can follow up without fear of blood-curdling rejection. Would you like to have dinner with me tomorrow night?*

She waited, her thumb tap-tap-tapping the side of the phone. This was a bad idea that she desperately wanted to be a good one.

Date one. What time?

Seven-thirty. McDonald's okay?

Perfect. Only if you buy me a happy meal and let me keep the toy. See you tomorrow. Xo.

Finn put her phone back in her pocket and looked up as a shadow crossed her.

"Looks like you might have found yourself a crayon, at least, if that smile is anything to go by." Gertrude squeezed her shoulder. "I'm calling it a day. It's too hot, and the Wingers aren't watching closely enough."

Finn caught Gertrude's hand and tucked it in the crook of her arm as they walked back to the parking lot. "Are you okay?"

Gertrude nodded slowly. "Growing old isn't for the weak, kiddo. You keep going even when it feels like your body is made of old spaghetti covered in grits." She gave a choked, somewhat sad, laugh. "And that's what you look like, too."

Saying anything in response would have been disingenuous, and Finn wasn't one to sugarcoat or deny. Her mother had always said to deny an old person was old was to deny their experience of the world.

"You have my number if you need anything." Finn knew better than to ask if Gertrude wanted help. She had her pride.

"I do, and maybe one day I'll take you up on it." She squeezed Finn's bicep before letting go. "Now, it's time for you to pick up that crayon." She got into her car and waved as she drove away.

Finn lowered the tailgate of her truck and sat on it, swinging her legs as she looked up romantic restaurants in the area. When she settled on one, she called and made a reservation. How long had it been since she'd been on an actual date? The resulting calculation sent anxious butterflies into overdrive. Years. Was she still up to it? Especially with a woman like Angie, who was probably used to the very best of everything.

Finn jumped in her truck and headed toward the gym but another part of the novel she'd been struggling with came to her in a flash, and she flipped a U-turn to head home instead. She parked at an awkward angle and ran into the house, desperate to get the new flood of words onto the page. It didn't matter that it wasn't perfect. It was there, and now she had something she could edit at some point. When she looked up later, the only light in the house came from her computer screen and the streetlamp outside. She'd gotten lost in a flow, and time had sneaked from beneath her tapping fingers.

Stretching, she felt the muscles in her back pop and grind, making her wince. Times like this, she wished she had a dog to walk. Somehow, simply going for a walk in LA felt weird. Not at the beach, though. She changed into a sweatshirt and grabbed her keys. At the last second, she took her abuela's letter from the table and tucked it into her back pocket. If she could get hold of Pablo, the beach might be the perfect place to do some final reading.

The empty stretch of beach off to the side of PCH was perfect. No pier, no long promenade. Just stairs leading down to a large patch of peachy sand. No doubt it was popular with local sunbathers during the day, but now, as the moon stared at its face in the ocean mirror below, the beach was beautifully empty.

She sat in the cold sand and video-called Pablo. He answered, unshaven and with dark circles under his eyes.

"Jesus, primo, you look like shit." Finn leaned forward as though it would help her see him more clearly. "What truck were you dragged behind?"

"The project down on the east end has gone sideways. We've been working day and night to get it back on track." He yawned hard. "Sorry I missed your calls. I'm assuming you're fine, since you're calling me from a fucking beach in California."

"Pablo, what do you remember about my mother's death?" If she hadn't been made nauseous by the question, his expression would have made her laugh.

"What?" The camera shifted as he moved to sit up. "Why would you ask?"

"Just tell me."

He squinted at her. "Probably the same things you do. I remember you weren't allowed to see her while she was sick. Your father kept her in the back room and said it would be too upsetting for us to see her that way. Then she was gone." He rubbed at his eyes and gave another jaw unhinging yawn. "You didn't get to say goodbye."

She pinched the bridge of her nose. That was what she remembered too. "What if I told you I think she's still alive?"

The camera flashed multiple directions until he picked up the phone again. "That's crazy."

"I'm sure I saw her at the cemetery. She was hiding nearby, just like me. She was with some woman who pulled her away." As she said the words out loud, she was sure it was true.

"We had a funeral for her." Pablo's frown created a deep V between his eyebrows, making him look fierce. "Why would your father go to that kind of trouble?"

Finn shrugged. "Why does he do anything? Pride, avarice—"

"What is avarice? Never mind, I don't care. Have you read your abuela's letter yet?"

Finn pulled it from her pocket and waved it in front of the camera. "I was hoping I could do it with you. But you don't think she knew, do you? She wouldn't keep that from me."

He nodded toward the letter. Or, he would have, if he'd been beside her. She knew what he meant.

"Okay." Trembling, she slid her thumb under the flap. The sight of her abuela's neat, steady handwriting made the tears well in her eyes before she read a single word. "I don't think I can do this."

"You don't have to." Pablo's tone was gentle, his expression sympathetic. "But you've never been a coward, Finn."

"Dick." She took a deep breath and began to read aloud in Spanish.

My dearest child,

There are so many things I've wanted to tell you over the years. So many times I would smile and wish I could share a moment or thought with you. Although Pablo knew where you were, I couldn't take the risk of reaching out to you. I know you needed to leave, and I didn't want your bastard father to find out we'd been talking. I'm sure he tapped my phone just in case you ever got in touch, so it's good you didn't. Still, I missed your sharp wit and sharper tongue. You are the grandchild I prayed for, and you should know that I'm so very proud of you. It took great courage for you to escape this place, and I know the world will be better because of it. Pablo gave me your books to read, and I wanted to tell the whole world you were my grandchild. You have made me proud.

I didn't know if I should tell you the next part, and I still don't know if it's wise. But I've lived with the secret too long, and I have to believe that you will be strong enough to know what to do with the information.

My love, your mother did not die of an illness. She died of a broken heart. You see, your father bullied her into marrying him *when she was too young to really know herself. By the time she understood who she was, it was too late. She had you and your sisters to take care of, and your father rarely let her out of his sight. I've always thought it was because he knew her heart resided elsewhere. She'd fallen in love with a woman she met, a politician who often opposed your father. When he found out, he kept her prisoner in her own home and made excuses, so he didn't look bad. He was always a soulless, prideful, evil man.*

She died locked away from her children and the woman she loved. He allowed me to speak to her only once, to convince her to let go of the woman and renew her faithfulness to him. She would no longer be let out without a guard to watch over her. But I told her to run, to hide, to live her life.

Instead, she passed away. I believe she simply gave up. The woman she was in love with disappeared as well, never to be heard from again.

I hope you can forgive me, child. You were too young to deal with this information at the time, and I wanted you to run, to hide, the way your mother should have. You did, and my heart has always been full of joy that you got away. I tell you this story because in my heart, I believe that your mother would want you to know the truth, even if there's nothing you can do about it. You should know that she was happy, for a while. And she loved you so very, very much.

Pablo tells me you keep people away; dearest, love is the reason we exist. We live so we can make the world better by loving so brightly it can make the stars seem dull in comparison. Your father took enough from you. Don't let him take the gift of a long life filled with love too. You deserve more. Where the heart leads, your soul will follow. Follow your heart, my love.

I will watch over you from my place in heaven, where I'll wait with your mother until we see you again. Be brave, be strong, be open.

Love,
Your abuela.

Finn lay back on the sand and let her tears slide down her cheeks and onto the beach. "So it wasn't my mother then. I was so sure."

Pablo wiped the tears from his cheeks too and set the phone down so he could make coffee but still talk to her. "I don't know. Like you, she only saw your mother the one time. Is it possible she got away?"

"If she did, then he's probably been hunting for her all these years. There's no way his ego would allow her to go off and be happy."

"Like you." He rested his head against the cupboard. "At the job the other day, I heard your old name come up. One of the guys on the crew I'm running did some work out at your father's place. The roof, I think. He said he overheard your father ask some scary-looking guy in a suit if there was any word on you."

Finn shot up and wiped at her eyes. "And you didn't think to fucking tell me that right away?"

Pablo raised his coffee mug. "You know full well he wasn't going to stop looking for you. What's it matter if you know it for sure? All it will do is freak you out, and you'll go running off again."

She wanted to argue, but he was right. Somehow, though, knowing in a vague, unconfirmed way was better than knowing for certain. "What do I do?"

He sat at his coffee table and slurped from the mug that proclaimed *Builders know how to use their hands*. "Go on living. Work out like you're trying to be the next cover model for Muscle Magazine. Keep having sex with hot women at the beach. Write books that people want to give you awards for while you hide away in the dark. This doesn't change anything."

She couldn't agree. She pictured the woman in the cemetery.

Her mother could be alive. That could change *everything*.

Chapter Sixteen

ANGIE SMOOTHED HER HANDS down the sides of the soft black dress. It fit like it had when she'd bought it several years ago, and she was grateful for the reminder she was still in decent shape.

The doorbell rang and she hurried to answer it, the tap of her heels loud on the marble floor. When she opened the door, she was sorely tempted to throw the heels and dress aside and drag Finn straight up to her bedroom.

In black slacks, a black button-down shirt, and a deep blue silk tie, Finn looked every inch the woman from Angie's sexual fantasies. Her short, thick hair looked freshly cut and no longer touched her collar. Finn's dark eyes seemed to grow a shade darker as she looked Angie over. When their eyes met, Angie's knees went weak.

"If I weren't determined to know more about you, I'd say we should skip date one and go directly to date five."

Angie turned away to keep from saying that Finn could find out more about her in the morning. She picked up her purse and coat. "Then it's a good thing you're not in charge, isn't it?"

Finn gave her that maddening half-grin. "I'm willing to sit back and watch. For the moment."

Chills ran up Angie's arms at the idea of Finn watching her. "Shall we?"

"Hamburger Happy Meal, coming up." Finn motioned toward her truck. "I'm happy to drive, but maybe you want to take something more upmarket?"

"If you don't mind driving my car, we could show McDonald's some style. I've had enough of LA traffic for one day." She reached into her bag and hit the remote for the garage door, which opened to reveal her three rides.

Finn began to laugh. "A Prius, a Lexus Hybrid SUV, and a Tesla." She glanced at Angie and back at the cars. "I thought you'd have a Porsche in there."

Angie crossed her arms. "Being a celebrity doesn't mean I don't care about the planet. We need to pay attention to what we're leaving our kids—"

Finn took her hand, stopping her diatribe. "I think it's fantastic, Angie. I love when people surprise me, although we'll need to discuss the weirdness of you having not one, but three environmentally friendly cars, which seems to defeat the purpose. Anyway, which would you like to take tonight?"

"You choose."

Finn led her to the Lexus. "Let's take the biggest one. The McDonald's drive-through can get mean. We may need to bump people out of the way." She held Angie's hand as she climbed into the passenger seat.

Angie smoothed her dress once again. Finn's touch, the way she was so smooth and calm, was making Angie feel exactly the opposite. Was the backseat big enough—the thought was cut off by Finn getting into the driver's seat and setting them in motion. Once again, Angie noted that Finn was comfortable with luxury. She didn't seem at all out of place in the custom-built car. The tie she wore was expensive, and Angie was certain the shoes were Ferragamo. She'd worn one of their dresses to the Golden Globes last year and had become familiar with their designs.

They joked some more as they made their way to dinner, and Angie didn't ask where they were going, although she did look at Finn in alarm when she slowed down as though to pull into the McDonald's parking lot. Then she gave her that sexy grin and kept driving, and Angie wanted to crawl into her lap.

They pulled up in front of Cara Restaurant, and Finn took Angie's arm after the valet had opened her door.

"I've always wanted to come here. I just never have." She loved the twinkling lights wrapped around beautiful olive trees, and Angie sighed at how pretty it was. They were led to a table at the far end of the courtyard. Candlelight flickered and danced over the wall of vegetation beside them.

"Not quite as good as an old-fashioned cheeseburger, but hopefully you'll find something to suit you on the menu." Finn pulled out her chair for her and handed the hostess Angie's coat.

"Can I just say," the hostess said, "your last movie made me believe in relationships again. I love everything you do, and I'm so glad you're here tonight."

"Thank you, that's very kind." Angie smiled but groaned inwardly. Hopefully this fan wouldn't put it out on social media that they were there.

The hostess nodded and backed away, and Finn leaned forward. "Do you get tired of that?"

"Being recognized?"

Finn tilted her head from side to side. "Not so much recognized as fawned over. Does it get old?"

"Sometimes," Angie said. "It would be nice to go out and not have to worry that a fan like that one will tell other people I'm here."

"Like they did at the coffee shop the first time we met."

"When I threw money at you, according to Luna." Angie felt the heat rise to her face. "I'm sorry about that, by the way."

Finn handed Angie the wine menu. "I admit it was a first. But you seem to be a lot of firsts for me."

Before Angie could ask what she meant, the waiter came over. She glanced at the wine menu and then handed it back to Finn. "I'm not picky, and I'm also not a wine expert. You choose?"

Finn glanced at the menu and then handed it back to the waiter. "We'll have the Russian River Pinot, please."

At Angie's questioning look, Finn smiled and took her hand. "I love Northern California. The natural beauty is something else, and the Russian River area has always been a favorite of mine. Do you know there are more lesbians in Guerneville per square inch than in anywhere else in the world?"

Angie laughed. "You're making that up."

"I am. But it does seem like the flannel and boots capital of the world. Have you been there?"

"Not yet, but with that description, I should definitely make it my next stop." She took a sip of water, needing a moment to breathe. Being with Finn was so easy. "What took you to Guerneville in the first place? The plethora of lesbian company?"

Finn's laugh was deep and open. "Hardly. Most of them look like me, and I'm definitely into women who *don't* look like me. Women with long hair and curves. Women who look amazing in heels." Her eyes sparkled, her meaning clear.

Angie gratefully sat back as the waiter poured their wine. Finn did the obligatory tasting and nodded her appreciation, and after the waiter left, she held up her glass. "To date one of many, I hope."

Angie raised her glass and took a sip of the wine. It danced on her tongue, smooth and crisp. "That's gorgeous."

Finn nodded. "When I first moved to California, I travelled the state to figure out where I wanted to live. I started at the Oregon border and worked my way down, stopping in various towns and cities to get the feel of them. In Guerneville, I stayed in an old log cabin that had a river running in front of the house. The giant redwoods, the ferns that change color in the fall. It was really special."

"But you didn't stay there."

"I needed more variety. A little more weirdness to inspire my writing." She tipped her glass slightly at Angie. "Like celebrities getting accosted in a café while their daughter tries to crawl into the espresso machine."

"I don't imagine there was a lot of that in a little town up north." Angie picked up her menu when she noticed the waiter watching them from a distance. "Have you eaten here before? Any recommendations?"

"I have, and the tuna is fantastic. Anything here is great, really."

They were quiet as they made their choices, but Angie had to reread the menu several times. She simply wanted to keep talking. When the waiter came over, she was no closer to a decision, so she ordered the tuna. It didn't really matter what she had, as long as she was alone with Finn.

"Speaking of Luna," Finn said after ordering the apple-roasted chicken, "where is she tonight? And why did you answer your own door?"

"You don't miss much, do you?" Angie looked at her over the edge of her wine glass. She needed to slow down or the whole night would go to her head.

"Sorry, it's a hazard of my trade. I notice a lot." Finn topped up their glasses and waited for Angie to answer.

"Amazingly, Luna asked if she could go to a weekend science camp thing. She never wants to go to anything with other kids, and I almost said no just because I wasn't prepared for the question." She hesitated over her honesty with a person who had an awful lot of secrets. "And I answered my own door because I gave my house staff the night off. With Luna out and me on a McDonald's adventure, it didn't seem necessary to have everyone around." It was a half-truth, but it would have to do. She wasn't about to say that she didn't want the staff around if things went further with Finn tonight. "It's my turn. What's your favorite childhood memory?"

Finn flinched almost like she'd been hit, and she sat back, closing off in every manner of speaking. It was like she pulled a shutter down around her. "Why don't you tell me yours instead?"

Angie sighed. "Okay, tell me *something* about you. Something we don't already know."

"I'm a bird watcher." Finn's shoulders seemed to relax a little. "I hang out with a group called the Wing Watchers, which is led by a woman named Gertrude who looks a lot like a tody, a little green bird we have in the DR."

"So what's your favorite bird?"

Finn laughed and the tension eased even more. "I don't have one. I just go along because they're quirky and I like nature." She sipped her wine, but her gaze never left Angie's face. "Now, tell me why you have three cars instead of one."

"I bought the Prius several years ago when I was shooting a movie here in LA. I was doing a ton of driving, and I didn't want to be in something flashy that caught anyone's attention. Plus, there was the environment thing. Then I decided I wanted something bigger, something with more bulk when I was driving Luna around. The Lexus is what the nanny and Luna's bodyguard usually take her out in. I feel safer with her in that."

"Okay. Those two make some sense. But then why the Tesla?"

"Honestly? My ex bought it. She wanted the Model S because it was pretty much AI on wheels. She could practically watch a movie while she was on the freeway." The wine soured a little on her tongue. "I keep meaning to sell it, but I never have the time."

"Surely you have someone who could handle that for you?" Finn's penetrating gaze didn't waver. "Maybe you're not quite ready to let it go?"

Dinner arrived and Angie took a deep, steadying breath. Once the waiter was gone, she smiled at Finn. "Talking about exes is date two material. Date one should never include ex-girlfriends or explanations about bad habits."

Finn took a bite of her chicken and murmured her appreciation, making Angie focus on her tuna. It was, as Finn had said, delicious.

"Fair enough. No family, no exes, no bad habits on display. That leaves us with..." Finn continued to eat, clearly pretending to think. "Favorite colors? Favorite songs?"

"I love the deep red you get with roses, and I like general pop music." Angie winced. "God, how boring is that?"

Finn shook her head. "Nothing wrong with either of those. I love the turquoise you get in the Mediterranean Sea where it's shallow enough you can watch the fish swimming past the rocks, and I listen to classical music when I write because if there are words, I'll focus on them instead of creating my own."

Angie sighed. "That's so much better than my answer. Is that what it is to date a writer? Everything I say will sound flat and uninspired in comparison?"

"Dating should never be about comparison." Finn sipped her wine, her eyes dark with promise. "It should be about complementing each other. Like the perfect wine with your dinner, or that perfect bit of cloud sliding over a full moon, or the right sheets to fall into at night while holding each other."

Angie swallowed hard and tried to remember how to chew. No woman had ever made her feel so...so...she had no idea what she was feeling, but she liked it. A lot.

Their light banter continued throughout the rest of the meal, which was finished with specialty coffee and a shared butterscotch pot de crème.

"That was amazing, thank you." Angie finished her glass of wine and was glad there was none left in the bottle. She already felt a little lighter in the head than she should.

"My pleasure. Thank you for joining me tonight." Finn took her hand and kissed her knuckles. "I haven't had a night like this in a long time."

Angie giggled and put her hand over her mouth, mortified. She composed herself and grinned back at Finn. "I find it hard to believe someone as sexy as you doesn't take out a new woman every night of the week."

Finn's eyebrow twitched. "There you go with that sexy thing again. Stroking my ego that way could be dangerous."

She ignored the soft warning bell that chimed when Finn didn't deny the dating assertion. "I could stroke something else instead." The words were out before Angie could consider them.

Finn's eyes darkened, and her hand tightened on Angie's. "I think that could be arranged." She held up her hand and motioned for the check. "Shall we?"

It was only as they were leaving that Angie realized she'd had her first night out in years where she hadn't been approached by a single fan other than the waitress. It was a heady feeling, and although she noticed a person or two watch them leave the restaurant, no camera phones were out, and no one stopped them. She'd have to come back here, if it meant this kind of privacy. Maybe Finn would take her out again.

At the feel of Finn's hand on her lower back, she shivered.

"Cold?" Finn murmured, her breath warm against Angie's neck.

"A little," Angie said softly, pressing into Finn, who was standing close enough that Angie could feel the solid warmth of her.

Finn pulled her close, wrapping her arms around her from behind. "Can't have that."

She let go when the valet pulled up with the Lexus, and Angie nearly groaned out loud at the loss.

The silence on the way back to Angie's was full of expectation, promise, and uncertainty. Finn's thumb ran over Angie's knuckles, and she kissed the top of Angie's hand, her wrist, her fingertips as she drove. By the time they were at Angie's garage she was a wet, desperate mess. They got out, and Finn walked Angie to the door.

But when she opened it, Finn didn't follow her in. Instead, she pulled her into a long, deep kiss that made Angie's knees weak, and if she hadn't had her arms wrapped around her, she might have melted into a puddle at her feet.

They parted, and Finn rested her forehead against Angie's, her hand still resting on the back of Angie's neck. "Thank you for an amazing night."

"You could come in?" Angie tried to keep the plea out of her voice.

"I could. But that's what I would do with any other woman." Finn stepped back and pressed Angie's palm to her mouth. "And you're not just any woman." She let Angie's hand slide from hers as she walked backward to her truck. "Good night."

Angie gave a little wave as Finn got into her truck and drove off. She closed the door behind her and gave a sigh that extended all the way to the tips of her heels. There was no way on earth she'd sleep without dreaming of Finn's demanding kiss and the way her body felt solid and hot. Angie moaned out loud, kicked off her heels, and headed upstairs. Tonight, she'd take care of her own needs. But she'd be dammed if she'd let Finn off the hook next time. And the thought of there being a next time made her heart race in a way it hadn't in a very, very long time.

Chapter Seventeen

LUNA PUT ANOTHER NICKEL in her pocket. "Are you letting me win? Because that would suck."

Finn shook her head and reshuffled the tiles. Her concentration was anywhere but on the game at hand. Rather, she couldn't get her mind off the game playing out in her life. Her wild attraction to Angie, the mystery around her mother, and her damn agent who kept calling to ask her to reconsider the award and to ask about the next novel. And then there was Luna, a kid she was growing attached to.

"Obviously not. Letting someone win isn't kind. It means you don't respect them or their ability. I respect you and your ability. You're winning fair and square."

Luna gave a devious smile. "Soon I'll beat you every time."

"Ambition is good as long as it doesn't cloud your thinking." The words brought up memories of her father, and she gritted her teeth. She'd gone years with barely a thought of him and now he was messing with her head daily. "Your mom said you went to a science thing over the weekend. How was it?"

Luna was quiet as she shuffled the tiles longer than was necessary. "It was good, I think." She glanced at Finn and then back to the table. "How do you know if people like you? If you fit in?"

"Big questions for afternoon coffee." Finn took a drink of her now cold latte and grimaced. "I guess you know if people like you, because they want to hang out with you. They talk to you and enjoy your company. They want to know things about you, and they want to share things about themselves with you. Any of that sound right?"

Luna played her turn, and they sat in silence for a few more moves before she looked up. "But what if they're just being nice?"

"Hmm." Finn made a move and then tilted her head toward Delia. "Do you think she likes me?"

Luna looked at Delia for a minute. "I think so. She talks to you and laughs a lot. Plus, she brings you coffee even when you don't order it."

"And should I think she's doing it just because she's trying to be nice? Or should I believe that her actions are genuine because she hasn't given me any reason to think otherwise?"

Luna frowned and pushed her glasses up. "Explain."

"Okay." She made her move, but Luna didn't look at the game. "I think it's really easy to doubt people. Thinking negative thoughts is always easier than thinking positive ones. It's built into our DNA. Evolution has taught us to be constantly aware of danger in order to survive, and now, in a society where we no longer worry about being eaten by tigers or bears, we worry about our social order instead. But in this case, evolution is wrong. We should trust that people are who they say they are until they show us that they're something else. If people wanted to hang out with you, if they wanted to talk to you and you had fun, then take it at face value. Don't assume the worst. You do that enough with other stuff, right?" As was so often the case when she gave Luna advice, the hypocrisy of it made her stomach turn. She'd learned the hard way that people often hid who they really were.

Luna nodded, looking thoughtful. "But a lot of that other stuff is because of other people."

"Part of that is probably to do with how you were brought up. Your mom has always been the center of attention, which means you have too, in a way. And the celebrity world often shows that it doesn't have sunshine coming from its butt."

"Gross." Luna grinned, looking lighter than she did when she came in. "I wish Mom talked to me the way you do."

"Do you talk to her the way you talk to me?"

Luna stared at her for a long time, and Finn nodded at the table. "Your move."

They finished the game in silence and then Luna went to get another drink. While she was gone, Karen sauntered over and sat in her place. Finn sat back. There was a predator hiding behind those blue eyes, one that would pull you under the moment you weren't paying attention. She was the epitome of what Finn meant about the celebrity world having claws. She dressed like a harmless Bohemian, but beneath was a tiger waiting for a meal.

"I don't suppose you'd want to take me to dinner some time?" she said, glancing over her shoulder, clearly to make sure Luna wasn't within earshot.

"I'm afraid I'm already seeing someone. Sorry." She tried to keep her words civil, but she knew women like this. Clarity was more important than politeness.

"Seeing someone doesn't mean married." Karen's hand lightly skimmed Finn's thigh, stroking in a way that wouldn't be misconstrued.

"I'm a fan of serious monogamy and intellectual compatibility. I'm enjoying both with the person I'm seeing." She and Angie had gone on one date, and monogamy hadn't been mentioned in any capacity. But she wasn't about to discuss that with Karen. "I'm sure you can find someone who shares your sense of non-monogamous adventure and intellectual...stability."

Karen's eyes narrowed, and she stood. "No need to be rude. I get it." She practically stomped back to the table she'd been encamped at and picked up her phone. The door to the coffee house swung open hard as she stepped outside, already talking to someone.

"Geez." Luna carefully set down their two mugs. Her hot chocolate had a mountain of whipped cream on top. "I leave you alone for two minutes and you send my nanny into a tantrum."

"My apologies." She wasn't sure what else to say. Did she tell Luna that her nanny was a viper with a nice smile?

"I thought she'd be okay because she likes interesting music and she talked to me like I wasn't a dumb kid. But she's actually a lot like the popular girls at school." She licked the top off her mountain of whipped cream. "No sunshine coming out of her butt after all."

Finn sputtered in her latte. "Please don't say that in front of your mom. I'll get banned from the compound."

Luna picked up a spoon when she couldn't lick any more whipped cream off without sticking her face in the mug. "Do you like my mom?"

Finn was immediately thankful for her darker complexion that would hide the flush in her cheeks. "Of course I do."

"No, I mean, like-like. Like, would you date her?"

Luna's tone was neutral and didn't give away how she'd feel about that, and her expression was impassive too. "You're getting awfully good at hiding your emotions behind a mask. Should that be concerning?"

Luna's mask slipped and she grinned. "I've been practicing. There's this podcaster. She's a socio-archaeologist who interviews people in different communities, and she says it's important not to let your personal feelings show so the people don't shut down and stop talking to you."

"She has a point, but don't stop being the very cool open book you are. There's a lot to be said for vulnerability and being transparent."

"You change topics a lot without answering people's questions. That's something I want to learn too." Luna gave her a penetrating, all-knowing look that only a nearly-teenager could pull off well.

"Okay, first, tell me how you would feel if I like-like your mom?"

Luna spooned the last of her whipped cream before she answered. "Before, I think it would have made me mad, because you're my friend, not hers."

"And now?" The very last word she thought of when she thought of kissing Angie was friend.

"I think she's been lonely since Chris left. She doesn't do

anything but work and worry about me. But around you, she laughs a lot." She shrugged, a light frown still etching her features. "So you can like-like her if you want to, but you have to promise not to hurt her. And you have to promise not to stop being my friend too." She held up her pinky. "Promise?"

Finn hesitated. Could she promise either of those things? If she picked up and left the way she had in the past, that promise would be as broken as Luna's trust. Pablo's words floated back to her. At some point, she had to stop running. "Promise." She pinky swore and smiled back at Luna. "Now, what are you going to do about your no-butt-sunshine nanny?" Finn asked, swiping the tiles back into their bag.

Luna shrugged again and started to gather her things. It was time for her skate lesson. "She stays out of my way and doesn't talk to me a lot, and I like that. So I'll let her hang around for a while. She can do her thing while I do mine, and Mom doesn't have to worry. It's a win all the way around."

Finn couldn't argue with that, although she had a feeling Angie wouldn't be happy with that kind of relationship. "You do you. Are you going to see your science friends again?"

Luna bit her lip and pushed up her glasses. "One of the girls has invited me over on Friday to check out the geology display she's building for her science fair."

"Geology and archaeology are best friends. No one gets between them." Finn crossed her fingers to show how tight they were. "Sounds like a good time."

Luna slung her bag over her shoulder. "Yeah. Believe they're good until they show you otherwise. Right?"

Finn gave a mock bow. "The student learns quickly from the wise teacher."

"Weirdo. See you later."

Finn watched as Luna went outside and got into the waiting car. Karen, still on her phone, barely acknowledged her as she got in and slammed the door behind her. Finn's phone rang and she picked up, glad for the distraction. "Hey, primo. I feel like I've talked to you more in the last month than I have in the last decade."

"That's probably true, and it's all your fault. I'm loveable, and you've missed out." Pablo coughed and then came back on. "I had an idea to pass by you."

"No. Whatever it is, no."

"Shut up and listen. I think I figured out who the woman was that Abuela was talking about. The one your mamá was in love with. I've sent you her information, and I think you should try to find her."

"First of all, Abuela said she hasn't been seen since Mamá died. She could be dead too, and if she is, you know who made it so. Also, why would I want to find her? So she can tell me she loved my mamá, and that love got her killed? What good would it do?"

"You think you saw your mama in the cemetery. If you did, then this woman might be the way to find her. Wouldn't that be worth it?"

Finn bit her lip. The thought had already occurred to her, along with a million others. "Pablo, if she's been alive all these years, why didn't she reach out to me? Why did she leave us and never once try to get us away from him?"

He was silent for a moment. "I guess you won't know until you find her and ask. Check your email." He hung up without saying bye.

Finn closed her eyes and sighed. Only a short time ago life had been so much simpler. She watched people, she watched birds, and she wrote. No family complications, no enticing look into real attraction, no kid to let down.

Chris. Now she had a name to go with the ex who put the sadness in Angie's eyes. She pulled out her phone and typed in Angie's name along with the name of her ex. Only one photo appeared, and Finn zoomed in to look closer.

The woman had short hair styled to within an inch of its life. Her green eyes were cold, like frost on autumn grass. Angie smiled for the camera, but Chris looked almost bored. The fact that out of the thousands of photos of Angie out there, this was the only one of them online was baffling. Who wouldn't want to be seen with Angie at every opportunity? Then she remembered what Angie had said about not wanting to be with a woman who had secrets. Perhaps, like Finn, Chris didn't want to be caught on camera for some reason.

That was something Finn understood all too well.

Chapter Eighteen

ANGIE HUNG UP AND rested her chin in her hands. The last week had been non-stop readings, rehearsals, and wardrobe fittings. She'd thought she'd have another month before it got crazy again, but things were moving fast. There was one thing she'd been determined to take care of at the first opportunity, before the usual madness began, and it was done. She took a deep breath and reminded herself it was the right thing to do.

She went to the stairs and called up. "Hey, Luna, can you come down for a second?"

Luna's door opened and two pairs of feet came running down the stairs. Luna was followed by her new friend from science camp, Cari. Seeing Luna laugh and be a somewhat regular kid had made Angie's heart ache with happiness.

"What's up?" Luna said, sliding onto the barstool. Cari did so as well, a little less gracefully.

Angie pushed over a folder of paper. "Have a look."

Luna flipped it open and pushed up her glasses as she started to read. Within seconds, she slid from the barstool and threw herself into Angie's arms. "You really mean it?"

"I really do. I've called and spoken with the lead archaeologist on the dig, as well as the person in charge of young volunteers. They've both agreed to keep an eye on you, and they've got all my contact information. You're going to Turkey."

Luna squealed and jumped in circles. Her friend looked on, smiling and laughing.

"That's so cool. I wish my parents would let me do something like that. They're making me have a stupid party on a boat for my birthday." Cari's shoulders hunched a little, and Luna sat down beside her.

"Have you told them what you really want?" Luna looked at Angie. "Finn reminded me that sometimes we have to try harder to talk to people instead of assuming they won't hear us."

Yet again, Angie felt indebted to Finn for changing the course of her relationship with Luna. "It's a good reminder for all of us, I think." Angie handed Luna the folder. "There are some other details in there you need to know. We'll book the flights together tomorrow. Karen and your bodyguard are going with you." At Luna's expression, Angie held up her hand. "There's no argument here, honey. They can stay in the background, but I want adults who know you there to watch over you in case you need anything. I know you'll be thirteen, but that's still young. Compromise?"

Luna rolled her eyes, but she was still smiling. "Fine. They won't want to hang out on the dig site anyway." She took Cari's hand and tugged at it. "Come on. Let's go figure out what I need to take with me."

They raced back up the stairs, leaving Angie alone in the kitchen. A moment later though, Luna darted back in and threw her arms around Angie's waist.

"Thanks, Mom."

Angie hugged her back, holding onto the precious moment. "Anything for you."

Luna let go and raced upstairs again.

Angie settled onto the couch and pulled out her phone.

Date two should happen soon if you still want more time with me. It won't be long until I'm filming on location.

She'd had a daily text from Finn, but she'd been too busy, and too exhausted at night, to meet up. The texts always made her smile though. Sometimes they were bad jokes, sometimes they were quotes from people like Shakespeare, sometimes it was just, *Hope you have a great day, beautiful.* There'd been no pressure for a second date, no extreme flirting. It felt genuine, something Angie wasn't always sure how to respond to. Any of the characters she played would have known how to respond, but the real person she was...well, who was she? Thanks to Finn, she was trying to figure it out.

Date two. Is that KFC or Burger King? I'm not sure what the next step up from McD's is, but I guess I'll figure it out. Tomorrow, seven thirty?

Actually, I'd like you to choose a place you think is special. Somewhere that says something about you. Getting to know Finn was hard. Maybe this was a way in.

Subtle. I've never had a woman so determined to get to know me. I'm up for the challenge, but let's make it six thirty instead so we have time. See you tomorrow, beautiful.

Angie set the phone down and did a little dance in place. Things were better with Luna, she had the role of a lifetime, and now she was dating a woman who made her feel like she could dance on clouds. Life was good.

Doubts began to intrude the way they always did. Would Luna be safe so far from home? What if something happened to her? She still didn't know much about Finn except that there were things Finn wouldn't talk about. And the movie role... Well, that seemed to be going well. Elodie was a consummate professional and the directors were solid, if a little abrupt sometimes. Unlike other movie sets, she didn't feel degraded, and there didn't appear to be any sexual harassment among the crew. As always, it seemed to be the most stable part of her life.

She picked up the script and lay back on the couch. When things were crazy, work could always be counted on to distract her.

***

At six thirty the following night, Angie heard the doorbell and her pulse instantly sped up. Finn's husky voice made her shiver before she was even in sight, and then Luna came in ahead of her.

Finn handed her the huge bouquet of deep red roses, a small smile touching her eyes.

"My favorite color. Thank you." Angie inhaled the fragrant aroma and quickly found a vase. Her tummy fluttered at the romantic gesture, but even more so at Finn remembering that detail from their first date.

Luna looked them both over and then flopped onto the couch. "Remember your curfew and make good choices." She turned on the TV and made a shooing motion.

Angie leaned down and kissed her head. "Be good. I'll be home soon."

Luna just made a go away motion again as she put on a *National Geographic* documentary.

Finn grinned. "Want us to bring anything back, Luna?"

Luna looked away from the TV. "A peanut butter milkshake, please."

"Done." Finn held the door open for Angie and followed her out to the truck. "Your chariot, bonita."

Angie accepted Finn's help up into the truck and then tucked her long, flowing silk skirt around her legs. It was unseasonably warm, which meant she could keep her summer clothes out just a little longer. Not that they ever really went away in southern California. She adjusted the straps of her tank top to make sure they covered the thin black bra straps.

"Where are we off to tonight?" Angie asked when Finn turned onto the main road.

"It's a surprise, if that's okay?"

When they got on Hwy 2, Angie searched her mental map. "Into the mountains?"

"Not this time." Finn glanced over. "You look beautiful, and absolutely perfect for where we're going."

"You're looking pretty damn good yourself. That color looks amazing on you."

The deep blue button down looked so soft, Angie wanted to run her hands over it, but that would probably be distracting the driver, which was never good.

"You said you'd be leaving for your film location soon," Finn said, lightly tapping the steering wheel. "Any idea when?"

"The weekend before Luna leaves for Turkey." Angie smiled a little at Finn's look of surprise. "I had to let her go. And," she said, placing her hand on Finn's thigh, "thanks to you, we're talking more than we have in a really long time." She squeezed, liking the way the muscle bunched under her touch.

"You'd have gotten there eventually. Sometimes an outsider can just give a little nudge, that's all." Finn took the exit.

"You're taking me to a Dodgers game? The closest I ever came was a movie I did about dating a baseball player." Angie motioned toward the stadium they were passing.

"As a lifetime lover of pelota, it saddens me greatly that you don't appreciate the most beautiful sport in the world," Finn said, her hand pressed to her heart. "However, we won't be rectifying that tonight."

When they came around the corner, it was clear where they were headed. The park ahead of them glowed with neon lights and the feel of a thumping bass made the windows rattle. "A street fair?"

Finn shook her head as she concentrated on parallel parking on the crowded street. "Would I take you somewhere so common? No, bonita, this is the Caribbean Culture Festival." She finished parking and turned to Angie. "You said you wanted to get to know me better. Did you know less than two percent of Dominicans live on the West Coast? Once a year I get to come and indulge in sancocho, mangu, and merengue." She jumped out and ran around to open Angie's door. "Welcome to a little window to my life."

Finn took a bag from behind Angie's seat and then pulled out something covered in white feathers. "The colors this year are blue and white. This way you won't get recognized, and you can simply relax and enjoy." She slipped the mask's loops behind Angie's ears, lightly skimming the sides of her face as she did so. Angie looked in the side mirror. White sparkles surrounded her eyes, inlaid in a pure white mask that came to points on the side, almost like white horns. Bushy, soft white feathers came off the sides. When she turned to Finn, she saw that Finn was wearing one almost identical, except it was pale blue.

Angie happily took her hand and followed her through the gate into a world where color, scent, and music blurred into one another, creating a sensory overload in the best way. An enormous dance area had been set up under a tent, and couples were moving to the Latin Caribbean beat. Women in stunning outfits ranging from small, ornate bikinis to full sequined dresses strutted confidently through the crowd.

They stopped at a stage where there was a costume contest going on. Beads, bejeweled outfits, arm bands, thigh bands, boots. Angie's neck ached as she craned to take it all in.

Arm in arm, they went to various food stalls, where Finn explained some of the different options and even told Angie a memory of her own associated with that food. She mentioned her grandmother several times and every time, her eyes misted over a little before she turned away and moved on to the next thing.

When they made it to the dance tent, Finn held out her hand. "Can you dance?"

Angie watched the dancers on the floor, moving like the music was part of their DNA. "Not like that."

"Okay, can you follow?" Finn's sexy half grin and the challenge in her eyes made Angie take her hand.

"Let's see how well you lead."

Finn laughed and swept her into the moving crowd. Angie had learned to merengue when she'd shot the film in the Caribbean, and the steps came back quickly. Finn moved with grace and a sexual energy that drew Angie in and made her want to match Finn's rhythm. When the beat changed to a dance she didn't know, she grinned as Finn slowed and showed her the steps, her hips moving almost hypnotically. Angie had heard the saying that you could tell if someone would be good in bed by the way they danced, which meant Finn would be somewhere near god territory.

They moved to the beat, the bass thumping through Angie's veins, Finn's thigh pressed between her legs and then her butt pressed against Finn's crotch as they spun and swayed. Sweat beaded on her neck and dripped from her temples, and she'd never felt so free.

Eventually, she leaned closer and shouted, "I'm going to die of thirst!"

Finn laughed and took her hand, leading her from the dance floor and across the lawn to a bar set up in the back, farthest from the crowds. It was strangely quiet.

"This is the no-alcohol area. Always the best place to escape for a minute." She placed a lingering kiss on Angie's lips. "Be right back."

Angie rested on the bench, her thighs aching. Dancing with Finn had been like having sex, fully clothed in the middle of a crowd. Her whole body felt swollen with desire. She tried to focus beyond it to get some semblance of control, so she didn't pull Finn under the picnic table and beg to be taken then and there. Figuring it was safe enough where they were, away from the crowd and in a shadowed area, she took off her mask and wiped away the sweat on her face.

The lake, with its large fountain in the middle, shimmered with the lights from the festival. She'd never been to this area, but it had been in the news as a place of contention. Gentrification was knocking at the doors of the poor community here, and the residents were fighting but losing their homes. If they lost the fight, would festivals like this one still happen here? It was too deep a thought for the carefree night, and she shook it away.

Finn came back bearing three plastic cups of water and a cardboard container of plantains covered in cinnamon. "Doing okay?" She pulled off her mask and then straddled the bench beside Angie.

Angie drank half a cup of water before answering. "Amazing. This is incredible. You grew up with this?"

"I did. My favorite was Cabarete Carnaval, which is held on the beach. All of this," she motioned toward the festival crowd, "but right by the ocean."

"And do you usually wear the thong bikini?" Angie laughed at Finn's horrified expression.

"Can you imagine?" She shuddered. "This stud has never been caught in a bikini, I promise. But in the DR, we wear different types of masks. Some dress up like the devil while others run from their whips."

Angie winced. "I wouldn't want to randomly get whipped while walking through a crowd enjoying myself."

Finn leaned forward, her lips only inches from Angie's. "But if it wasn't random? If it was planned?" Her hand slipped under Angie's skirt and along her thigh, her fingers hot and strong.

"If you don't stop that, I'm going to beg you to take me right this instant, and damn public indecency laws," Angie whispered against Finn's lips, which quickly pressed against hers.

The kiss wasn't sweet. It wasn't gentle. It was merengue, summer nights, dancing on the beach in the rain kind of hot. Finn's hand moved away from her thigh only to pull her closer.

"Take a ride with me?" Finn murmured, pulling away only slightly. "Anywhere."

Instead of taking them to the main exit, Finn found them a quiet one not far from the no-alcohol area, and they were back at the truck in moments. Silence seemed the only option, but Angie slid to the middle of the bench seat, and Finn drove with one arm around Angie's shoulders. She got back on Hwy 2, this time headed toward the mountains, and then pulled off a well-hidden side road. She pulled the truck into a small parking area that overlooked the city below. Caribbean music floated up on the warm LA breeze, and the city itself was a magical glow in the distance.

As soon as the engine cut off, Finn turned and captured Angie's mouth in a kiss that left her breathless and begging for more. She turned and lay back on the seat, then moaned at the feel of Finn's weight on top of her, Finn's thigh pressed hard against her clit.

Finn's hot mouth was everywhere. Sliding over Angie's neck, her shoulders, her chin, her cheeks. Moving lower, over her collarbone and then gently sucking Angie's nipples through the thin tank top, making her arch and cry out, her hand tangled in Finn's thick hair.

Finn's hand slid up her skirt, her fingernails trailing lines of soft desire all the way to her hip.

"Please." Angie twisted, trying to get Finn's hand to where she wanted it.

Instead, Finn dropped her head to Angie's stomach, breathing hard and not moving. She fumbled behind her awkwardly and popped open the door, then slid out of the truck.

"Finn?" Angie sat up self-consciously, rearranging her tank top and ultra-aware of the wet spots over her nipples. Finn didn't answer, so Angie scooted out of the truck.

Finn leaned against the truck, her hands on her knees.

"Are you okay?"

Finn turned suddenly and pressed Angie to the truck, their bodies in contact all the way down. "Fuck no, I'm not okay. You're the most beautiful woman I've ever been with. You're driving me crazy, and I want to fuck you so bad, it physically hurts."

Angie waited. "But?"

Finn cupped Angie's face in her warm palm. "But I don't want to mess this up and going too fast can definitely mess this up." Her other hand skimmed Angie's side. "I don't want our first time together to be with us squished up in my truck. I want to take my time. I want to see you naked when you're begging me to take you." She placed soft, hot kisses along Angie's neck. "I want to taste every inch of you, then turn you over and start again while I take you from behind."

Angie whimpered, her knees weak and her tummy somersaulting. "So, take me home."

Finn shook her head, this time with a smile in her eyes. "Not yet. Not in a hurry or having to worry about staff or kids hearing you scream." She stepped back and took a shaky breath. "I want it to be perfect. Something you'll always remember."

Angie wanted to stomp her foot like a frustrated kid. "Fine. Then take me home so I can take care of myself while I think about you doing it for me."

Finn groaned and closed her eyes. "That's mean."

"Deal with it, stud." Angie walked around to the other side of the truck, but in truth, Finn's desire for it to be something real, something more than just a momentary fling, made her heart sing.

Chapter Nineteen

FINN SCROLLED THROUGH THE information Pablo had sent over. The woman he'd pinned as the one her mother had been in love with—that thought was jarring in itself—was unquestionably the one she'd seen in the cemetery. Older, a little grayer, but the same short hair, short build, and penetrating dark eyes.

Alive. Her mother and her mother's lover were alive.

But where were they? Had they flown in from somewhere too, the way Finn had? Surely they didn't still live in the DR? Somehow, they'd known about her abuela's death, so that meant they were either still on the island, or they were in touch with someone who knew how to get hold of them.

Someone, somewhere knew where they were.

She flopped back onto the couch. That look in her mother's eyes before the woman had pulled her away was one she wouldn't forget. Sadness, grief, desperation, surprise, shock. Could a moment of expression hold so many emotions? Or was she imagining it?

There was no question of her returning to the DR to do the searching herself. Her life was here, and she wouldn't risk her father finding out she was in his vicinity. Salty words traveled fast on tropical winds. All it would take was one person who recognized her to spread the word.

But hiring a private investigator would be easy. The bigger question, one she hadn't yet found the answer to, was whether or not she wanted to pursue it. Fear was a strong motivator and as someone who studied people, Finn knew what it did to the psyche. God knows, she'd let it run a good chunk of her life. Could she hold it against her mother? But then, Finn hadn't left four daughters behind either.

Swearing, she googled local investigators. She wouldn't be able to trust one from the island, because her father used them regularly to spy on people. An hour later, she'd hired one and sent the photos of her mother and her mother's lover to him. He promised he'd be on the plane to the DR the following day.

With that momentarily off her plate, she could turn her attention to the other complications in her life. Namely, her dating life.

Taking Angie to the carnival had been a spur of the moment decision based largely on the dreams assaulting her all night. Running from an unseen foe, walking lonely through a cemetery to watch a funeral where no one attended, and her name was on the headstone.

It was neither subtle nor surprising, and she was a little disappointed in her subconscious for being so obvious and uncreative, but maybe she needed it to be blunt so she understood. Her abuela's words haunted her as well. *He's taken enough from you.* And so, the carnival. She tended to avoid any connection with the small community here in LA. There was always the slightest chance she'd be recognized, and she couldn't take the chance. But with a mask and a beautiful woman in her arms, she hadn't been able to resist.

And what a fucking night. The amount of self-control it had taken to send Angie inside with nothing more than another hot, demanding kiss was superhuman and deserved a whole plethora of awards. She'd explained to Angie her desire to go slow, but that wasn't the whole of it, and she felt an iota of guilt at the minor omission.

The truth was that sex with Angie was bound to be out-fucking-standing. But what then? Sex that hot, with a woman who set her on fire both intellectually and physically, would lead to vulnerability. To connection. And Finn didn't have the inclination for either of those. Or, she hadn't until now.

The phone rang, and she groaned at the sight of Paige's name. "I thought if I avoided you long enough, you'd forget about me until I sent you something new."

Paige huffed. "My job is to be tenacious, Finn. Can you imagine this bullheadedness in any other job? I don't think so. First of all, how is the new manuscript coming along?"

Finn looked at her open laptop, where she'd stopped in the middle of a scene that wasn't quite working. "Pretty well, although I'm loath to admit it to you. I'm thinking I'll have a first draft ready in the next two months." She held her phone away from her ear as Paige squealed.

"That's amazing news, which I'm going to gently pass on to the awards panel."

Finn groaned obnoxiously into the phone. "Paige, I already told you—"

"Yes, yes. Hermit writer, secrets, safety, humble, etcetera. The panel have decided they don't care. They're going to give you the award in absentia and say you weren't able to be there to receive it in person. Which is what in absentia means, in case you didn't know."

"You know I don't want the notoriety."

"And if that was the case, you should have written far more mediocre books that no one would pay attention to." There was the ruffling of paper. "Finn, I can't pretend to understand why you'd turn this down. But it truly is a beautiful book worthy of this kind of acknowledgment. It will drive sales through the roof, and that money will help you continue to be the hermit you're determined to be." Her tone was gentle, which was always an indicator that she was handling her. "And that means that this next bit is going to send you into a tailspin."

Finn's stomach lurched. "What now?"

"A studio has approached your publishing house about making the book into a movie."

Finn hung up.

Maybe Paige was right. Maybe she should give up being a writer and go to work in fast food instead. No one would give her a second look, and she could fade into the patchwork of humanity, just another thread in the cosmos. She glanced at the box of books that arrived. Her author copies of her latest book. Not the one up for the award, but one she was proud of as well. No. She couldn't move on to stacking shelves. Without the ability to tell stories, she'd lose what made her, her. She'd be normal.

"Dire." She got up, disliking the sound of her voice in the empty room. She picked up her phone.

Last night was sublime. Date three soon?

The response was almost immediate, like Angie had been waiting for her text.

Only if you promise not to send me home with an aching clit again.

Finn's fingers hovered over the phone, but she couldn't figure how to respond. A couple of options would be too crass, and others wouldn't be nearly suggestive enough.

Okay, Romeo. Don't strain that big brain of yours. Date three on Saturday?

Finn blew out a relieved breath. *Seven?*

I have the day off from work. Could I entice you to spend the whole day with me?

I think you could entice me to leap off a mountain without a parachute just for a chance to see you smile. Ten thirty? Was that cheesy? It looked cheesy when she reread it. Where was the award-winning novelist now?

Smooth talker. See you at ten thirty. Xo

With that conversation done, Finn moved to her desk, but the walls closed in today. She needed light and air for the next chapter. She put her writing gear in her backpack, jumped in the truck, and headed out. First stop, the gym. That was the only thing keeping her sane as her libido tried to take over her life. Then coffee with a view and hopefully a flood of words.

***

Four hours and an equal number of bad cups of coffee later, Finn flexed her fingers and stretched the stiff muscles in her back. The afternoon light was fading, and a breeze made her shiver. She pulled her sweatshirt from the picnic bench she'd been sitting on, and her phone fell out. She hadn't given it a thought since she sat down. The words were flowing, and the scenes were drawing themselves out in her head second by second. She could hardly keep up as she served as a conduit for the story.

She happened to glance at the screen and then froze at the number of missed calls. Three from Luna, four from Angie. Two voicemails.

"Weirdo Finn, I need you. Call me back right away." Luna's voice sounded small and scared.

Pulse beginning to race, she listened to Angie's message.

"Finn, I'm so sorry to bother you, but we could really use your help. Luna's hurt herself and has had to go to the emergency room. I'm at a reading and I'm at least two hours away, if not more because of traffic. I've called and given the hospital your name, just in case you can get to Luna before I do. Call me back when you can? Thanks."

Finn shoved her stuff into the backpack without looking at it and ran for her truck. How badly was Luna hurt? Angie sounded fairly calm, but she was an actress, after all. Who knew what she was feeling under that bravado?

She called Angie back, but it went straight to voicemail. "Hey, I'm sorry, I just got your message. I'm on my way to the ER, and I'll call you as soon as I get there." Next, she called Luna, who answered.

"Finn? Are you coming?" Luna still sounded small and scared.

"I'm on my way, hija. I just got the message. What happened?"

"I was skating like normal, then this creepy paparazzi guy started taking photos and asking me all kinds of questions. My bodyguard got him to go away, but it messed up my concentration and I hit the concrete. I think I broke my ankle." She hiccupped as she began to cry.

"Hey now. It's going to be okay. Where's Karen?"

"I don't know." More hiccups to accompany the crying. "I don't usually care where she is, but when I got hurt, she was nowhere to be found. Except for the bodyguard, I was all alone."

Finn's heart ached at the pain in Luna's tone. "We'll kick her ass for that later, okay? For now, I want you to try to stay calm. I'll be there in about fifteen minutes, okay?"

"Okay. Have you talked to my mom?"

"I've left her a message letting her know I'm on my way. We'll both be there soon."

"'Kay." She sniffled. "Get here fast, okay?"

"Promise."

They hung up, and Finn tapped the steering wheel at a red light. "Come on. Get out of the way, dopey. Do you need an escort?" she shouted as the person ahead of her failed to get going the second the light changed. She broke a number of laws in the short time it took her to get to the parking lot of the hospital, but she didn't care. She gave her own name then Luna's at the Emergency desk but was told she wasn't there. She'd been moved to a private room.

When Finn frowned, the nurse pointed at Luna's last name and parent information without saying anything.

Of course. They didn't need Luna recognized and the paps surrounding the hospital. How quickly she forgot the significance of an important last name. Finn loped up the stairs to Luna's room, where the bodyguard was conspicuously waiting outside her room. He nodded at Finn but didn't say anything. In fact, she couldn't remember seeing him ever speak to Luna. It wasn't like the movies, then, where the guards were chummy with their charges. Too bad. Luna could use more people in her corner.

Luna was on her side, curled into a ball, her foot at an awkward angle. Her cheeks were blotchy, and tears streamed down her cheeks. When she saw Finn, she struggled into a sitting position.

Finn sat on the edge of the bed and hugged her back when Luna put her arms around her and cried. She stroked her hair, briefly wondering how she'd come to be part of this little family. "Shh, hija. It's okay. You're not alone. I'm here. Your mom is on her way."

Eventually Luna's tears subsided. She sat back and scrubbed at her face. "Sorry."

"Hey now. You never need to say sorry for hurting and definitely not to people who care about you. Let's look at that ankle."

Finn rose and peered at the oddly twisted foot. "Yup. That's a bad one. Probably have to amputate. We'll call you Stumpy, and you can start swearing like a pirate."

Luna giggled and wiped at her eyes. "Mom would have to let me. It's probably a rule."

"Definitely."

The doctor came in and smiled gently at Luna. "How're you doing?"

"Finn's here now." Luna said it like it was an explanation, which it was, in a way.

The doctor nodded at Finn. "I see that." She held up some X-rays and popped them on the wall screen. "And now I can tell you and Finn that you broke this bone," she pointed to a clearly fractured spot, "and we need to set it and put a cast on it."

Luna looked at Finn, her eyes wide. "Will it hurt?"

Finn took Luna's hand. "Yup. For a minute or two."

The doctor nodded. "You've broken bones before?"

"A couple times." Finn didn't feel the need to go into when, or how, or who'd broken them for her. "But for a kid who's going to Turkey to do a major dig, all by herself, this is nothing. You're tough, right?"

Luna pushed up her glasses, her lip trembling slightly. "Yeah. I'm tough. But you won't leave, will you?"

"You kidding? I wouldn't miss you being all hero-like." She squeezed Luna's hand and got a small smile in response.

"All right. We're going to gather everything we need and then we'll be back to start."

The doctor left, and Finn sat back down on the bed beside Luna. "Need anything?"

"I wish Mom was here."

"She'll be here soon. Can I ask a weird question? Why didn't your mom call your dad to come be with you?" They hadn't discussed Luna's relationship with her dad, but Finn figured he was still around in some capacity.

"His girlfriend got a part in some horror movie, and he's with her in Maine." She shrugged and looked at some point beyond Finn. "He probably wouldn't have come anyway. I've only seen him twice in the last year."

"Got it. His loss." Finn pulled out her phone. "Now, as everyone knows, anyone in the hospital gets whatever food and special treats they want when they get out. So, we'd better get prepared."

The distraction worked. They spent time scrolling through various dessert options and ridiculing one another's choices. By the time the doctor came in, Luna looked almost like her normal self.

The doctor and nurses set everything up, and Finn took Luna's hand once again when they injected her with anesthetic. Where the hell was Angie? "Okay, hija. Look at my face and squeeze my hand as hard as you need to, okay? I'm strong enough to take it. And remember to breathe."

Tears filled Luna's eyes, but she hardly made a sound as they set her ankle and then began the casting process. Finn stroked her head and murmured how brave she was, and then Angie came in, looking wild and out of sorts. She rushed to Luna's side, and Finn quickly relinquished her position.

"Hey, baby. I'm so sorry it took me so long. The freeway was a mess." Angie looked at the doctor. "How is everything?"

The doctor filled her in, and Finn sat in the guest chair by the window. Now that Angie was in place, Finn could breathe again. She hadn't had to care for a child since she'd tried to protect her sisters, and that had been a very long time ago. The memory of looking after her sisters was a deep gut punch. She'd done everything she could over the years to forget them. Not because she didn't love them but because she did, and like their mother, she'd left them behind. She'd barely glanced at them at the funeral, unable to bear the guilt.

"Thank you so much, Finn."

Yanked from the painful memories, Finn focused on the room. Angie and Luna were looking at her expectantly, though Luna was looking drowsy from the painkillers the doctor had given her.

"Of course. Any time."

"Mom, I can still go to Turkey, right?" Luna's voice was soft, her eyes drifting shut.

"Of course. We'll work around this, don't worry." Angie held Luna's hand as she fell asleep.

Finn didn't know what to do. Stay and be supportive, or go and leave them to it because she wasn't part of this family and she'd done what she was asked to do?

"I can't tell you how much it means to me that you did this." Angie let go of Luna's hand and moved to Finn's side. "When I realized her dad was in another state, you were the first person I thought of. And on my way here, I thought about how weird that is. We haven't known you long, but I already feel like you're someone we can count on." She took Finn's hand in hers. "That's something really rare in our world."

The trembling that had started the moment Angie took her hand continued to spread through the rest of her. "Angie, I–"

"I know, Finn. You may not stick around. You made that clear, but while you're here, before you run from whatever you're running from, I hope you'll let us in."

Finn stood. "Want coffee? I could use one. And a Danish, if the cafeteria has any. Or something else? Carrot sticks? A pudding cup?" She backed out of the room, her hands shoved in her pockets, so Angie didn't see them shaking. "I'll get a couple things."

She practically ran from the room and headed down the hallway without paying attention to where she was going. By the time she stopped to lean against a wall and compose herself, she had no idea where she was. It took another ten minutes to make her way to the cafeteria, where she got them both coffee and then loaded up on a bag of food, including a Danish that looked like it might need to be resuscitated.

She took her time getting back. Hospitals were good fodder for character work too. Vastly different than the coffee shop chatter and more deeply real. The elevator stopped and a woman got in. Bags under her eyes, lank hair, and rumpled clothes made it clear she'd been here for a while. In her hand dangled a thin gold chain with a small heart pendant.

"Pretty," Finn murmured without thinking.

The woman looked at her blankly, then down at the necklace, as though she'd forgotten it was in her hand. "I suppose. He gave it to her for their twenty-fifth anniversary. His wife got a new car to go with her new house. But his mistress got this." She held it so the heart caught the light. "Funny what people will settle for just so they don't feel alone." The door opened, and she got out without another word.

Settle. It was a word without much positive connotation. *Settle down* meant be quiet. *To settle down* meant to be rooted, to lose your freedom. *To settle* meant to accept less than you hoped for. It meant spending twenty-five years with a man for whom you were always second best, a second thought, second choice.

Musing, she headed back to Luna's room and found Angie sound asleep beside her in the bed. She set the coffee and food on the table, gave them a lingering look, and headed out. Settling was exactly what Angie and Luna would be doing by keeping Finn in their lives. But she couldn't find it in herself to walk away. Like the selfish man who'd kept a mistress on the hook for more than two decades, was she willing to keep them in her life just so she didn't feel alone?

She was waiting for the elevator when someone touched her arm.

"Don't go."

She turned to see Angie looking adorably sleepy. "You don't need me now. Everything is okay."

"I may not *need* you, but I *want* you to stay. And I know Luna will want that too. I could use help getting her into the car, what with her crutches and such. Come back to the house with us and stay for dinner." She held Finn's hand, her eyes never leaving Finn's. "Please."

Damn beautiful women and their soft voices and gorgeous desire for connection. Angie had a zillion staff at the house who could help, not to mention the lurking bodyguard who remained by the door, so her reasoning wasn't sound. But what did that matter? "Sure. Okay." She followed Angie back to the room and took one of the seats. Angie curled up by Luna again.

"Promise you'll still be here when they say we can leave?"

Finn rose and moved to Angie's side. She brushed the hair from Angie's cheek and then kissed her softly. "I promise."

As Angie fell asleep and Finn watched from the uncomfortable guest chair, she wondered why she kept making promises she wasn't sure she could keep.

Chapter Twenty

ANGIE OPENED THE FRONT door while Finn walked slowly with Luna, coaching her along on her crutches. Progress at the hospital had been slow when it came to paperwork and getting Luna released, and it was late. Luna looked exhausted and Finn didn't look far behind.

Once they were inside, Luna looked at the stairs and then at Angie. "I forgot how many there were."

Finn looked between them. "If you trust me not to drop you, I can carry you up. You can tackle these tomorrow."

Luna looked grateful and Angie nodded. "Thank you. I seem to be saying that a lot lately."

Finn bowed low to Luna. "If you would be so kind as to indulge my desire to show off how strong I am, I would be much obliged, young warrior of the wheeled board."

Luna gave a tired giggle. "So weird." She held up her arms. "Show off then."

Finn gently picked Luna up, and Angie took her crutches. As she followed them up the stairs, she couldn't help but think that this was how life should be. A supportive partner there to call whenever things went sideways. Someone Luna could talk to. Someone who felt safe, kind, and open. Well, not open. Not really. But what facts did Angie need to know about Finn's past? That didn't tell her who Finn was now. And Finn was someone incredibly special.

She set Luna on her bed and turned away.

"Finn?"

She turned. "What's up, hija?"

"Will you still be here in the morning?"

"Um…" Finn looked at Angie.

"It's late, and we have guest rooms. It's silly for you to drive home tonight."

"Guess so, kid. See you in the morning."

Finn left, and Angie helped Luna get ready for bed. When she was tucked in, Angie sat beside her. "Honey, I know you like Finn. And I really like her too. But she told me that she moves around a lot."

"You think she'll leave?"

"I think it's a possibility. Maybe not now, but one day. I just don't want you to get hurt, that's all. Sometimes it's better to know that people may leave your path."

Luna looked tired as she turned over. "Like you thought Chris would stick around." She snuggled into her pillow. "Not everyone leaves, Mom. Sometimes love is real. You just have to remind people, that's all."

Her eyes closed and Angie smiled. "That's a nice way to look at it."

She made her way back downstairs, her back aching from the uncomfortable position lying beside Luna. Her stomach growled, irritated at being given only an old pastry and half-burnt coffee for dinner, especially after she'd worked all day.

Finn was sitting on the couch, her eyes closed. "All good?"

"All good." Angie moved to the fridge. "I'm starving. Want something?"

"I'd eat uncooked rice with a topping of prunes right now." Finn rolled her head to look at Angie without raising it from the couch. "Want help?"

"I've got it. Relax."

It was quiet as Angie went about making them omelets with a side of bacon. There was no rule that said you couldn't have breakfast at midnight. It had been years since she'd cooked an actual meal but doing it felt good. It was easy to forget how capable you could be when you had to do so little.

"I'm going to kill Karen if she's not already dead somewhere. That would be the only excuse for her not being there when Luna fell." She took her anger out on flipping the bacon.

"I'm assuming you haven't heard from her?" Finn asked, her eyes still closed.

"I've left a ton of messages, and she hasn't called me back." She turned to look at Finn. "How could I have been so wrong about her? What does that say about me as a parent?"

Finn pushed herself up from the couch and took a seat at the island instead. "It says you're human, and you can't read into people's souls. Seems pretty ordinary to me, if you don't mind me saying so."

Angie sighed. "I suppose. I'm going to call Helen to see if she'll come help until we find someone else. I don't suppose you want the job?" She grinned when Finn shook her head vehemently.

"God in heaven, no. I nearly killed twelve people trying to get to the ER, and this was just a broken ankle. The world wouldn't be safe if I had to keep up with her every day." Finn spun a fork around in circles on the countertop. "Also, I feel like this might have taken the place of date three, which means we can now talk about exes. Can I ask about yours?"

Angie grimaced. "That was the least smooth you've been since we met, but yes." She flipped the omelets and then plated the food. "Chris and I met at a fundraiser. She was all fire. Passionate, intense, charismatic. We hit it off and moved in together three months later." She carried the plates to the table and sat across from Finn. "At first, it seemed fine. She wasn't really a kid person, but I figured she'd come around once she got to know Luna and saw how great she was."

Finn nodded and kept eating, letting Angie talk.

"But it was strange. Any time the paps came around, she'd make sure to stay off camera. If I came into a room, she'd put her phone face down or close the laptop. There were warning bells, but she insisted she was just being respectful and giving me all her attention right away." She laughed humorlessly. "Deep down I knew she was keeping things from me, but I couldn't figure out what. Eventually it became clear she wasn't warming to Luna at all, and she'd go as far as to suggest we go away on trips together without Luna. That created plenty of arguments, as you can imagine, and she started acting weird. Staying out late, not calling, that kind of thing."

"She sounds like a certifiable asshat." Finn ate her bacon, looking at Angie thoughtfully. "What happened to end it?"

"There was a photo of us that made it into the big wide world. Two days later, my agent said someone was trying to get in touch with me, saying that they had information I should know about Chris. Normally I'd ignore something like that, but with the way she'd been behaving..." Angie rolled her neck, trying to ease the tension building in it. "So, I called the woman. Long story short, Chris was wanted by the police. Four different women had fallen under her spell, and she'd taken all of them for thousands of dollars. Forgery, fraud, the list went on. That's why she avoided the cameras. She was avoiding being caught."

Finn's eyebrows rose. "Damn. What did you do?"

"I didn't have to do anything. The police came knocking the next day, arrested her, and I haven't seen or heard from her since. Fortunately, we hadn't gotten to the point of shared accounts, and I'm extremely private about my money, so she hadn't gotten her hands on anything. In fact, she was already making plans to move on to another wealthy woman. That's what she was doing on her phone and such, making plans with someone else. Seems she knew she wasn't going to be able to con me the way she did the others."

"Damn." Finn had finished her meal and pushed the empty plate away. "Humans can be a black hole of never-ending dog shit. I'm so sorry that happened to you, but I'm glad it didn't turn out worse than it did."

Angie went to clear their plates but Finn shook her head, indicating Angie should stay put. She began doing the clean-up.

"The worst part of it was how it made Luna feel. Like she didn't matter. Like I *chose* someone who would treat her that way." Angie let the guilt infuse her the way it always did when she thought of that time period. "And she was right to feel that way. Her dad is a world-class narcissistic jerk, then there was Chris, now Karen." She hugged herself, trying to ward off the cold shame. "When it comes to my daughter, I do nothing but screw up."

Finn wiped her hands on the dishtowel and pulled Angie into her arms. "Being a parent is the hardest job in the world, and your boss is a little human who doesn't always know what they want or need, and you just have to give it to them, even if you have no idea how."

Angie rested against Finn's shoulder, breathing in the light spice of her cologne. "You always know what to say." She pulled back slightly and looked into Finn's eyes. "Will you sleep next to me tonight?" When Finn's eyes darkened, Angie grinned a little. "Not for that. I just want your arms around me. Is that okay?" Asking for something so simple shouldn't have been so hard, but it still made her wince inside.

In response, Finn took her hand and led her upstairs. Angie went into the bathroom and slipped on her pjs, a simple tank top and shorts set. Hardly the sexy apparel she thought she'd be wearing the first time she had Finn in her bed, but it would do. When she came back into the bedroom, Finn was already in bed. The tight black tank top showed off her biceps and Angie reconsidered the cuddle-only invitation.

Finn patted Angie's side of the bed. "We need to turn off the light so I can't see you looking at me like I'm your favorite dessert."

Angie slid into bed and turned her back to Finn right away. "Big spoon?"

"Damn right." Finn pulled her close, wrapping her arm securely around her waist. "Sleep well, beautiful."

Desire burned hot, but exhaustion dampened the flame. She wiggled her butt to get closer, and Finn groaned.

"Seriously, Angie. I was heroic today and shouldn't be punished for it." She kissed the back of Angie's neck, leaving a trail of goosebumps. "Go to sleep and stop torturing me."

Angie sighed happily and let herself sink into the warmth and safety of Finn's embrace. She would deal with tomorrow, tomorrow. For now, she was right where she wanted to be.

***

Angie woke alone. Finn's pillow was cold, and Angie shivered not just from the temperature, but from the idea that Finn had already left. She'd been having delicious dreams and as she'd come to, she'd hoped to put a little of them into play for real.

She pushed herself out of bed and then bit her lip. Finn's button-down shirt was still neatly hanging over the chair and her shoes were still beneath it. Smiling, she hurriedly threw on her robe and went to Luna's room, but it too was empty.

As she made her way down the stairs, she heard laughter and voices and recognized more than just Finn and Luna's. "Helen!" She launched herself into her arms. "I was going to call you this morning, but I overslept." She looked at the time. "Oh my god, I should have been at the studio an hour ago."

Helen held up her hand. "Stop and breathe, darlin'. First of all, Luna called me as soon as she woke up this morning and I came straight over, bearing gifts." She motioned at the huge stack of pancakes with bowls of chopped strawberries, nuts, and chocolate beside them. "Second, you left your phone down here last night and when Luna saw who it was, I answered and let them know what had happened. They told you to take the day off and let them know what you need." She poured Angie a cup of coffee and gently pushed her into the seat next to Finn. "Third, we'll discuss the situation with Karen after you've eaten, showered, and compiled a list of meals you might want Susan to cook this week. I've already called and told her what's going on, and she's planning on using her room in the house until Luna is up and around again."

Angie leaned into Finn's embrace as she started to cry. "You're such a godsend, Helen. We've missed you so much."

"I've missed you too." She looked at Luna fondly, then winked at Finn. "And it seems we have other things to catch up on as well." She looked at her watch. "Now, I'm going to go unpack in my old room."

"What about Karen's things?" Angie looked at her phone. Nothing from the wayward nanny.

"They're already gone, Angie. I don't know when she decided she was leaving, but she knew before this happened with Luna." She gave Luna's shoulders a squeeze. "I'm sorry, sweetheart. She wasn't worthy of this family."

Helen left, and Angie did her best not to show her fury. "How are you feeling today? How's the ankle?"

Luna finished chewing an enormous mouthful of pancakes. "Finn didn't sleep in the guestroom last night."

Finn started choking on her food.

Angie slapped her on the back until she stopped coughing and used the time to figure out what to say. Finn was always really honest with Luna. Maybe that was the way to go. "No, she didn't. She slept in my room. I wanted the company."

Luna looked surprised at the direct answer and then grinned. "Company? Is that what the kids are calling it these days?"

Finn coughed.

"All right. Knock it off before you kill Finn. How are you feeling?"

Luna looked down at the cast. "This sucks, but it doesn't hurt too much. Getting around the dig site on crutches is going to be hard though."

"It will. Are you sure you want to go? You could put it off till next year?" At Luna's crestfallen look, Angie kept going, even though her protective instincts were begging her to stay silent. "You don't have to, and it's completely your choice. I'm just saying it could be a possibility."

"But you won't stop me from going?" Luna's gaze was penetrating, as though she was determined to see through the ruse.

"I won't. You're smart and capable, and you know what you can and can't do. Maybe," Angie said, trying to find middle ground she was comfortable with, "you should contact the people at the dig. Tell them what happened and see what they think. No one will know better, right?"

Luna nodded, looking at her plate. "Okay. I can do that."

Angie pulled Luna's iPad from the table. "Are you comfortable? Or do you want to sit on the couch?"

"The couch, please. I can feel my heartbeat in my foot this way." Luna carefully got off the stool and accepted the crutches from Finn.

They got her settled on the couch with pillows under her foot, then Angie and Finn returned to the kitchen. It was the first moment Angie had to really look at her, and she was sorely tempted to drag her back upstairs.

Her black tank top hugged her torso, defining the rigid muscles beneath and showing she had a six pack. She'd mentioned going to the gym several times, and she clearly spent a good amount of time honing her body. A beautiful tattoo of a delicate looking purple flower twined around her upper arm. Her bicep twitched as Angie ran her fingertips over it. The jeans hung low on her hips in a way that should only be allowed in ads for lesbian porn. Somehow, her bare feet completed the sexy look, and Angie became a mindless puddle of lust.

"Babe, you're killing me," Finn whispered in her ear.

"It's entirely your fault for standing in my kitchen looking… looking…like this." Angie waved her hand over Finn's body.

"Should I cover up?" Finn moved closer, her voice low.

Angie tilted her head in answer, and Finn lightly brushed a kiss over her lips.

"Gross. At least go in another room."

Luna's voice broke the moment, and Angie rolled her eyes and stepped back.

Finn laughed and the tension left her shoulders. "I should go home and change. I have work to do today as well."

"You're leaving?" Luna sounded panicked and shifted so she could see Finn, but she was at an awkward angle.

Finn squeezed Angie's hand and then went and sat on the coffee table so Luna could see her. "If I don't go home and shower, you'll never get the stench of me out of the house. And it's not exactly like I can borrow your mom's clothes, is it?" She flexed, making Luna scoff.

"You'd look ridiculous." Luna pushed up her glasses. "But you'll come back? I probably can't go to the coffee shop for a while. You'll have to come here."

Angie leaned on the counter, watching the exchange. She didn't want to interfere in this friendship that clearly meant so much to Luna, even if she too wanted to beg Finn to come back sooner than later.

"I have a life, you know. What about my pets? Who will look after them?" Finn's smile showed she was teasing, and Luna relaxed into the couch.

"We both know you're too weird to have pets. And people who have pets always share their photos and stories about them, and you've never said anything about one."

Finn shook her head. "I have an image to keep up as a spy, remember? My pet sloth will be extremely lonely. He and the iguana barely speak to each other. I'm their only hope at socialization."

Luna laughed. "So weird."

Finn stood. "I promise to come back, but I really do have to work and take care of some things. But we pinky promised, right?"

Luna nodded. "See you soon."

Finn ruffled her hair. "I'm at the other end of the phone." She went back to Angie and pulled her into her arms. "And as for you," she whispered into her ear, "cuddling you last night was the sweetest torture I never want to endure again without having fucked you senseless first."

Angie's knees went weak, and she held onto Finn's shoulders to keep from falling at her feet.

"So with that thought, I'll be taking my leave." Finn slowly slid her hands from Angie's waist, a wicked grin on her lips. "I'll call you about date four and to see how the patient is doing."

Angie simply nodded. If she opened her mouth, she'd beg Finn to stay. She'd give her a robe to wear and wash the clothes she had on, just to keep her nearby. And they could definitely remedy the shower situation.

"Killing me," Finn said softly, backing away. "See you soon, bonita."

Moments later, Angie heard the front door close, then the truck start and drive away. She leaned her head on her arms on the counter and debated going upstairs to take care of herself while imagining the things Finn could do to her.

"Can we watch *The Lorax*?" Luna asked.

Angie looked up. Well, watching cartoons would certainly take the edge off her desire too. And that was the one movie Luna turned to when she was anxious or sad. She picked up the strawberries and chocolate and brought them to the couch. She lifted Luna's foot, sat down, and placed it on her thigh. "Let's do it."

There would be time for Finn later. Right now, she needed to be in full mom mode. As the movie began and her thoughts drifted, she wondered just how much time she and Finn might have together. She'd be going away to film soon. Would Finn be there when she got back?

Chapter Twenty-One

FINN COULDN'T KEEP UP with the story flooding through her. The characters were living the experience, and she was just a vessel, someone to record their emotions and actions as they battled their demons. All she had to do was not interfere and the tale would unfold as it was meant to.

She wrote until the characters needed a break, like the actors on a stage. Her stomach growled but the empty fridge offered nothing but mustard and outdated salad dressing she couldn't throw out, because then there'd only be mustard and that would be too sad. She ordered pizza, unwilling to go out and ruin the buzz of creation.

Writing had helped distract her from the horny thoughts that Angie inspired, but now that she was taking a break, they rushed right back in like a tide yearning for shore. First, though, she called Luna.

"I thought I'd check in on our heroic warrior of the wheeled board. How are you fairing?"

There was a moment's hesitation. "Mom's upstairs."

"Weird answer to that question. If I want to talk to your mom, I'll call her on the phone to which she's tethered. I'm calling you to see you how you are."

"That's cool." It was easy to hear the smile in Luna's tone. "I'm okay. Bored, mostly. My friend from science camp is coming over, and she's going to stay the night."

Hearing that Luna had an age-appropriate friend was a relief. "Sounds like good stuff."

"Are you coming back tonight? We could all watch a movie."

"I think I'm going to sleep in my own bed tonight. But I'll be back over soon, I promise."

"Okay. My friend is here. See you." Luna hung up without waiting for a response.

Finn gave it fifteen minutes and then called Angie.

"Luna told me you called, and I was going to be seriously pissed off if you didn't call me too. It's way too strange to be competing for your affections with my daughter."

Finn laughed. "I wanted to give you time to get them settled. Like I told her, I'll call each of you on the technology to which you're attached. How are you doing?"

"I feel like a teenager obsessed with sex. You?"

"Same. Want to get together again soon?" There was no question she was done waiting and wanted Angie on her back, naked and crying out her name.

"I have to get back to work. Some of the script has been reworked after the table reads, and we need to have another run at it. Are we still on for a full day out together? Luna wants to go to her friend's house on Saturday."

That meant no time restrictions, which would be perfect. "Saturday it is. See you at ten thirty. And bring a swimsuit."

That gave Finn a few days on her own, which made her feel slightly adrift. When had she grown so used to their company and so unused to being alone? This business with Angie and Luna was a slippery slope, and no matter how hard she dug her heels in, she simply kept sliding right toward the vision of family they offered, one she'd never known.

As if responding to her thoughts, Pablo's name appeared on her phone as it started to buzz.

"So?" he said when she answered.

"So what?" She propped her feet on the table, ready for the conversation to come.

"What have you decided to do?"

"I've hired a private investigator." She looked at her watch. "In fact, he should be there by now."

"You hired off-island, right?"

"Obviously. Just because I've been away doesn't mean I've forgotten. And you know I'll call you when I find out anything."

"I know." He paused. "I have news."

"Never good news. Why is that? Why can't you call to tell me you've won the lottery, or there's evidence that we're not heading toward global disaster?" Her stomach sank. She'd been having such a good day too.

"Your sister is getting married."

How could that be? Her sisters were all too young. She faltered when she thought about how long she'd been away. "Celia?"

"Marrying the oldest Pérez boy." Pablo's tone was neutral, not giving anything away about how he felt.

"Because his father is my father's closest ally. Jesus. Did she have any say in it?"

Pablo sighed. "I don't know. He keeps them away from people except when it comes to the press. They're allowed to go shopping, but they always have guards with them, and you know what that means."

"They can't say anything that won't get back to him." Finn rubbed at her neck, trying to release the tension. "Thanks for telling me. I can only hope she'll be happy, whatever the situation."

"Anyway, let me know what you hear. Love you."

Finn relaxed against the couch, but then jumped up and gathered her computer and notebooks. She needed coffee and fresh air.

***

"And so I said to her, there's one of her and one of me. Why does she get to say the toilet seat has to be down? Why can't she be the one to have to put it down when she wants to go, instead of me having to put it up?" Steven shook his shiny bald head as though truly vexed.

Finn sipped her coffee, made special by Delia who said she'd added a dash of good juju, and was very glad that this wasn't an argument she would ever need to have in her home.

"Who do you think is right?" he asked.

"I think you could compromise. You do it half the time, and she does it half the time. Then nobody wins, and you're both satisfied."

Strangely, he looked agreeable to that solution. "That's a great idea. Compromise is life, right?" When she just nodded, he squinted at her. "Why don't you have a girlfriend?"

"I do. Several, in fact. Two wives, two girlfriends, one mistress, one femme domme, and a non-binary, asexual companion."

He blinked at her as though trying to determine whether or not she was serious. She kept her expression neutral as she sipped her coffee and watched Gertrude whisper-shout details about the ferruginous hawk watching the group from where it perched on an old oak tree branch.

"You could be serious with us sometimes, you know? You don't have to constantly make stuff up." He kicked at a pile of rusty, crackling leaves.

"How do you know some of what I say isn't true? The best stories are somewhere between truth and lies."

"That sounds like something someone who makes a lot of stuff up would say." He shrugged. "I like you anyway." He lifted his binoculars and focused on the hawk.

Finn ambled along behind the group, letting her mind wander. Unerringly, it continued to wander right back to Angie and the way she felt in Finn's arms. By the time the Wingers were flying away toward their separate homes, Finn felt a little lighter.

"So have you found your color?" Gertrude asked when she and Finn were the last two in the parking lot.

"I have. It's a lot brighter than I expected, and I'm a little worried about it drawing attention though." That was more honest than she'd planned on being. Maybe relaxing in nature wasn't a good idea after all.

"And people who like to stay in the shadows don't like to draw attention." Gertrude hoisted herself up to sit beside Finn on the tailgate. "Maybe that means it's time for you to join the rest of us in the box of crayons."

Finn watched a bird of prey circle lazily overhead. "What if that could mess up the other colors?"

"I feel like we're beating this metaphor to death, but fine. Mostly, other colors combine to make brilliant new ones. Even the black crayon can't completely hide another color, so worrying about that isn't any good." Gertrude closed her eyes, her face tilted toward the sun. It caught the lines in her face and showed the roadmap of her life.

"My choice seems to be run and let someone very special down or stay and let things get potentially messy." Boiled down to such simple options, Finn could see that only one was the way to go.

"Running has to come to an end sometime. It's okay to do it for safety, or because you know that's what's best at the moment. But running forever takes an awful lot of time and energy. What a waste of something finite. Use what you have wisely, child. It slips away before you know it." Gertrude slid down from the tailgate with Finn's help. "Maybe bring your friend one day. It would be nice to meet her."

Finn waved. As simple as it would be to invite Angie to something like a long wander with the Wingers, would she want to do something so ordinary? Did super celebrities go on bird walks? From what she'd learned, Angie had little time to do anything other than work. But she'd been spending plenty of time with Finn and Luna over the past weeks. Did that mean anything?

Refreshed but not necessarily wiser, Finn went home and started writing again. The next couple days were the same. She woke, had coffee, showered, hit the gym harder than usual in order to work out the frustration of being sexually aroused for as many minutes as there were in the day, and then went home to her desk and let the story flow. Even the quick snags were worked out without much hassle, and she was grateful not only for being able to write again, but also for the reprieve in thinking about Angie and Luna. She texted them regularly and popped in to see Luna for lunch one day. Angie was working, but Helen was there, as was the chef, Susan. They joined her and Luna for a game of tiles, and Susan was quick to pick up Finn's strategy, which made for a more intense experience.

By Saturday, Finn was almost desperate to see Angie again, and the moment she opened the door, she took Finn's breath away. She wore a delicate sundress in pale blue with a deep V-neck that showed off her cleavage and made Finn salivate.

She got out and opened the truck door. "You look beautiful." She gave her a soft kiss as she got in.

"And you look like a true Californian."

Finn wiped her palms on her cargo shorts. "I have a change of clothes for later."

"I like the look. Casual and sexy." Angie held up a large, square handbag with that rustic-made-to-look-worn look. "I've got a swimsuit and change of clothes too. Where are we headed?"

"I called in a favor from a friend. Do you like boats?" If Angie said no, the day's plans were going to go to hell fast.

"I love sailing. There's something about being on the ocean that's so freeing." Angie rolled her window down and let her hand play in the wind. "Where are we sailing to?"

"Can I surprise you?"

"You always do." Angie's smile was mischievous.

They talked about Luna and her plans, along with how Angie's movie preparation was going. The drive went quickly, and Finn gathered the things she had prepared.

"Are we moving in together on this island and you forgot to mention it?" Angie asked, surveying the cooler, huge picnic blanket, towels, and bag of sundries.

"Me moving anywhere requires about fifty boxes of books." She studied the pile of things, wondering if she'd overdone it. "I just wanted to be prepared."

Angie touched her arm. "I'm teasing. I love the thought you've put into this."

Finn kissed her, unable to resist, and then looked up when someone called out.

"Angie, this is Paige, my agent. Paige, this is—"

"Jesus, Finn. You said you wanted to bring someone. You didn't tell me you wanted to bring *the* someone." Paige held out her hand and shook Angie's hand with both of hers. "I had no idea our recluse knew the most beautiful actress of our time. I didn't know she knew anyone, actually. I thought she'd show up with a mannequin."

Finn rolled her eyes, but Angie's laugh made the teasing worth it. "My loving agent helped me get the boat and captain for today. Because she's actually right, I don't know anyone but the two of you. And Luna," she amended.

"Well, you know the two most important people then, and that's all that matters." Paige turned away and gave the crew directions, and the things Finn had unloaded from the truck were efficiently stowed on the boat. "Also, I know the captain personally, as well as his crew. They know where their bread is buttered and won't breathe a word of this."

Finn took in Paige's dilated pupils, her quick breathing, her pink cheeks. There was no question there'd be a serious Q&A session at some point. But it wasn't going to be now. "Thanks, Paige. We owe you one."

"You *owe* me about three hundred pages of one, and I'm going to hold you to it." Her eyebrows rose. "In fact, I could use this to get you to accept—"

"Bye, Paige." Finn let the warning slip into her tone, and Paige sighed theatrically.

"Fine. Bye. Have fun." She blew them a kiss and hurried off to her car, probably to harass another client.

"Shall we?" Finn held out her hand and helped Angie onto the boat.

The captain and single crew member were nice, and they kept to themselves, which was exactly what Finn wanted. She and Angie sat at the front of the boat, soaking in the sun. When Angie took off the sundress and stretched out in her white bikini that showed off every curve, Finn nearly stopped breathing. She glanced over her shoulder to see the captain and crew member staring as well. She couldn't blame them. A goddess was on board, looking for all the world like she had no idea what effect she was having on the people around her.

The captain gave her a brief smile, shook his head, and looked away. The crew member busied himself elsewhere.

Finn sat beside Angie. "Can I put suntan lotion on you?"

"I've already put it on everywhere but my back." Angie rolled over and gathered her hair over her shoulder. "Thank you."

Finn's mouth was as dry as desert sand as she rubbed the lotion into Angie's soft, toned skin. There wasn't a blemish on it. Not a freckle, not a mole. She took her time, enjoying the way Angie seemed to push into her touch.

"Tell me about your tattoo," Angie said, her words slightly muffled by her arms.

"Morivivi." Finn said, thinking of the flower that graced her upper arm. "The flower of death and life. It was my mother's favorite, and I got it in memory of her." An action, apparently, that might have been unnecessary. "It protects itself when it's touched, drawing in, and then opening back up when it feels like the danger has passed."

"When did you lose her?"

Finn slid her hand over Angie's back. She had enough suncream on now so she wouldn't burn if they landed on the sun, but she couldn't stop touching her. "When I was seventeen."

"Do you have siblings?" At Finn's hesitation, Angie said, "Vague facts are safe, Finn."

"You have a way of getting me to tell you things. Okay. I have three sisters. I found out a couple days ago that one of them is getting married soon."

"Will you go to the wedding? Can I go with you?" Angie turned on her side and rested her head on her hand.

"No." Finn winced at the way that came out. "I mean, I'm not going, for reasons I don't want to get into. But if I were going, yes, I'd most definitely ask you to be my date."

Angie grinned. "That's better. Now I don't have to throw you overboard."

"The only problem with taking you to a wedding would be the fact that you'd outshine the bride, which is never a good look. We'd have to get your makeup artist to make you look like an old hag. Then I'd take you home, we'd get into the shower, and voilà! I'd have a young goddess in my arms, like a fairytale." She trailed her fingertips over Angie's hip and along her thigh.

"I played Nanny McPhee once. She starts out all old and warty and then is beautiful by the time the children have learned her lesson and she heads off into the sunset."

"I watched a clip of that. You did a great British accent, but you had on way too many clothes for my taste." Finn gave Angie's bikini strap a little tug.

"Before we get indecent in front of an audience, want to tell me where we're going now?"

Finn lay on her back beside Angie. "Anacapa Island. Once home to Frenchy LeDreau, who lived there as a hermit for thirty years. Imagine living on an island all alone for three decades and then coming back to California in the sixties?"

"The culture shock must have been like dropping onto a new planet." Angie, still on her side, laid her hand on Finn's stomach. "And are we going to tour Frenchy's old hideaway?"

"I can be obtuse, but even I know that wouldn't be romantic." Finn put her hand over Angie's, liking the way it felt there. "When we dock at the only dock on the island, the guys will take the kayak down from the back of the boat, and then we'll go kayaking over to Arch Rock, where we'll snorkel and play with pinnipeds, hopefully. Then we'll head to the one beach available at exactly the right tide time today and have lunch. The guys will be dropping the cooler and blankets off while we adventure." She looked over. "Is that okay with you? If not, we can always just sail around the Channel Islands and watch for dolphins, or sharks, or whales. Or flying fish."

Angie's hand slid up Finn's tank top, and her fingers played over the ridges of Finn's abs. "It sounds wonderful, but maybe we skip the snorkeling and go straight to the private beach."

The captain ducked out of the cockpit. "We'll be docking shortly. There are some dolphins playing in our wake, if you're interested."

Angie leapt up and grabbed Finn's hand. "Come on."

They made their way to the back and watched as the dolphins jumped, rolled, and raced along them behind them, their slate, rubbery looking bodies highlighted with pinkish-white racing stripes vivid against the white water.

"Dolphins are a species who mate for fun and not just for procreation," Finn said, leaning on the side.

"They're also polygamous." Angie leaned over to get a better view. "How do you feel about polygamy, Finn?"

"I think in an apocalyptic situation, it may be the only way to rebuild the human race. I hope to be dead before that happens."

"So you're not a fan?"

"Of an apocalypse? Or of having to carry children in order to breed more humans?" Finn grinned when Angie looked over her shoulder and gave her an exasperated look.

"Of having multiple partners or not being strictly monogamous." She laughed when a dolphin blew water at her.

The yacht slowed, and she put her hands around Angie's waist. "Oh, look, we're here." She picked her up and spun her around, her heart racing at the sound of Angie's laughter.

The plan went exactly as Finn hoped, and it wasn't long before they were sliding out of the kayak and into the water. Finn tied the kayak in place by a boulder and then took Angie's hand. They floated along, pointing out an unusual-looking eel here, and then a bluebanded goby and a giant kelpfish over there. The kelp forest swayed in the water like dancers, and Angie flapped at the water to get Finn's attention when seals appeared like fat wraiths in the emerald kelp.

Eventually, Finn glanced at her watch and saw that it was time for lunch. She didn't want to miss the opportunity to picnic with Angie in a private cove.

They swam to the kayak and pulled themselves aboard, not so gracefully, and then Finn paddled them around to the cove. When the arch came into sight, Angie leaned forward, almost tipping them over.

"Isn't that amazing?" she said, looking over her shoulder at Finn.

It was at that precise moment that Finn knew she had a mental image she'd never forget. Angie, backlit by the sun in her white bikini, the forty-foot rock arch behind her, and the sea crashing against it. Magic. Pure, undiluted magic that touched Finn's heart as easily as snow caressed spring flower petals.

Unnerved by the surge of emotion, she paddled silently into the cove. The huge picnic blanket had been laid out. Towels were neatly stacked at the corner, and next to it was the cooler. At the edge of each corner was a long-stemmed red rose placed head-up in the sand.

"Was this your idea?" Angie asked, not looking away from the picture-perfect scene.

"That depends." Finn went to the towels, shook one out, and wrapped it around Angie's shoulders. "If you like it, then yes. If you don't, then no. I blame the captain."

"No one has ever done anything like this for me." Angie held the towel close to her, and she still hadn't looked away.

"I like being the first," Finn murmured into her ear, before going to get her own towel. She was nearly knocked over when Angie flung herself at her.

"Thank you." Angie tilted her head and kissed Finn, softly at first, and then with more passion.

Finn let the towel drop and pulled Angie to her. She knelt, pulling Angie down to the blanket. She reveled in the salty taste of her skin, the way her neck arched to give Finn more access. She pulled the string at the nape of Angie's neck, allowing the material to slip off, exposing Angie's breasts.

Finn moved forward, her weight pressing Angie to the blanket. Angie spread her legs, allowing Finn to kneel between them as she lightly sucked in Angie's nipple and moaned at Angie's soft cry. Angie threaded her fingers into Finn's hair, keeping her in place. She sucked harder and felt Angie's hips raise, pressing into her stomach. She left one nipple and went to the other, lavishing the same attention on it as she caressed the other breast.

"God, Finn. Please..."

Finn pulled off her sports bra, then lay back down. The feeling of Angie beneath her, the sounds she made as Finn tasted every inch of her just the way she'd wanted to was driving her to delirium. It wasn't enough. She couldn't get enough fast enough. She pulled Angie's bikini bottoms off and moaned when she put her palm over Angie's hot, wet center.

"Tell me, bonita. Tell me what you want from me," Finn murmured in Angie's ear as her palm pressed against Angie's clit. She needed to hear it. Needed to hear the goddess under her say it was Finn she wanted.

"Please, Finn." Her hips rose and fell against Finn's hand with increasing urgency. "Please fuck me. Show me you want me."

Finn moaned and pushed three fingers into her and at Angie's cry, she felt herself grow that much closer to getting off herself. She pushed deeper in response to Angie's pleas, to the way her body pushed into Finn's touch. Faster, deeper, harder. Angie begged, writhed, called Finn's name, and it was the music of the spheres, sensual cosmic beauty that filled Finn's soul to the point she was sure she'd explode, her essence unable to contain the beauty and eroticism of what they were sharing.

Angie's fingernails dug into Finn's back as she stiffened and gave a hoarse cry, her eyes shut tight, her back arched, and her core clenched hard around Finn's fingers. Finn twisted them just so and Angie bucked again, and then again. Angie's thigh was hard against Finn's clit, and at Angie's final orgasm, Finn ground down and let go, throwing her head back as her orgasm hit hard and deep.

They lay that way for a moment and then Finn slipped out, rolled onto her back, and pulled Angie against her. Angie rested her head on Finn's shoulder and draped her leg over Finn's.

Angie shook her head. "That was—"

"Yeah." Finn held her close and kissed her head. "Yeah."

Angie traced the lines of Finn's abs, making her shiver even under the hot afternoon sun. "You make me crazy. I can't stop thinking about you. Even at work, where nothing ever distracts me, I find myself thinking about you. And now, after this..."

Finn, already turned on again, rose. "I've been thinking about you too, and I think I mentioned one way in particular." She pressed Angie to her stomach on the blanket and then lay on top of her. She gathered her hair in one hand and pulled it out of the way so she could place kisses on her neck, then she slowly made her way down Angie's spine, paying special attention to the curve of her back, to the way her hips felt under her hands. She put one hand on Angie's shoulder and pulled her to her hands and knees, and with her other hand, entered Angie once again, this time a little harder.

Angie pressed against her, gasping. "Fuck. Yes. Please, yes."

That was all Finn needed. She took Angie deep and slow, pushing hard, her thumb pressed against her clit with every thrust. Angie rocked against her, calling her name, begging with inarticulate sounds for more.

Finn moved faster, keeping in tune with Angie's body as she climbed inexorably toward her climax. When she did, she rose up, pushing hard onto Finn's fingers, and Finn held her in her lap, letting her ride out her climax.

Angie leaned into Finn, her body limp.

"Are you okay, mi amor?" Finn nestled into Angie's neck, not wanting to let any space between their bodies just yet.

Angie didn't respond, and Finn turned Angie's chin so she could see her face. At the tears sliding down Angie's cheeks, she froze. "Have I hurt you? Are you okay?"

Angie took a shuddery breath. "I'm beyond okay. I'm... overwhelmed. In awe. I don't know. Finn, that was... You're..." She gave a little sob and pressed closer.

Finn pulled out of her and shifted them to the blanket. Once again, she wrapped Angie in her arms. Although there weren't any tears in her eyes, she knew what Angie meant. She felt it too.

What the hell was she going to do now?

Chapter Twenty-Two

ANGIE STRETCHED LIKE A cat in the perfect spot of sunshine. Her body ached in the best way.

"Any more food before I pack up?" Finn asked, resting on her elbows and looking sexy and relaxed.

"I'm full, thanks." The simple combination of deli meats and cheeses, along with bottles of Cubanista beer, had been perfect when they'd finally stirred themselves from their post-sex nap. As she watched Finn languidly start piling things into the cooler, she wondered at the feeling of overwhelming passion she'd felt earlier. In all the times she'd been with someone, she'd never had that happen.

"Have you ever been in love?" she asked suddenly.

Finn stopped what she was doing and looked over her shoulder. "Why do you ask?"

"Just curious." That wasn't quite true, and she knew they both knew it. But saying those words? That wasn't something to do. Not yet.

Finn continued packing up their things, and then plucked a rose from the sand and lay on her side next to Angie. She drew the rose petals along Angie's skin and smiled at the goosebumps that followed.

"No. I've never been in love. As you know, I move around a lot. That means my relationships tend to be on the brief side. A night, maybe two, but nothing more. They're functional." She looked into Angie's eyes, her gaze unwavering. "You're the first person I've dated seriously in a very long time. You're the first person to make me want to stay in one place."

"And would you? Stay?"

Finn sat up and wrapped her arms around her knees. "Honestly? I don't know, Angie. I don't want to make promises I can't keep. There are things in my life I haven't told you. Things that are complicated." She looked at Angie, who was sitting up beside her now. "And what about you? Aren't you always at work? Do you have time for something serious?"

Angie wanted to say of course she did, but wasn't that what Luna had accused her of? Not having time because she was always working. Chris had thrown that at her as an excuse to seek attention elsewhere. "I guess I feel like you're making me consider some new things too."

Finn's smile was soft and sweet. "Then maybe we just see where this takes us. No expectations or strings." She took Angie's hand in hers and kissed her knuckles. "No promises to break, just us seeing what we become."

Somehow, it felt a little lacking, but Angie made sure not to show it. "I think that sounds like a good place to start."

Finn checked her watch. "The boat should be here any minute to pick us up and gather the things." She stood and pulled Angie up and into her arms. "You're the kind of magic people only know from fairy tales, Angie. You're beautiful, kind, and sweet, and sex with you makes me think there's a god out there somewhere who wants us to know what ecstasy is."

Angie let the words fill the tiny hole that appeared in her happiness at Finn's lack of commitment. She returned Finn's kiss, wrapping her arms around her neck and pressing against her.

Finn lightly bit Angie's bottom lip. "We don't have time for another round, but I'll take you up on that offer when we've got four walls around us."

As if on cue, the yacht rounded the corner and blew its horn. They lowered an inflatable boat, and the crew member rowed out to them. The three of them loaded the picnic materials and then got in and headed back to the yacht.

Angie took her bag below deck and showered off the salt and sand. Nothing could wash away the sense of Finn's touch though, and the feel of it made her smile as she dressed and headed back to the main deck. The sun was setting, and she sat between Finn's legs with Finn's arms wrapped around her from behind.

As the boat pulled back into the harbor, Angie turned to Finn. "Can we go back to your place? I'd like to see where you live."

"You just want to make sure I don't have a husband and seven kids waiting at home." Finn grinned and nipped at Angie's earlobe. "It isn't as neat, clean, or big as your place. Is that okay?"

"How snobby do you think I am?" She returned Finn's kiss with the ardor already rebuilding.

"I think you're probably one of the most down-to-earth celebrities the world has ever known."

The boat docked, they thanked the captain and his crew member, and Angie saw Finn hand over an envelope and shake their hands. She knew to tip, even though they'd probably been paid well for the trip. Once again, she was reminded that Finn was comfortable around this kind of wealth, which seemed such a contrast to the solitary life she led.

They got into Finn's truck, and she was surprised when she realized she had no idea what city Finn lived in. "Where do you live, and how did you end up there?" Angie asked.

"I live in Crescent Heights. When I decided to live in LA, I found the areas of the city where I could be close enough to humanity to be useful to my writing but still be surrounded by trees. I highlighted areas on Google Maps that seemed to dead-end, and I drove around those dead ends looking for houses for sale. Impractical on many levels, but it gave me great knowledge of the city." She grinned. "How's that for a direct answer?"

"I'm so stunned I don't even know how to respond. I think I'm in shock."

Finn laughed and concentrated as they drove up the curving streets of the foothills. The houses were big and set back from the street, growing more so the further up they went. When they got to a clear dead end, Finn turned into a long, steep driveway.

"Remember, I'm not a celebrity." She turned off the engine but didn't move to get out. "Maybe this is a bad idea. Maybe we should go to your place, since Luna isn't home."

Angie opened her door and jumped out, then slammed it and moved to the front of the truck, where she put her hands on her hips and waited. She wasn't about to let this opportunity to know Finn a little more pass by. She could see Finn sigh as she turned to get out.

She took Angie's hand and led her to the house, but Angie stopped and took it in. The house was large and had a massive rooftop terrace that overlooked the city beyond. The covered porch had two rocking chairs that looked almost new, and the garden was landscaped with rose bushes and big, beautiful trees. Finn tugged on her hand and Angie got moving. Once they were inside, she turned in a slow circle to take it all in.

There was no carpet. Smooth white flooring reflected the light and showed the sculptures displayed on pedestals along the walls. As she followed Finn into the living room, she smiled at the stacks of books here and there. Some on this table, some on that one. A large fireplace took pride of place in front of a couple comfortable-looking couches.

"Drink?" Finn stood with her hands in her pockets, her shoulders high as she looked at Angie's feet.

"Are you really so uncomfortable having someone in your space?" Angie asked, running her fingers over a beautiful wall sculpture of a face that was seeming to unravel.

"Well, I don't have anything to base it on, since there's only one other person who visits me."

Angie looked up. "And your functional, brief relationships?"

Finn finally smiled. "Their place or a hotel. Or wherever fits the brevity of the moment."

"And who is the other lucky person to come visit? Paige?"

Angie moved on to a glass orb set on a windowsill. No doubt it would catch the light and send streams of color through the room.

"My cousin, Pablo. Drink?"

Angie nodded. "Whatever you're having."

Finn left the room, presumably to go to the kitchen, and Angie continued to look around. Finn had never said anything about being an art lover, but the nature of the pieces she'd collected made it clear her tastes were both eclectic and refined. Angie had been around enough art snobs and people with money to recognize expensive pieces.

Finn came back in with two bottles of beer. "Sorry, I don't have much in the house."

Angie accepted the bottle and tapped it against Finn's. "Finn, who are you?"

Finn frowned and sat on the arm of the couch. "What do you mean?"

"I mean you're comfortable around wealth in a way that suggests it's a world you know." She gestured toward the wall sculpture. "You like expensive art, and you have a house in a location that probably cost a small fortune by non-wealthy standards. But you live a mostly solitary life, and you drive an old truck when you could clearly afford something far more expensive. You won't talk about your past, and you keep a big aspect of your present completely private."

Finn looked at her as she sipped from her beer, her expression thoughtful. "Do those things bother you?"

Surprised, Angie shook her head. "Bother me? No, I don't think so. Not a lot, anyway. Maybe? I'm not sure. But it makes you a mystery I want to solve."

Finn took a deep drink and then stood and held out her hand. "Let's begin by answering some of those questions in my bedroom."

Angie took her hand. "None of those questions involved anything to do with sex."

"We can pretend." Finn led the way.

***

Angie stretched and sighed happily at the soreness in her body. She hadn't had a workout like the one last night in any gym session. Maybe she needed to trade that in and just have sex with Finn every night. She'd made Angie come over and over again, and when she'd used her mouth instead of her fingers, Angie had felt the room spin as she'd forgotten how to breathe.

When she'd woken later, she'd returned the favor. Finn allowed her to touch and taste her at her own pace and watching her let go of her usual laid-back demeanor as she'd cried out Angie's name had been the sexiest thing she'd ever encountered.

Now, as she watched Finn sleeping, she felt content in a way she'd never felt before. Like the world had stopped to let her soak it in, to be fully present instead of always looking at the next item on her calendar.

She needed the bathroom and a drink. She slowly got out of bed, trying not to wake Finn. Once she'd finished in the bathroom, she headed to the kitchen and started a pot of coffee. They'd have to drink it black, since there wasn't anything but mustard and salad dressing in the fridge, neither of which would help the coffee. She made a mental note to get her PA to have a grocery order sent over. She didn't use one between films, preferring to do some things herself, but now that she was back in work mode, it was time to make use of her once again.

While she was waiting for the coffee to brew, she looked at the stack of magazines on the table. *Railroad Enthusiast* sat on top of a copy of *Classical Piano Today*. She laughed and picked one up, and then an open letter caught her eye. Without thinking, she leaned closer to look at the insignia at the top. She set down the magazine and picked up the letter.

At a noise behind her she turned. Finn stopped mid-stretch when she saw what was in Angie's hand. Her eyebrow quirked, and a small frown formed between her brows.

"An Atwood Award?" Angie flapped the letter. "You've won the Atwood Award?"

Finn sighed and took the letter from Angie's hand before she could make it any further and read the title of the book nominated. She tossed it back on the table.

"It's no big deal, and I won't be there to accept it. I tried to decline it so they could give it to someone else, but they're stubborn bastards."

Angie looked at the letter and back at Finn. "That would be like a scientist declining a Nobel Prize. Finn, an Atwood Award is the biggest literary award outside the Nobel for literature. I'm not a writer and even I know that. How could you turn it down? *Why* would you turn it down?"

Finn turned away. "Drop it, Angie. Please."

Angie's frustration bubbled to the surface once again at Finn's secrets. "I just want to understand."

"And I told you. I'm a private person with a past. That," Finn nodded at the letter, "could potentially lead my past to me. And I can't–won't–have that happen."

"So you hide. You refuse to step into the light because of the shadows of your past?"

"Hey, that's pretty good. I should use it in a book." Finn's dry tone set Angie on edge.

"Finn, what could possibly be so bad that you'd let life pass you by this way? You're clearly incredibly talented and good at what you do." Angie looked around at the house. "More than I can guess at, probably, even with your Atwood Award."

"Can you really not imagine what kind of past someone would have that they'd want to outrun? Is it so hard to imagine wanting to leave the person you used to be behind?" Finn ran her hand through her hair and didn't make eye contact. "I need you to let it go, Angie. I make decisions on my life based on things you can't understand. That's how it has to be. Accept me as I am and know that my life has to be pretty much the opposite of yours. Please."

Stung, Angie moved past Finn and into the bedroom, where she threw on her clothes. "I told you, Finn, that secrets have hurt me in the past. I thought I could let it go, that your past doesn't define the woman you are today." She yanked one of Finn's sweatshirts over her head and motioned at her, even though the sleeve covered her hand. "I was wrong. Whatever that is, you're letting it affect your present and your future. You're still in hiding, and you're letting amazing things go by because of it. Those are some big secrets, and if you can't share that part of you with me, even after..." She shrugged and blinked back tears. "I think we need to reconsider."

Finn's jaw clenched as she stared at Angie, her eyes hard. "I warned you. I never lied to you."

"I'm not saying you did." Angie pulled out her phone and ordered an Uber. "But I *am* saying that secrets scare me, and what I'm feeling for you scares me, and that combination is fucking terrifying." She wiped away the tears threatening to slide down her cheeks.

"Angie, come on," Finn said, moving toward her. "Let's talk this out."

"No, Finn." Angie backed up a step. If Finn touched her, held her, she'd relent. "Until you're ready to trust me with who you really are, until you're ready to stop letting your past haunt you...until you're ready to stop running, we can't be together." She finally let the tears fall. "Because I'm falling for you, hard, and I know you warned me. I know you told me you may not stick around. But god dammit, my heart doesn't understand."

She brushed past her again and went outside, where the Uber was already waiting. She turned and looked back to see Finn standing in the doorway, her expression stricken. But she stayed silent and made no move to stop Angie from leaving. She waited one, two more seconds, then got into the car.

It pulled away, and Angie covered her face as she cried.

Chapter Twenty-Three

THERE WERE NO WORDS. Finn couldn't think of a single word, let alone a sentence, that could define how much it hurt to watch Angie walk away. She'd hoped it wouldn't end this way. She'd allowed herself to believe, for a beautiful, surreal moment, that she could have a life, where her past was gone, and her future held something magical.

Estúpida. She'd been a fool. She sat on her porch in the rocking chair, the empty one beside her rocking on its own in the breeze, mocking her loneliness. Her phone buzzed and she saw Luna's name, but she couldn't bear to talk to her right now. She'd pinky sworn that she wouldn't stop being Luna's friend. But with the look on Angie's face, with the way she felt about Finn's well-guarded past, how could that bit of friendship continue?

Her phone buzzed again, and this time it was Pablo. She ignored it too, but then it buzzed again, and again.

"What?" she snapped.

"Okay, no need to ask if you've seen it then."

Her stomach lurched. "Seen what?"

"Go to *Celebrity News* online. I'll wait."

Finn went to her laptop and did as he said, her fingers aching with tension. "Fuck." The huge photo was of her and Angie at Carnival, huddled together on the bench, along with one of them dancing in a way that made it clear they weren't just friends. Below it was photo after photo of the two of them in different locations. A couple were even at Angie's house and included Luna. All of them were unguarded, real photos that could only have been taken from the inside. The bastards even attached another article with photos of Luna skateboarding and asked questions about what it must be like to be the plain-looking child of such a gorgeous celebrity couple. They showed her constantly alone and suggested that there might be mental health issues involved. "Fucking Karen."

Finn's name was attached but thankfully, it was clear they didn't know anything about her. That made it a little worse as far as the gossip and speculation went.

"So, something else made you answer the phone like your balls are caught in a vice. Sorry to add to it. Prima, I've always been jealous of your status with the ladies, but you've outdone yourself this time."

"Yeah, well, it's over so don't be too envious. I wouldn't tell her about my past and she walked out." The truncated version didn't hold nearly the emotion of the real thing.

"Why not tell her?" he asked.

"You know why."

"No, actually, I don't." He swallowed something loudly and burped. "Telling her who you were wouldn't change her opinion of you. It isn't like she'd go running off to your father to tell him where you are. He's not going to go after a movie star. I know you felt like it kept everyone safe, but if you look at it really logically as the grown-up you're supposed to be, it doesn't make a lot of sense."

"Yeah? And now? My face is splashed all over the place. How long till he finds me and makes a mess of my life?"

"You're not a kid anymore, Finn." Pablo's tone was gentle, a sure sign he was about to say things she didn't want to hear. "If you let him mess up your life now, then it's your fault. You've outgrown him. Your past is hurting you because you can't let it go. Let it go, prima."

"You're right. I have to go." She hung up, knowing he'd forgive her.

She scrolled through the photos online. Angie looked beautiful, no question. But it wasn't just that. Finn looked happier than she remembered being at any time in her life. And they looked damn good together.

A text came in.

My lawyer is working on getting the photos taken down so we don't shatter your precious privacy. Karen signed a confidentiality agreement, but it may be too late to stop the tide. Sorry.

The perfunctory tone deflated Finn even more.

Is Luna okay?

I'll take care of her, don't worry.

Finn winced. *I'm sorry, Angie.*

Me too. I hope you figure things out. Take care.

Finn threw her phone on the couch. She couldn't have messed this up any worse if she'd actually tried to. She needed to get away, to get some distance from all the things clouding her mind and clogging her soul.

She threw together a duffle bag of clothing, gathered all her writing materials, including the magazines she might need for research, and locked the door behind her.

And then the cameras started flashing, and questions came thick and fast through the air like arrows.

"What is the nature of your relationship with Angie Davis?"

"Are you and Angie Davis a couple?"

"How long have you been seeing Angie?"

"What do you do for a living? How did you two meet?"

Reporters stood in her yard, cameras rolling, and microphones turned toward her as they shouted questions her way. She gritted her teeth and pressed through them to her truck, nearly slamming a mic in the door thanks to an overzealous reporter who strayed too close.

Taut like an overfilled water balloon, Finn threw the truck in drive and edged forward, forcing them out of the way and keeping her eyes straight ahead to avoid the cameras focused on her.

After all she'd done to keep her address private, all it had taken was her name tied to Angie's and they'd found her home, her sanctuary. This was exactly the shitstorm she'd been wanting to avoid from the moment she left home at eighteen. She'd let her guard down, and now she was going to pay the price. So why was it the one person she wanted to talk to was the one person who'd brought her world down around her?

***

Treebones Resort in Big Sur was Finn's home away from home. Usually, she only went there once a manuscript was ready for the next draft. The new scenery and some time away from it helped her edit with fresh eyes.

Now, it felt like a refuge.

Maggie, the longtime owner, gave her a warm smile and strong hug. "I had a feeling you'd be turning up here any time now. Your place is free, so go on down. Want me to have your usual grocery order set up?"

Finn rested against the doorjamb. "I can't tell you how much better you've just made me feel. Yes, please. I'm going to be in hiding for a while. I don't think the paps will come here, but—"

"If they show their slimy butts around here, I'll throw wet breadcrumbs and sic the seagulls after them. They'll be gone quick enough." She handed Finn a slip of paper. "And I've put down a different name for you anyway. Won't be any record of you being here."

Finn glanced at the register receipt. "Maribel Madrigal." She laughed. "I'll take the name of a cartoon character anytime. Thanks, Maggie."

Maggie made a shooing motion. "Go on, get settled. Come have a drink with me one night if you need a break or someone to talk to."

Finn passed the first autonomous tent and continued on to the second, which was also the furthest accommodation on the property. The half egg-like structure with an unobstructed view of the Pacific made her sigh with relief. Although Maggie called it a tent, it was bigger than some apartments she'd been in and was warm and cozy inside. She let herself in and dropped her bag on the couch. Her shoulders relaxed and the tension in her neck eased.

This place was off the grid. No internet, no TV. Just Finn and her writing. By the time she headed back to reality, everything would have blown over. She just had to wait it out.

She unpacked her few things and got the desk set up as her writing station. She'd often used writing as a distraction when she was growing up, immersing herself in the stories she created rather than live in the volatile world around her. She'd do the same now.

A knock came and she accepted the bags of groceries from the resort worker, who barely looked at her before loping off back toward the lodge. Finn put everything away in the small kitchenette and was reminded of the sad lack of food in the fridge at home. The sad lack of anything, really.

She threw on a favorite old sweatshirt with a creepy original Mickey Mouse on the front and sank into the Adirondack chair on the front deck. The ocean was the only sound, thanks to it being incredibly expensive *and* off-season.

Unfortunately, the silence allowed her mind to wander, and as it did, the tears that filled her soul finally overflowed from her eyes. How had things gone so far? And why didn't anyone understand her reasons for wanting privacy? Even Pablo, who knew her well enough to know what she'd been through.

Was her abuela right? And what about Pablo and Angie? Gertrude and her box of crayons? Was everyone right but her? How many people had to tell you something before you heard the truth of it? And then, there was her mother. What was she supposed to do about that information? She flashed to the woman at the cemetery with the haunted, surprised eyes. Was it her? And the woman with her, could it have been her lover?

She scrubbed away the tears and went inside. She'd put today to bed and maybe wake with some clarity tomorrow.

It turned out that was easier said than done. She lay awake, following the lines of shadows that seemed to skate over the domed ceiling thanks to the clouds sliding over the moon outside. The roar of the ocean reminded her of Angie's cries mingling with the sound of the water lapping beyond them as they'd fallen into a sensual sacred moment from which they'd emerged newly born and vulnerable.

Was it only yesterday? Where was Angie now? How was Luna handling the extra attention? She could still picture her the day they'd met, anxiety clouding her pale features as the press pressed in. She punched the pillow and then pulled it over her face to keep from yelling at the gods. Finally, she got up, made a pot of coffee, took her laptop outside, and wrote by the light of the moon.

Dawn sent long, thin slices of the palest pink across the sky, and she tried to blink the grit from her eyes. With her conscious brain exhausted, her subconscious had taken over and the rest of the novel had flowed like wine, bittersweet and rich.

But the last chapter eluded her. How did the story end? She couldn't see it, even though she was so near the finish line.

The ocean lifted and fell, tinged pink by the sunrise. She let it lull her, soothe her, and she slipped inside to bed.

Chapter Twenty-Four

ANGIE AND LUNA SAT in the car one street over from Luna's school. The bodyguard drove and Helen sat in the passenger seat. Silently, they all watched as the principal tried to get the paps to move their vans away from the school, although he was doing it with such a smarmy smile, it was no wonder they weren't listening to him.

"Home school?" Luna asked, pushing her glasses up but not looking away from the scene.

"New country?" Angie countered, earning her a small smile.

"Neither," Helen said from the front seat. "Luna, you're going to march right in there with your head held high. You tell them whatever you want to tell them, just don't swear. And Angie, you're going to work. Then you're both coming home to one of Susan's amazing meals, and we're going to work through your trip itineraries." She turned and gave them a stern look. "You're not runners. You both know what running away from things gets you. Face this head on. Let other people run if they want to, but not you two."

"Yes, Helen," they said in unison, and then they laughed.

"I'm going to regret this, but drive around to the next side street," Luna said, and continued to give directions until they were next to a thicket of trees behind the school. "There's a gate back here that no one knows about. I'll go in this way and avoid the cameras." At Helen's look, she shrugged. "I'll hold my head up high *inside*. Let them hang around being asshats with no one to sink their teeth into."

"This is how you were leaving school because of the bully." Angie craned her neck and could just see the silver of the fence.

"A bully who doesn't go to school here anymore, thanks to you." Luna gave Angie one of her rare hugs. "See you tonight."

"I'm taking your mom to work, and then I'll be back in case you need me," the bodyguard said.

Luna nodded, got out of the car, and wandered off into the cluster of trees.

Angie looked at Helen. "Was it a good idea to say that Finn runs away? I think Luna's still convinced Finn is some kind of hero."

"Luna is fully aware that Finn has run away. Saying it out loud doesn't change that. She's allowed to know that Finn ran and to still believe she's a good person. The two things don't cancel each other out." Helen turned back to face forward. "You've played enough complicated characters to know that people aren't just one thing or the other."

Angie rested her head against the window and thought about that. "But if you can't be sure of who the person is, if they let their life be consumed by something you know nothing about…"

"Still doesn't make them a bad person. Flawed, maybe. Misguided and in need of therapy, probably. But not bad."

"Are you saying I should accept her as she is?" Angie really wanted Helen to say yes, that's exactly what she should do. At least that way she'd have advice that would make it feel okay to find Finn and try to make it work.

"No. I'm not saying that. You're right. She's letting something from her past waylay her present, and that's not acceptable. If she was living a full life and was open to the world around her, then I'd tell you that her past didn't matter. But she's made it matter, and she's shown you that she runs when she's faced with conflict. That's not a good look on anyone." Helen reached back and patted Angie's leg. "Sometimes you have to just wait these things out."

Angie nodded, and no one said anything else for the rest of the drive to the studio. Helen got out and gave Angie a strong hug.

"Focus. You have a job to do, so go do it. The world out here will fall into place one way or another."

Angie held on, leaning into her maternal strength. "Thank you. I don't know what we would have done without you."

"You'd have found a way." Helen held Angie at arm's length. "You're stronger than you realize, sweetheart." She got back in the car, and it drove off, leaving Angie standing outside the studio.

She squared her shoulders. Helen was right. She had nothing to be ashamed of. So she was dating a hot woman no one knew anything about. That wasn't a crime. No one had to know that she'd tried to email and call Finn to see if they could talk, but the email had bounced and the phone had gone straight to voicemail. She'd dropped by her house and saw the tell-tale signs of multiple cars in Finn's driveway. She'd clearly been set on by the paps as well, and she'd taken off.

Would she come back? Or was that it? She'd warned Angie and Luna that she moved a lot. But surely she didn't leave a houseful of things behind? Angie thought back to their conversations. Finn said moving required about fifty boxes of books, and the beautiful art in her home wasn't something that could be left without thought.

That meant she'd be back at some point. If nothing else, Angie and Luna could say goodbye properly. If, of course, Finn let them know she was back.

Angie breathed in the scent of the studio. Metal, paint, cleaner. This was a world she understood, and it would be good to lose herself in it for a while.

***

The day of rehearsals finished, and Angie rolled her neck. The emotions for this film were intense and required far more depth and thought than she'd ever had to use before. At one point, when she wasn't hitting the mark for the anger required, Elodie had taken her aside.

"I saw the rags." Elodie's touch was gentle on Angie's arm. "That invasion of privacy is a lot like a surprise enema, isn't it? And looks like maybe it was damn near as messy?"

Angie swallowed against the sadness and nodded.

"And they brought your daughter into it as well?"

Again, Angie just nodded.

"So they fucked your love life, and they targeted your daughter. How does that make you feel?"

Angie stared at the floor and let the emotions rise. "I'm ready."

Elodie nodded sympathetically, and the resulting scene had the director raising his arms in victory as Angie screamed at the sky in rage and frustration.

"That's what we knew we'd get when we wanted you for this part." Bert Forster threw his arm around her shoulders. "Keep digging into that, and we'll have award noms coming out our collective asses."

Angie stopped when the door opened. "Luna? Is everything okay?"

Luna looked around as she moved toward Angie on her crutches. "Everything's fine. I can't skate, Finn's gone, and Cari is busy. I didn't want to be home alone, so I asked the driver to bring me here. Is that okay? I thought we could ride home together."

Angie pulled her into a tight hug. "Of course it's okay. This is the director, Bert Forster. And this is my co-star, Elodie."

Luna's face lit up. "I love everything you do. I wish I was as good at physical stuff as you are. I can't even skate without breaking something."

Elodie smiled. "Hey, I've broken twelve bones doing my own stunts. That's the cost of doing what you love. Your ankle is just the first of many if you keep living the way you want to."

Angie winced but Luna laughed, and her chin lifted a little. "I like that. It sounds like something Finn would say."

"Yeah, it does." Angie smiled weakly and saw the empathy in Elodie's eyes. "We'd better get home or Susan will have our heads."

"Susan?" Elodie asked, her eyebrows up. "Already moved on?"

"Gross. Susan cooks our food, and she's totally not mom's

type." Luna started her crutch walk toward the door.

Angie sighed and closed her eyes for a second. "I have to grab my stuff. I'll be right there."

Elodie turned to her, arms crossed. "Life is complicated, isn't it? As in, we don't always know who it is we're in bed with."

"Subtle, El." She bit her lip, remembering a story about Elodie. "You were in the military, right? I don't suppose you have any friends in the information business?"

"I might have a few contacts I could reach out to." Elodie kissed her cheek. "But be sure that's the road you want to go down, okay? Sometimes letting someone tell you in their own time is better than digging up their dead."

Angie blinked away the tears. "I hear you. You're right. It isn't my place, and I wouldn't want it done to me."

"Talking things out is good." She gave her a sympathetic smile. "See you Monday."

Angie got her bag and checked her phone. Still nothing. But what did she expect? She told Finn they couldn't be together if she couldn't be honest, and Finn had made it clear her past was off limits. Unless Angie was willing to capitulate, there was no middle ground.

She tried her best to keep up a cheerful presence at dinner. Susan and Helen joined them, thankfully, and that kept the conversation going even when Angie's thoughts drifted back to Finn.

After Luna and Helen had retired for the night, Angie curled up on the sofa and listened to Susan humming in the kitchen as she cleared up. She'd nodded off when she felt Susan's hand on her shoulder.

"Hey."

Susan handed her a mug of chai tea. "Thought you could use this before bed."

"Thanks." Angie noticed the way Susan's fingers touched hers as she handed over the mug.

"I can't imagine what you're going through right now, Ang." Susan sat on the coffee table in front of her. "I've known you for a long time, and I know your inner circle is made up of those of us who have a room in this house, and Barb."

Angie felt the tears well in her eyes. "Pretty sad, huh?"

"Not sad, no. But a little lonely, I'd guess?" Susan smiled sympathetically. "I just want you to know that I'm around if you need an ear, okay? I've had my share of woman troubles, and maybe I could help." She grinned. "Or, if it comes to that, I can give her a case of food poisoning for messing with my friend."

Angie laughed and wiped away the few tears that escaped. "Please don't make anyone ill on my account." She tilted her head, pretending to think. "At least, not *really* ill."

Susan tapped the side of her nose and winked. "Understood." She held Angie's hand. "Seriously, though. Remember that you're not alone in this world, okay?"

Angie squeezed Susan's hand. "I can't tell you how much I appreciate the reminder. Thank you."

Angie watched her walk from the room and then dropped her head to the pillow. If only she was attracted to Susan. That would simplify things, given how kind and open she was. But ultimately, all she wanted was Finn. Unavailable, frustrating, gorgeous, mysterious, Finn.

Helen was right. All she could do was wait. But for how long?

Chapter Twenty-Five

THE WEEK PASSED IN a blur of black and white. The final chapter of the book Finn had been working on continued to elude her, so she'd turned her attention to something new, something that had woken her in the night and demanded attention. The characters were fleshy and ready, and she'd barely been able to keep up with them as they demanded she tell their story.

With no phone service and no internet, it was easier to shut off from the world beyond the ocean in front of her and the occasional trip to the main house to have coffee with Maggie. There were few other guests this time of year, which meant Finn could breathe as she lounged in front of the fire with Maggie, with no need to worry about being recognized.

"So what's your plan, Finn?" Maggie asked, sipping the expensive Writer's Tears whisky Finn always brought with her. "You clearly can't live here indefinitely. Well, you could, but that would be silly."

Finn stared into the flames reflected in her glass. "The answer is obvious, but it scares the hell out of me."

"That answer being?"

"I have to be okay with my family finding me. And I have to tell Angie where I come from, so she's ready for whatever fallout that may cause. She may not want to be with me after I tell her."

Maggie snorted. "Please. You've built your family into some kind of mythic monster. But they're just people. And if Angie doesn't want to be with you because of it, then she doesn't deserve you." She tilted her head as she sipped her whisky again. "But that doesn't sound like the woman you've described to me."

Finn was fully aware she'd done nothing but talk about Angie and Luna in the time she'd spent with Maggie, and it only served to underscore how much she wanted them in her life. How much she wanted a life outside the shadows, if not in the limelight.

"But," Maggie smiled at a passing guest and waited till they were gone, "simply being okay with your family finding you seems awfully passive, don't you think? Why not take that bull by the horns so you're not always waiting for that boot to drop?"

Finn sat for a while, pondering that question. Slowly, she shook her head. "Because I've been waiting for that boot to drop since I got out. I left for valid reasons, but everyone is right. They don't have to continue to dictate my future. If my family makes contact, I'll deal with it. But it may never happen." The weight pressing on her chest since Angie had left her house began to lift. "I need to move forward, not look back. Along those lines, I did hire a private investigator who was going to the DR to see what they could find. So far there hasn't been anything, but you never know, right?"

Maggie tipped her glass. "There's the woman I knew was in there. So, back to my main question. What's your plan?"

Finn stood and wiped her hands on her jeans. "I'll head out in the morning."

***

The drive was made longer by virtue of the new characters vociferously demanding Finn's attention. She made use of three different truck stops in order to put down what they were saying and doing as the scenes played out along the dotted lines of the highway. Where she'd normally stop at Morro Bay to have lunch by the water or stop at Elephant Beach to laugh at the enormous, beached seals, this time she could concentrate on only two things. Talking to Angie and the book imploring her for attention.

She went straight to Angie's house, but a feeling of unease lodged in her ribs when the guard who waved her in looked puzzled. When she pulled up in front of the house, Helen was waiting in the doorway.

"You're late." She turned away, leaving Finn to follow.

"I'd say better late than never, but that isn't always true. Like ambulances, for instance." Finn was rambling but the house felt too empty.

Helen sat down at the kitchen island and motioned for Finn to take the other seat. "You might be too late altogether. Like an ambulance that doesn't make it in time."

Finn's shoulders dropped. "Tell me?"

"They've left for their trips, Finn. Angie is off to Japan and Luna is off to Turkey. Because of all the hoopla, they decided to go early. Luna is going with Angie for a little while first, then she'll fly to Turkey from there. Neither will be back for at least a month."

There was silence as Finn contemplated Helen's information. A month from now the furor around their relationship would have died off. The paps would have moved on to new prey. Maybe it was good to have that time apart? At the idea of having Angie and Luna gone, thinking Finn had left them behind, she knew that wasn't the case.

"However." Helen folded her hands, waiting for Finn to look at her. "They're staying at a hotel near the airport tonight."

Finn slid from her seat and pulled out her phone. "You're an angel." She held out the phone with the maps app open. "Please?"

Helen tapped it in and handed it back. "I'll let her security team know you're coming. The rest is up to you." She held up her hand for Finn to wait, then went into the living room and picked up a wrapped package. "This is from Luna. She said to make sure to give it to you when you came back." She raised her eyebrow. "She had no doubts you'd come back."

Finn smiled, her heart thumping. "She's a smart kid. Way smarter than me."

"That wouldn't be difficult, under the circumstances." Helen's smile was gentle, though her words weren't.

"No, it wouldn't." Spontaneously, she pulled Helen into a hug. "Wish me luck." She let go and raced from the house, glancing at the map. Forty-two minutes. She'd make it in thirty.

***

Her desire to make it in less time than the map suggested was thwarted by the ever-present hellscape of LA traffic, where jams appeared and dissolved like strange portals in time. She allowed herself the balm of swearing loudly at the offending line of red lights. She'd also unwrapped the package from Luna, which brought tears to her eyes. An amazing T-shirt that would fit her perfectly, with the Tracy Chapman *Fast Cars* album cover emblazoned on the front. She'd forgotten she'd asked Luna to make her one, but trust Luna to remember and deliver. By the time she made it to the hotel, she'd replayed what she wanted to say a hundred times, none of which made her feel ready for the conversation about to play out.

If, of course, Angie would see her.

She went straight to the reception desk and gave her name, saying she was expected. A quick phone call meant she was escorted to the elevator, where the receptionist pressed her keycard to the panel before pushing the button for the top floor. She gave Finn a quick smile before exiting, and somehow Finn knew she wouldn't be calling the paps.

When the doors opened, a guard was waiting. He walked the few steps to the main door, knocked, and then let Finn in before closing the door behind her.

She stood in the whitewashed, polished hallway, unsure what to do next.

"Yes?" Angie called from another room. "Who is it?"

Finn's body tingled at the beauty of Angie's voice, and she forced herself to move forward. So Helen had told the guards, but not Angie. That meant Helen wasn't totally sure Angie would see

Finn either.

Finn looked around the corner to see Angie waiting, her expression bemused as she waited for someone to respond. When she saw Finn, her eyes widened, and she put her hand to her chest.

"Oh."

"Oh." Since nothing was flying at her head—yet—she moved forward. "Helen let me know where to find you so we could talk."

"We?" Angie crossed her arms.

"Me. I. So I could talk. To you." Finn sighed and pinched the bridge of her nose. "Is Luna here?"

"She's at the Flight Path Museum. She'll be back in about an hour, so you'd better start talking."

Finn bit her lip. "Okay. I—"

"Sit down. I feel like the principal listening to a naughty child."

The idea of role-play flitted through Finn's mind and she very nearly grinned, but that wasn't the mood she was going for. She sat across from Angie and rested her elbows on her knees. "I was born in the Dominican Republic—"

"I know that."

Finn winced. "Bear with me, please?" When Angie huffed and sat back, she continued. "My given name was Diana Maria Rodriguez. I have three sisters. My father is Marco Rodriguez, the head of the Partido Reformista Social Cristiano, a far right-wing government sect." She waited, but there was no recognition in Angie's expression. "It isn't surprising you wouldn't know his name. Dominican government issues don't get talked about a lot outside of Washington. He was in power for a long time before he was voted out. His policies were devoid of humanity, and he was nothing more than a thug with power." Talking about him made her stomach clench. "Even though he was voted out, he stills hold massive political sway."

"Your mother?"

Finn sighed. "We'll get to that in a second, if you don't mind?"

At Angie's nod, she forced herself to keep talking. "We grew up terrified of him, my sisters and me. He was violent, and you never knew when some whim would make him want to mentally torture you in some way. Tell you that he'd kill your sister if you brought shame on the family or kill your dog if you didn't smile just right for the press. I took the worst of it." Her breath shook in her chest as old memories crashed through well-worn barriers. "Can I have something to drink?"

Angie jumped up. "Of course." She went to the bar area and brought back a bottle of water. "Unless you want something stronger?"

Finn took a long swig. "I need to be able to drive, but thanks. I'll drown these memories in alcohol later." She smiled a little when Angie sat beside her on the couch, so their legs were touching. "Sure you want to hear more?"

"All of it. Everything." Angie took her hand. "You're safe with me."

"He hated how independent I was. He hated that I'd stand up for my sisters and even jump in front of them to take the hit aimed their way. No matter how often he came at me, I'd always get up and look him in the eye so he could see how much I hated him. When I turned eighteen, he told me either I would marry one of his cronies' sons, or he'd kill me. It would set an example for my sisters either way. I escaped the following morning and made it to America. I filed the name change papers in the DR right before I left so it would be almost impossible to find me. I left the DR with my new identity already in place, and that's who I've been ever since."

Angie's eyes were wide and her grip on Finn's hand was fierce. "And you've been running all this time?"

Finn sank back into the sofa. "He's still looking for me. He wants control in every possible way, and the fact that I escaped will be something he can't let go. He'd rather have me dead than living happily somewhere."

"Jesus." Angie took Finn's water bottle and drank before

handing it back.

"Yeah." She took Angie's hand and stared at their entwined fingers. "You can see why I needed my privacy, why I was scared that he might find me."

"Of all the possibilities, that wasn't one I'd ever thought up." Angie squeezed Finn's hand, making her look up. "I'm so sorry if you being in the papers has put you in danger."

"I admit, that was a big concern. But I was worried about you and Luna getting caught in his crossfire too, Angie." She tried to still the internal shaking that was making it hard to breathe. "If anything happened to you two because of my past..."

Angie was silent as she stroked Finn's fingers, and Finn let her think. If this was the last time they'd be together, she wasn't about to rush it.

"Thank you for worrying about us," she finally said. "And you're right, it is a concern. Tell me about your mother?"

Finn's shoulders rose again, not helping the budding headache. "She died when I was twelve. One morning, he told us she was sick, that we couldn't see her because it would upset her. They fought all the time, and my mother stood up to him as best she could, but none of us were a match for his level of crazy. She died, and we never got to say goodbye." Finn remembered the funeral and the way her father had practically vibrated with fury. Now she thought she knew why.

"So you mean she escaped by dying?" Angie's brow was furrowed.

"That's the weird thing. One of the weird things? Anyway. When I went to my abuela's funeral, there was a woman in the cemetery, also watching from the shadows. She was wearing the shawl my grandmother made for my mother. And she was with another woman." Finn scrubbed at her face and then told Angie what her abuela's letter said.

Angie walked to the window overlooking the city and the ocean beyond. She was quiet for a long time, giving Finn the chance to try and memorize every inch of her, the very essence of her. The way her brown hair glinted in the sunlight like it was streaked with gold, the way her slight waist curved into her perfect hips, the way she tilted her head and her eyes moved like she was watching something. She was beauty personified and Finn wanted to remember her just like this, always.

She turned away from the window, her eyes alight. "So, your mother escaped her imprisonment to go away and be with the woman she loved. And now she knows you're still alive, and you know she's still alive, and your face is in the celebrity news, which means she might be able to make contact."

Finn had been so focused on her father's wrath, she hadn't quite made that connection. "I suppose that's true. I hired a PI to try to find her, but I've had a text to say that there's no trail to follow in the DR. But you're right. Maybe she'll find me instead. The paps certainly managed to find my address with no problem."

Angie winced. "I'm truly sorry about that—"

"Don't, Angie." Finn got up and went to her, taking a chance. She put her hands on Angie's waist and breathed easier when Angie didn't pull away. "I knew who you were and the life you lead. It yanked me out of my comfort zone, but that's a good thing. You were right. I've been letting the past influence my life. I got away from him physically but let him continue to dictate my life, my choices, my decisions. It has to stop."

"But what if he comes after you?" Angie's tone was low, fear crimping the edges.

"Then I'll deal with him." She smiled as she thought of Angie's logic. "And maybe being so publicly tied to a celebrity isn't a bad thing. I can't just disappear without someone noticing, right?"

Angie's expression was thoughtful, and she bit her lip. "I suppose that's true. I'd certainly notice."

The tension was back in Angie's posture, a subtle shift that shuttered the emotion in her eyes.

"Tell me," Finn said softly, sliding her hands away from Angie's waist.

"Luna." Angie's eyes were sad, but she didn't look away from Finn's gaze. "If it were just you and me, then we could take this on knowing the risks. But Luna... If anything happened to her—"

"Right." Finn nodded, and her shoulders dropped in defeat. That tiny flame of hope extinguished like it was buried beneath a snowdrift of disappointment. "And that's why I didn't want to get involved with anyone. Especially you and Luna. But I couldn't help it."

"I'm not saying we can't happen, Finn." Angie pulled Finn into a hug and nestled her face against Finn's neck. "But what you've told me is a lot. I need some time to process, okay?"

Finn nodded, breathing in Angie's scent. Her perfume, her shampoo, the very nature of her beautiful soul. "I understand, and I didn't expect anything else. I just owed you the truth." Gently, she pulled away, though it made her heart ache to do so. "You'll tell Luna what she needs to know?"

Angie's arms dropped to her sides. "Of course."

They stood there staring at one another for what felt like too little time as well as an eternity. Finn stepped back, trying to smile, trying not to let it show that her heart was slowly cracking like glass with too much pressure on it.

"I hope your shoot goes well. And tell Luna to kick some ass in Turkey, okay?"

Angie didn't say anything. Tears made her eyes glassy, and when they fell, it took every ounce of strength in Finn's soul to keep from going to her. But trying to reapply a Band-Aid was never a good idea once it had been ripped off.

"Bye, Angie," Finn whispered, and let herself out of the hotel room.

Chapter Twenty-Six

ANGIE LOOKED OUT THE window at the clouds below, her thoughts a bewildering muddle of options and questions. She smiled at the chef who set down the quinoa salad in front of her and set Luna's order of halloumi sticks and fries on the table beside the couch she was lying on while she watched a David Attenborough documentary on the jet's big screen TV. She'd bought the extravagant jet after her first few blockbuster films made it nearly impossible to take a flight without being bombarded with people seeking autographs, selfies, or long conversations. She didn't want to seem ungrateful, but that was a lot when she just wanted a quiet flight or needed time to go over lines.

And at times like this, she was grateful for the silence.

"Mom?"

She snapped back to the moment and looked over.

"Is Finn going to stay away just to protect us? Because I've been thinking about that, and it pisses me off."

Angie winced a little. "Luna, watch your language, please. But it pisses me off too." When Luna had returned from her visit to the museum, Angie had made the decision to tell her the majority of what Finn had told her, minus the specifics of abuse. She'd alluded to the fact that he was a dangerous, violent man and that was enough information, as far as she was concerned. Luna didn't need the details of what Finn had been through to understand Finn's pain. Luna was mature and deserved to know not only the truth, but that there was a possibility of danger. Ignorance was never the answer to safety. Of that, Angie was sure.

They'd stayed up late talking about family, and Luna had fallen asleep on the couch. Angie, on the other hand, had lain awake, pondering the many questions she didn't have answers to.

"Luna, would you want to meet your grandparents?" she asked, still looking out the window. When she was met with silence, she looked over.

Luna's frown was deep, her expression uncertain. "Will you tell me why you don't talk to them?"

Angie moved from the plush leather chair to sit beside Luna. "They simply aren't very nice people. They wanted me to be successful, and when I was, and they saw how much money I could bring in, that's all they ever thought about. I became a way to make money instead of simply being their child. After I had you, they started to look at you the same way, and I wasn't about to let them do anything like that to my daughter." It was a simplified version of what she'd told Finn, but it would suffice.

Luna played with her food, moving it around the plate. "So you haven't seen them my whole life?"

"Pretty much. But they're your grandparents, and you're an amazing kid with an incredible brain, and you know who you are. And if you needed to talk or ever felt uncomfortable around them, then I'd be right by your side." The protective instinct she'd felt from the moment Luna was put into her arms resisted that idea, but she knew it was the right thing to do.

"Thanks." Luna pushed her glasses up and shoved her plate away. "I'll think about it, okay?"

"Okay. No pressure either way." Angie kissed the top of Luna's head.

"Do you think people can change? Isn't that the whole point of *A Christmas Carol*?"

Angie laughed. "I think circumstances can make people change, yes. I think life can take strange twists and turns and help you learn things." She took Luna's hand. "And I've been thinking. I want to say that I'm sorry."

Luna frowned again, her head turned slightly in suspicion. "For what?"

"I've put my career ahead of you way too often. I told myself that it was best if I left you at home when I was shooting on location, that it was best not to drag you around." As the new knowledge flooded through her, guilt rose right behind it. "But the truth is, I knew I couldn't focus as well if I was worried about where you were while I was shooting. And that was so wrong, Luna. I'm so sorry I missed so much." Tears slid down her cheeks, and she made no effort to hide them or wipe them away.

Luna lurched forward and threw her arms around Angie, who held her tightly. They rocked that way for a while, and then Luna pulled back to wipe her nose on her sleeve.

"Does this mean you won't go away so often?" she asked.

"I think maybe it's time for me to really take a break. After this movie, I won't sign on for anything. What would you like to do?"

"Can we travel? I want to see some of the places you've been. And I want to go to the Acropolis." Luna's eyes lit up.

"It's a deal." Angie went to the fridge, pulled out two bottles of water, and passed one to Luna.

"Can Finn come?" Luna didn't look up from the bottle she was opening.

"Oh, honey. I don't know. It bugs us both that she's protecting us, but she might not be wrong. It sounds like her father is a dangerous man."

"But we have bodyguards. All the time. And you have weirdo fans who send you all kinds of weird things." At Angie's look of surprise, Luna rolled her eyes. "Sometimes it's like you forget I'm in the house and I have ears. I hear you talking to Claire."

The mild rebuke wasn't subtle, and it hit its mark. "You're right. I do." She moved Luna's hair from her face. "We've got some time to think about it while we're off on our adventures. And about that, I wanted to ask you something."

Luna waited, eyebrows raised, and then made a "come on" motion with her hand.

"When you're done in Turkey, I'll probably still have a couple more weeks on set. How would you feel about hanging out with me in Japan instead of flying straight home? We could—"

Once again, Luna hugged Angie hard, then she jumped up like she simply couldn't sit still. "You mean it?"

Angie pulled out her phone, tapped on it, and handed it over. "Already booked. I hoped you'd say yes."

Luna grabbed her phone and remote-shared the information, then sat back down. "This is awesome. Will we really do stuff when you're not working? We won't just hang out in your trailer, will we?"

"Nope. But you have to take charge. You decide what tours you want to go on, what you want to see, all that stuff. We'll have someone arrange it around my work."

Luna's excitement as she launched onto Google to begin planning their adventure practically burst Angie's heart. It had taken way too long for her to understand that this, right here, was what was important. Finn had given up years with her sisters, possibly a lifetime with her mother, and ended up living a solitary existence. But Angie had Luna right here, right now, and life moved so fast.

Eventually, Luna fell asleep with the phone still cradled against her chest, and Angie put a blanket over her.

Susan smiled as she cleared their plates. "Sounds like you're mom of the year now."

"For now. She's heading into the teenager zone, so it probably won't last."

Angie was grateful Susan had offered to come along. At least this way she had a friendly face around while all this craziness was going on. But Susan wouldn't be on set with her, and Barb had taken a movie role in Australia and would be hard to reach for a few months. Once again, that left Angie without someone to turn to. Really, she wanted to talk to Finn. When she got back to the States, maybe they'd have figured out how to make things work.

Maybe.

Chapter Twenty-Seven

IF IT HADN'T BEEN for the new book forcing its way through Finn's fingertips, the weeks of silence would have driven her insane. Fortunately, she still had texts come in from Luna every few days, full of all the exciting things she'd done and found, and how she wasn't letting her cast get in her way. Her enthusiasm always made Finn smile and she never waited long before answering, wanting Luna to know she still had a friend back home, though it sounded like she was making plenty at the dig site. She'd also sent Luna a pic of her wearing the special T-shirt, and Luna had responded with *"That's cool."*

There was nothing from Angie though. Not a word. And Finn didn't send her any messages either. She'd put her cards on the table, and now it was Angie's decision about what to do next.

The phone rang, and Finn answered without looking at the display.

"How's my favorite writer on the planet?"

Finn laughed and pushed away from the desk. "How many of your authors do you say that to, Paige? All of them, I bet."

"All of them don't win awards and bring in the commissions you do." As always, papers shuffled in the background. "I wanted to check in and see how that next book is going."

Finn looked at the screen and allowed a bit of pride to bubble up from the depths. "Actually, really well. I practically can't stop most days. In fact, I'm not far off a finished first draft—"

Paige's squeal made Finn wince as she held the phone away from her ear.

"That's amazing news. When can I see it?"

"By the end of the month." Belatedly, she realized what she was saying. "Wait. The thing is, I think we're talking about two different books. I'm still waiting on the final chapter of the other one. This one, the one I'll have at the end of the month, that's a new one—"

Once again, Paige's squeal could have made dogs howl two counties over. "You've got *two* new books for me? I thought getting one would be a miracle."

Finn laughed. "Me too. This other one just popped into my head and wouldn't go away."

They talked about a few logistics for a moment, and then Finn took a deep breath. "Paige, do you think the Atwood Award folks would still want me to come to the actual ceremony?"

There was no squeal this time. Just a long, deep silence. "Tell me you're not fucking around, Finn. Tell me you're serious."

"I'm serious. I've made some decisions about my life recently, and this is a step I need to take."

"I have to go. I'll call you back." She hung up.

Finn shook her head and set down the phone. Although it was the right thing to do, it still left her shaky inside. The award was a big deal, and in truth, she wanted to stand on that stage and take it. She wanted to take it for all the little brown kids who loved to escape into stories but thought their voices wouldn't be heard. She wanted to show them that it could happen.

She went and grabbed an apple, then headed to the front door to sit out on the deck and get some fresh air. For the moment, her characters were quiet, and she could let her mind wander to other things. The paps were gone when she'd returned from Treebones and they had yet to return, though she'd had to change her phone number after it wouldn't stop ringing with requests for interviews. For now, she could sit outside without being bothered by anyone.

But when she opened the door, she froze.

A woman stood there, hand raised to knock. She stopped, her dark brown eyes wide as she looked at Finn.

"Mom?" Finn whispered, holding onto the doorframe so she

didn't collapse.

She simply nodded, slowly lowering her hand. Movement caught Finn's eye, and she looked to her left to see the other woman from the cemetery standing there, waiting expectantly. When she met Finn's gaze, she stepped forward.

"Carmina." She held out her hand.

Automatically, Finn took it, but she couldn't breathe. Couldn't stop staring. Couldn't think. Time slowed impossibly as she tried to make sense of things.

And then her mom gave a soft, strangled cry and threw her arms around Finn, and the world crashed back in. She held her and they cried together, there in her doorway, until Carmina gently led them back inside and closed the door behind them.

Her mom and Carmina sat on the couch, and Finn sat on a chair facing them. Blinking, she stood. "Drink?"

"Water?" her mom said, still staring at her like she was a dream that might fade any moment.

Finn took her time getting all three of them glasses of water. Her hands shook, and she had to take calming breaths before she could carry the tray back to the living room. An awkward silence ensued as they drank, and no one seemed inclined to speak first.

"You have a beautiful home," Carmina eventually said, looking around.

"Thank you." Finn finally found some words. "I'm glad you found it. After that day in the cemetery, I wondered if you'd try."

Her mom, looking equally shaken, nodded. "I'd heard from old friends that you'd disappeared, and seeing you that day..." She swallowed and wiped away some more tears. "I couldn't believe it. You were so close. But we ran, like we've been running for so long."

"Where have you been? We had a funeral." Anger, illogical and unwanted, rose like an intruder. "We needed you."

Her mom flinched, and Carmina took her hand. "Perhaps its best we start from the beginning?"

"I had a letter from Abuela. She said you were in love?" Finn said. At least this way they'd know she had some details.

"True." Her mom gave Carmina a tremulous smile. "We met while I was doing some charity work for the orphanage. It was like lightning. The moment I met her, I was in love with her. Sounds impossible, but it's true. We spent all our free time together, and eventually, well..." Her mom's smile was soft, full of love, and then it faltered and was replaced with an expression of pain. "I told your father I was leaving him and taking you girls with me. He'd had me followed, and he knew about Carmina. I think if I'd waited any longer, he would have had her killed."

Carmina grunted and her jaw clenched. "El Bastardo. That's what I called him from the moment I met him."

"Not to his face, obviously, since you're still here," Finn said, earning her a small smile.

"When I told him I was leaving, he had his guards throw me in the back room. He had the windows sealed shut from the outside and guards posted at the door. Not only could I not escape, I couldn't speak to anyone." She took Finn's hand. "I didn't know what he told everyone. I still don't."

Finn looked at her mom's hand, so small in her own. "He said you were sick, and that to see any of us would only upset you and make you sicker. Then he said you were dead." She shrugged. "That's it. You were gone, and he said he was all we had, so we'd better obey."

Tears slid down her mom's face. "You must have been so scared."

"That's the least of it. How did you get away?"

"One night, the guard opened my door. He told me I needed to pack and go, that your father was going to have me taken into the hills and murdered the next day. He said there was no time to get you girls, that we had to go right then, or we'd get caught. He'd been my childhood friend, and after he dropped me off at Carmina's house, he drove away and to my knowledge, never looked back. Carmina and I went underground, using a network that helped abused women. Your father raged through our friends, threatening to kill anyone harboring me."

"But our network was solid, and they kept us well hidden. We moved into Haiti where your father's reach didn't go." Carmina took over when Finn's mom began to cry again. "Your father tightened security around you girls, so that there was no way to get to you. The rest of the guards were faithful to him, and you were hardly let out. As hard as our network tried, there was simply no way to get you into the underground we'd been part of."

"We tried, hija. We really did." Her mom's expression was pleading.

"I believe you." The momentary anger was easily replaced with a deep sense of gratefulness. "I can't believe you're here though."

"We saw you in the magazines and online." Carmina grinned. "The photos of you with Angie Davis were easy to find, and we had a friend who managed to get your address, though it took time."

The hours passed swiftly as they caught up on each other's lives. They'd opened a small café in Haiti, bought a little finca with an olive grove, and lived a quiet, contented life. Finn told them about her journey to the States and how her writing had made so many of her dreams come true. She ordered take-out since there was still hardly any food in the house, much to their dismay. She also gave them a copy of her latest book, which she had yet to give to anyone. Her mother held it to her chest like it was a cherished prize.

"And so," she said, after finishing her third slice of pizza, "I don't know where we stand. I miss Angie like crazy, and the coffee shop isn't the same without Luna. They've become a family I didn't know I wanted, and now I feel empty without them."

Her mom looked sympathetic. "I'm glad you told her. Unless someone has had to run from their past, they can't truly understand where you're coming from. But at some point, we have to figure out that we're more than what we've been, more than how we were raised."

Finn got the guest room ready for them and said goodnight. She sat on the front porch, rocking and watching the trees sway in the chill night breeze. How strange life could be. She'd gone from a lonely, albeit successful, life in the shadows, to a life where the possibilities for more were so vast, they threatened to overwhelm her.

She'd always taken things step-by-step, planning the next move. Until she'd made it so far, and there were no more steps to take that wouldn't mean leaving the comfort of her safety zone. Then she'd stood still, watching the world from the sidelines.

Angie and Luna had made it impossible to stagnate any longer. Their openness, their desire to really be part of the world had infused Finn's own being like a flower that only blooms in the perfect conditions. And now, with her mom back in her life too... She blew out a big breath. What could she do next?

She went inside, got her laptop, and headed out again. The final chapter of the other book was calling to her, forcing her fingers to the keyboard. An hour later, she softly shut the laptop and closed her eyes.

Her abuela had said she had to follow her heart. If there was any chance in hell that Angie's path would cross hers again, she'd fight to see where their hearts might lead them.

Chapter Twenty-Eight

ANGIE'S HANDS GRIPPED THE steering wheel, clenching and unclenching as she stared at the modest two-story house in front of her. Her pulse raced and her stomach clenched, and her neck was clammy with sweat.

"Mom?" Luna's tone was gentle. "We don't have to do this right now. I can come back with Helen another time."

Yanked out of the memories that made bile rise in her throat, she tried to give Luna a reassuring smile but based on Luna's expression, it didn't work. "Thank you. But we'll do this together."

"Well, sitting here like creepers isn't going to get it done." Luna grinned and threw open her door.

With another deep breath, Angie followed her up the stairs. Luna rang the bell and then pressed close to Angie's side.

The door opened, and the woman's hand went to her chest as she stared at them, her lips almost immediately trembling.

"Hi, Mom." It felt so simple, so lame, but what else could she say?

"Roger! Roger!" Her mother continued to hold onto the doorframe with one hand and her chest with the other. "Oh my god. I can't believe—" She faltered. "Roger!"

He came hurrying into the foyer and then stopped when he saw them. "Jesus H." He swept past his wife and threw his arms around Angie, pulling her into a bone-crushing bear hug. "Angie. My girl."

He wept. Her mom was crying too. And Angie stood there, frozen in the surrealness of the moment.

"Hi. I'm Luna."

Her father pulled away and looked down at Luna, tears still falling down his plump, red cheeks. "How wonderful to meet you, Luna."

She held out her hand and he shook it, before drawing her into a gentle hug. Her mother stepped forward, finally, and hugged Luna too. Then she turned to Angie and raised her arms tentatively. "Angie."

Angie smiled a little and gave her a stiff hug before she stepped back and shoved her hands in her pockets.

"Come in, come in!" Her father waved them inside. "Iced tea? Soda? Coffee?"

"Iced tea, please," Luna said, looking around as they made their way toward the living room.

Emotion made it hard to breathe as Angie looked at the photographs covering the walls. From her as a child to photos clearly cut from magazines, to one of her and Luna at the Kiyomizu-Dera temple only a few weeks ago, there was hardly an inch of space that wasn't claimed by them.

The four of them sat at the kitchen table, and Angie couldn't meet their eyes as her parents stared at them, clearly unable to think of anything to say.

"I just got back from an archaeological dig in Turkey," Luna said, folding her hands on the table. "It was the most incredible trip of my life."

"Tell us about it." Her mother's smile spread like a cloud had lifted from her face.

Luna launched into the tale of the dig, how her cast had been frustrating, but she'd learned how to get around anyway, about the pottery shards she'd found, about how they determined age and what that meant for their understanding of the area's history. She hardly took a breath, but Angie knew Luna well enough to know she was paying close attention to how her grandparents responded.

"That sounds truly wonderful. What a remarkable young woman

you are," her father said, looking as proud as a grandfather should. "And you, Angie?" He motioned toward the picture showing them a few weeks ago. "You were in the area too?"

She shook her head. "I was in Kyoto, and Luna came to join me at my shoot when the dig finished. Then we did some sightseeing before coming back." She clasped her hands in her lap so they wouldn't see them shaking. "She wanted to meet her grandparents. I hope it's okay that we came by without calling first."

Her mother made a sound like a half gasp, half laugh. "This is the best surprise we could have ever hoped for."

"Angie, we're so sorry." Her dad reached across the table to hold her hand, but she kept them in her lap, and he pulled back. His expression turned sad. "We can't tell you how sorry we are. We've talked about it year after year, about all the things we did wrong and how we pushed you away. That's why we stopped trying to get in touch. You made it clear you didn't want anything to do with us." He frowned and picked at his cuticles. "I think...well, you're still acting, so we can't have been totally wrong, but—"

"And we know why you cut us off from Luna." Her mother gave a small, watery smile. "We were so wrapped up in the life we wanted for you, for us, that we didn't let you enjoy a childhood." Her mother put her hands over her face and began to cry in earnest.

Her father put his arm around her and kissed her head. "We have so many regrets. Losing you and Luna created a hole in us that would never heal. It hurt, and we didn't understand for a long time." When her mother elbowed him slightly, he took a deep breath. "But we get it now."

Angie blinked, uncertain how to take their heartfelt apology, although a little of it felt somehow backhanded. Could years of resentment and frustration be wiped away just like that? "Thank you. That means a lot to me." She looked at Luna. "I'll need time to process that, but I'm letting Luna decide what she wants her relationship with you to be from now on." Her jaw tightened. "But if you ever push her to do something she doesn't want to—"

"Never!" Her mother shook her head, wiping her cheeks on her sleeve. "I swear to you, Angie, if you come back into our lives, we'll be the supportive parents and grandparents you both deserve. We won't ask for a thing other than your time."

Her dad nodded, his gaze moving from Angie to Luna. "We swear."

Luna grinned. "I'm going to hold you to that."

The rest of the afternoon passed in a surreal haze of memories plunged into the present. Angie was mostly content to listen as Luna asked questions about what Angie was like as a child, what her grandparents had been doing for the last thirteen years, and in return, telling them about their life in Beverly Hills.

"And then there's Finn." Luna wiggled her eyebrows and giggled when Angie rolled her eyes. "Mom doesn't know it, but Finn is her soulmate."

"Oh, is she? Nice of you to tell me. I think that's something I'm supposed to figure out myself." Angie wasn't at all ready to allow her parents into that part of her life yet. As it was, the raw way things had been left between her and Finn meant they needed to talk before any mention of soulmates could be made.

"Look, I'll show you." Luna pulled out her phone and showed them photos of Finn. Some of Finn lounging by the pool, a few selfies of them together, and even one of her and Angie seemingly deep in conversation.

"She's the one in the magazine photos too, right?" her mom asked. "She's incredibly handsome, if I may say so."

"Hey now," her dad said, his eyes narrowed. "Don't you go switching teams on me now."

Her mom laughed, a sweet, open sound. "I'm married, not dead. I can see attractive, you know."

Angie shook her head. "Okay, enough. You're right, she's incredibly handsome. And many other wonderful things. But it's complicated."

Her dad reached across the table, and this time she let him take her hand. "Honey, life *is* complicated. It isn't the movies, where the story is linear and tied with a bow. It's messy and uneven, but god knows, it's short. Don't waste time and wish one day that you could get it back. Like we do." His eyes were glassy as he looked at her, clearly feeling the depth of his words.

"Mom, look!" Luna held up her phone and showed Angie a text from Finn. "Finn's getting an award tonight!"

Angie took the phone and bit her lip as she clicked on the link Finn had attached with the message, *how many stick people do you think I'll be able to draw thanks to this crowd?* So Finn had decided to go ahead with the very public award ceremony. The photo in the article, one of her sitting on some stone steps in front of an ocean somewhere, made Angie's heart race. An idea began to form, and she checked her watch.

"We need to go." She stood, and Luna jumped up too, her huge smile making Angie smile in return. "We'll call you soon and set up time to get together, okay?"

Her parents looked a little bemused, but they stood waving at the door as Angie and Luna ran out to the car.

Luna stopped before she got in the car. "Come to dinner next week. We'll send you the details."

They looked surprised and waved a little more vigorously as Angie pulled out of the driveway. She hit the Bluetooth on the dash. "Claire, I need a favor."

***

Finn shook out her hands in a vain attempt to rid herself of the octopus-like anxiety slowly consuming her confidence. From the moment she'd stepped into the venue that afternoon, people had been gracious and complimentary, and she'd never had to talk so much about her writing in her life. The process, the characters, the subtext. She barely had time to answer one question before they threw the next one at her. It was exhilarating in a way. But it was also overwhelming and more than a little unnerving.

She'd done a private reading for the Atwood Award committee, the five members who determined the winner of the annual award. They were considerate and intelligent, unsurprisingly, and the unequivocal praise they handed out made her want to hide under a table. The thought brought up a vision of Luna the first time they'd met, and she straightened. If Luna, with all her anxiety, could go off to Turkey by herself at thirteen, then Finn could damn well handle some praise and some folks talking about her writing.

She watched the announcer on stage and imagined the stick figure drawing she could do. Toupee perfectly in place though still perfectly fake, slacks perfectly creased and just a little too tight around the butt, big smile under bigger glasses. The image was calming. They were just people. People that people listened to, sure, but just people. Someone touched her elbow, and she jumped a little.

"Sorry," the woman whispered. "Someone in the audience wanted me to give this to you right away." She held out a slip of paper.

"Thank you." Finn waited until she walked away and then opened the note.

Elegant script slipped across the page like a river.

We're sorry we're not backstage with you on this incredible night, but we can't wait to see you hold up that award. Good luck and we'll see you at dinner. Love, Angie.

In Luna's less elegant scrawl, she wrote below Angie's note.

I fully expect a signed copy of my own. Kick butt and remember that you don't care what other people think. Just us, obvs. No jellies, just words. Love, Luna.

Finn laughed out loud, drawing a quick *shh* from a tech person nearby. They were here. She shifted so she could look into the audience, and there they were. Angie and Luna sat on the second row right beside Paige, and although Angie was watching the presenter who was talking about the important literary projects happening in the world, Luna was looking around. When she caught Finn's eye, she gave a little excited wave and shimmied in her seat. Angie glanced at her, and then to where she was looking, she smiled and gave a small, discreet wave.

Finn raised her hand and touched her heart, earning her a bigger smile from Angie and an eye roll from Luna.

Then she looked further down the row and saw her mom, Carmina and Pablo, also watching her. Carmina had leaned forward a little, clearly to see who Finn was looking at, and then she sat back and whispered something to her mom, who put her hand to her mouth and laughed. Pablo puffed up his chest and gave her thumbs up. Behind them, watching like a bird, was Gertrude, her purple-pink hair standing out in the sea of monotones. Beside her was a male companion, who she'd referred to on their last Winger walk as the next crayon in her box.

"With that, it is my absolute honor to introduce to you tonight the winner of the Atwood Award. Under her pseudonym, JJ Taylor, author Finn Montoya has gifted us with the kind of literature seen rarely in one's lifetime." He turned to face her. "Finn Montoya, everyone."

Applause erupted, and Finn stepped onto the stage. She swallowed hard at the bright lights, at the cameras filming, at the camera phones in the audience. There was no turning back now. She accepted the glass obelisk award and tilted it in thanks, then set it on the podium. She shook the announcer's hand, and he left her there, alone, in the spotlight.

For a moment, she couldn't speak. She could barely breathe. So many people were out there, watching her. Seeing her. When her gaze settled on Angie and Luna, the world calmed around her and everyone else faded away. When Luna made a come-on motion with her hand, Finn smiled. Everything would be okay.

"Thank you for your warm welcome." She took a deep breath, focused on the people in her life who made it worth living, and launched into her speech.

***

Finn tried to make her way through the crowd but found she was being stopped every few feet by well-wishers and people who wanted to talk literature. Finn looked over and around people, trying to spot familiar faces, but the dinner hall was packed. Paige held court with a select group of authors and agents, and she couldn't have been more in her element if she'd been a monkey in a banana tree. Finn did her best to keep from making eye contact, knowing full well that if Paige got hold of her, there'd be no escaping to get to the people she really *needed* to be with.

Just when Finn was worried she might lose her temper and start telling people they should be at home reading rather than drinking expensive champagne and irritating the bejesus out of her, someone tapped her shoulder.

"My apologies, but Ms. Montoya is needed for a meeting," the bodyguard, a brick wall kind of man, said in a surprisingly gentle tone. "Ma'am, if you wouldn't mind following me?"

Finn would have accepted a piggyback ride at this point, but she simply nodded and smiled an apology and stuck close to his backside. By the time they made it to the terrace, she was nearly getting that piggyback ride, so determined was she not to be waylaid.

When he stepped aside to reveal Angie, Luna, her mom, Carmina, and Pablo waiting by the rail, she gave him a hard pound on the back, probably a little too hard given her adrenalin rush. "Good man. Thank you."

Luna ran forward and hugged Finn hard. "You looked like a pig trying to find a way out of the slaughterhouse, so we sent Ben to get you out."

"Luna!" Angie pressed her hands to her face.

Finn laughed and hugged Luna back. "That's exactly what it felt like. Thanks for the save."

Angie came forward and the air left Finn's lungs. The long black dress with the deep V-neck showed off every curve and the heels made her nearly Finn's height. Her long hair was swept up, allowing for a view of her shoulders and neck that made Finn weak-kneed.

"Wow," she said softly as she leaned in to kiss her cheek.

"You can't look at me that way in public. It's indecent," Angie whispered in her ear.

"I'm feeling extremely indecent," Finn whispered back before pulling away. "I see you've met my family?"

"I hope you don't mind, hija. When we saw her, we had to say something." Her mom's gaze was searching, uncertain.

Finn pulled her into a tight hug. "Everything is great, Mom. I promise."

Her mom daintily wiped at her eyes. "I knew I shouldn't have bothered with makeup tonight."

Carmina stepped forward and shook Finn's hand. "Your speech was something else. You're a credit to the DR, and to your mother."

The words were simple, and yet Finn felt them to the very essence of the child who'd left her country so long ago. "Thank you."

Next, Pablo pulled her into a bone-crushing hug that sent the air squishing from her lungs. "I knew you'd get your head out of your ass eventually, prima." He laughed, then whispered in her ear, "And damn. For a woman like that, I'd face down every military from every country in the world."

"Release me before I have you arrested for groping me." Finn slugged his shoulder and then straightened her suit jacket.

"Disgusting. I don't know what she sees in you." He too straightened his suit and tugged at his tie.

"Finn, can we eat? I'm *starving*." Luna held her stomach like she was in physical pain.

"I'm not sure we'll be able to eat in peace, but we can try." Finn looked around and then back at Angie. "You're used to this kind of thing and I'm not. What's the move?"

Angie hooked her arm through Finn's. "Follow me."

Somehow, although people wanted to stop both of them to chat, and they did have to pause once or twice for photos, something about the way Angie commanded the space and moved forward meant people mostly just smiled and moved out of their way. She found a steward, who then led them to a table at the front of the room that had been reserved for Finn and her guests. Gertrude and her companion were already there, and Finn smiled at the fact that his tie matched her ruby red dress, which clashed terribly with her hair. It was perfectly Gertrude, and she accepted the warm hug gratefully.

She pulled out Angie's chair and nearly moaned out loud when Angie slid her hand over Finn's hip as she sat down. Luna slid into the seat next to her, and then Finn's family took the other side.

"Finn, do you like my suit?" Luna said, tugging at her jacket. "I asked Mom what you'd be wearing, and she said probably something like this."

"I think you look amazing, kiddo." Indeed, Luna's suit looked a lot like the dark gray suit Finn was wearing. But whereas Finn was wearing a deep purple button-down, Luna was wearing a T-shirt. "What band are we sporting today?"

Luna opened her jacket a little to reveal the design. "Joni Mitchell. Best songwriter of all time."

Finn nodded and tried not to squirm in her seat as Angie ran her hand up Finn's thigh.

"You look wonderful. And Carmina is right, your speech had me in tears." Angie's barely-there grin let Finn know she knew exactly the effect she was having on her.

The food was served amid constant conversation, and when they set down a plate of pasta covered in unshelled giant prawns, Luna blanched and Finn stopped the server. "Excuse me, I'm sorry, but Luna is a vegetarian. Is there an option available for her, please?"

"Of course." They took the offending plate away.

Luna slumped back in her seat, looking a little green. "Thanks,

Finn. They looked like red cockroaches."

"Agreed, mija." Finn's mom pushed the plate aside. "Prawns are popular where we come from, but Carmina has to cook them. I don't even like looking at them, let alone eating them."

Luna leaned forward. "Can we come visit you?"

Her mom flinched slightly and looked at Finn to answer.

"We've got some things to figure out before we head that direction, but my mom and Carmina can come visit us here any time they want to, okay?" She flicked a bit of her drinking water at Pablo. "Not him, though. He's a bad influence. He got me into all kinds of trouble when we were growing up."

"I demand to be told every story over pizza and ice cream one night." Luna nodded, her understanding of the situation clear. "And I was thinking, we have enough room for all your sisters to come live with us. Then we could all be here together." She didn't look up as the server put a dish of risotto in front of her, and she dug in with gusto.

Finn's chest fluttered at the sweet innocence of Luna's remark. If only it were that simple.

The rest of the evening passed in congenial conversation, with Finn occasionally being whisked away for interviews, autographs, and conversations. But she always kept her family in sight.

Family. This was her family. Her heart ached with the beauty of it. Angie's smoky gaze conveyed what she was feeling, and there was no question Finn wanted to take that dress off slowly and leave it on the floor somewhere.

Gertrude and her companion left, yawning and saying they had to be up early for a Wing Watchers walk. She extended an invitation to Angie as easily as she would a random person in a grocery store, and Finn smiled as Angie accepted with grace. As the night came to a close and they were some of the last people there, her mom touched her hand. "Can I ask you a strange question?"

Finn shook her head. "I refuse to tell you my favorite food or color. Those are private things meant only for the most intimate settings."

Angie pinched her inner thigh, making her jump.

"I want to know about your chosen name. Why Finn Montoya?"

Luna, looking sleepy, rested her head against Finn's arm. "Hey, yeah. What's that about?"

Pablo snorted and shook his head as he continued to pick at the bread and butter.

Finn felt the heat rise to her cheeks. "I read this book where the boy was brought up by a town drunk, but he kept his sense of adventure and his good nature."

Her mom smiled. "*Huckleberry Finn.* I used to read it to you girls at bedtime."

Finn inclined her head in acknowledgment of sweeter times. "And Montoya..." She grimaced. "My name is Inigo Montoya. You killed my father. Prepare to die."

Angie covered her mouth and blinked back tears of laughter. "You named yourself after a fictional character in a movie?"

"A suave, debonaire character good with a sword, intelligent and well-spoken, who had a need for vengeance that drove him through life."

Carmina put her arm around her mom as she started to cry. "Sounds about right. Guess we'll have to see that movie, eh?"

"You haven't seen *The Princess Bride*?" Luna mumbled, her eyes closed. "That's the worst thing I've ever heard."

Finn put her arm around Luna, so her neck wasn't at such a weird angle. "I think it's time for us to go." She stood and scooped Luna into her arms.

The bodyguards, always unobtrusive, were there in an instant, and Finn was able to quickly say her goodbyes thanks to having a sleeping child in her arms. They all piled into a waiting limo, and Finn didn't miss the look in her mom's eyes.

"It's so beautiful to see you with a family, hija," she whispered as she gazed at Finn and Luna.

"I don't know—" Finn started, not wanting to give Angie the wrong idea.

"She's really amazing with her. With both of us." Angie gently took Luna and shifted her to another seat, where Luna curled into a ball. "I hope it's okay. I've given the driver my address. We have the room, and it's late."

"We didn't bring any clothes," Carmina said.

"We've got enough in the house for everyone." Angie smiled. "It would mean the world to me if you stayed. We could keep getting to know each other over breakfast."

Her mom nodded. "If it's okay with Finn."

Pablo yawned loudly. "I don't care if it's okay with Finn. I'm totally sleeping at the hot celebrity lady's house. No one back home will believe it."

Finn was too overwhelmed to say anything, so she simply nodded and kissed Angie's knuckles. While they were in company, it would have to be enough. But the moment they were alone, she'd show Angie just how she felt.

Chapter Twenty-Nine

ANGIE GASPED AS FINN nibbled at the sensitive skin under her ear and along her neck. Goosebumps broke out as Finn's fingertips slid along her arms to her fingers and back up again, leaving a trail of desire in their wake.

"Mi vida," Finn murmured against her neck. "I want you."

"Please." Angie arched into her touch. "God, Finn. I need you."

But Finn wasn't in any hurry, despite Angie's pleas. She slid the zipper of Angie's dress down slowly, her fingertips following along on her bare skin, making her shiver with need. As she peeled the dress from Angie's shoulders to expose her breasts, her fingertips continued the gentle, arousing trail of fire. When Finn bent to suck Angie's nipple, her knees buckled. Finn's strong hands kept her upright as she sucked and lightly bit first one, and then the other.

She pressed her hands to Finn's head and begged, not caring that the words coming out didn't make any sense. Finn backed her to the bed and then lay slowly on top of her, pressing her to the mattress. She kissed a hot line from her collarbone to her breasts, again lavishing them with attention and driving Angie to the brink of madness.

"Finn, you're killing me." She writhed beneath her, the dress keeping her from pressing against Finn just where she needed to.

Finn knelt on the bed and pulled the dress away to reveal the lacy thigh-high stockings and matching G-string. She closed her eyes and tilted her head back. "Dios mío. You're so fucking beautiful." She lay down beside Angie and trailed her fingertips over her stomach and along the line of her panties, then over her hips to the tops of her stockings. "You're a goddess from the most

erotic dream I couldn't even conjure on my best day of writing."
She bent and began to kiss and nip her way over Angie's hip to the
flat of her stomach, and then moved lower, where her hot breath
against Angie's clit made her cry out.

"Finn, I swear to god, if you don't take me right this second..."
She trailed off, since there was nowhere to take that threat.

In response, Finn slid her fingers under the sides of Angie's
panties and pulled them off, before throwing them aside. Then
her mouth was on Angie's clit, and there were no words. Just the
sensation of Finn's hot mouth on her, the feel of Finn's hands under
her ass, holding her in place, the way her tongue felt as it stroked
her.

The orgasm hit too fast, too soon, and it wasn't enough.
Fortunately, Finn knew what she was doing. She moved up Angie's
body and pushed two fingers inside her, and Angie muffled her
cries against Finn's chest as Finn took her deep and slow.

"Mi vida," Finn murmured against Angie's hair. "Mi corazón."

Finn's musky cologne mixed with the scent of sex and her
words and pulled Angie's soul from her body as Finn's pace
sped up, and Angie begged in sounds for her not to stop. She
rode Finn's hand hard and pressed against her as the next orgasm
crashed through her. Finn pulled her tightly against her with her
free arm, not stopping her deep, hard rhythm until Angie sagged
against her.

Tears slid down her cheeks, and Finn kissed them away.

"Are you okay, love?" Finn asked, leaning on her elbow.

"That was... I don't..." Angie took a ragged breath and cupped
Finn's cheek. "I love you."

Finn's eyes widened slightly and then she dropped her forehead
to rest against Angie's. "I love you too. And I'll show you this way
and every other way for as long as you'll let me."

Angie tugged on Finn's suit jacket. "It's a little lonely being naked
on my own down here."

Finn grinned. "I kind of like it. It feels studly."

Angie pushed up and moved so she was straddling Finn's lap. "Yeah, well, you can show me how studly you are with a lot less clothes on. Actions speak louder than Zegna."

Finn made a sound of appreciation as Angie started unbuttoning her shirt. "You know your designers."

"And you look good enough to eat wearing this one. I might get them on speed dial."

Finn groaned as Angie slid her hands inside the shirt and palmed Finn's breasts. "Anything. Any fucking thing you want, I'll give you."

Angie got up and took off the rest of Finn's clothes, far faster than she'd divested Angie of hers. Looking at Fin laying there in a sports bra and tight boxers, her skin dark against the white comforter, Angie was reminded of works of art, though she couldn't think of any this exquisite.

She traced the bumps and ridges of Finn's abs. "I thought writers sat at a desk and drank and ate all the time. You don't get this body from doing that." She ran her tongue along the trail her fingers had taken.

"I refuse to talk about exercise with you right now." Finn put her hands behind her head. "But do with my body whatever you want. It's your toy."

Angie liked the sound of that. She'd never been with someone so willing to give themselves over to her, and it made the vulnerability of losing herself so completely to Finn's touch that much easier to allow. She finished taking off Finn's clothes and then settled on top of her. Finn wrapped her arms around her and looked into her eyes.

"I love you, Angie. And I'll do everything in my power to protect you and show you how much I adore you. I swear it."

Angie kissed her, long and deep, until they needed to come up for air, and then she lowered herself between Finn's legs. She breathed her in and flicked her clit with her tongue and smiled when Finn pulled a pillow over her face and moaned into it.

Angie settled in and sucked, teased, and licked until Finn's hips bucked and she came, one hand pressing the pillow to her face, the other tangled in Angie's hair as she held her tight.

Angie rested her head against Finn's thigh for a while as Finn stroked her hair, and then when Finn tugged gently, she rose and curled up in bed next to her. Finn pulled the comforter over them and pulled Angie close, spooning her tightly.

There were still plenty of questions to be answered. There were things to worry about and decisions to be made. But for now, for this beautiful moment in time, there was nothing but the love they'd declared and the feeling of peace in Finn's arms.

***

Angie woke from the dream that wasn't so much a dream as the seeds of a plan. She straddled Finn, who was sleeping on her back, and kissed her softly.

"If you wake me up this way, I hope you're ready for me to enjoy making you scream my name," Finn said without opening her eyes but moving her hand between Angie's legs.

Angie laughed and jumped out of bed. "I'll keep that in mind, stud, but right now, I'm going to shower and go down for breakfast. I'm calling a family meeting."

She stopped at the entrance to the bathroom and looked over at Finn, who was sitting up on her elbows, watching her. "Showers are lonely places—"

She laughed and squealed as Finn leapt from the bed, nearly tripping on the covers as she chased Angie into the shower.

Sex was quick but no less intense as Finn pressed against Angie's back and pushed deep into her as the hot water cascaded over them. When Finn went for a second round, Angie pushed her away, laughing. "Come on. I want to talk."

"If you want to talk instead of have sex this soon into our relationship, I think we can plan on seeing a therapist sooner rather than later." Finn grumbled as Angie tossed her a towel.

Angie pressed against her and wiggled. "Trust me, I don't want to talk more than have sex. But when I have something on my mind, I have to deal with it, or I stay distracted."

Finn shrugged but she was smiling. "Good to know." She looked at her crumpled suit on the floor. "Looks like I'll be a little rumpled at breakfast though."

Angie bit her lip and opened the closet. "When I made the plan for us to attend the awards, I asked my personal shopper to get you a few things."

Finn's predatory grin made Angie laugh. "So you planned on getting me into your bed last night, did you?" She grabbed her around the waist and swung her in the air. "Dirty girl."

She smacked at Finn's shoulders. "I'll show you just how dirty later."

Finn relented and let her go, then pulled some jeans and a shirt from the closet. "I like you choosing my clothes. There's something power-hot-femme in it."

Angie pulled on her favorite jeans and a T-shirt. "I think we'd better have a ton of sex before I go back to work again, or I'll get fired because I'll constantly be on my back at home instead."

Finn growled and moved toward her. "I like the sound of that."

Angie dodged and threw open the door. "Downstairs!"

Finn sighed theatrically. "Fine."

In the kitchen, Finn's mom, Nachelle, and Carmina were already deep in conversation with Helen, and Susan was looking at photos of Angie's trip with Luna. When they came in holding hands, Susan tilted her head, met Angie's gaze, and gave her a small, knowing smile. Angie smiled back and then turned to the others.

"I already made omelets for everyone else," Susan said, rising from where she sat with Luna. "I'll get yours on now."

"Thank you." Angie sat on a barstool at the island, and Finn took the one next to her. "I've got an idea, and I want to run it past you all."

"I'll go wake Pablo," Helen said. "Don't say too much you'll have to repeat."

Conversation stopped and everyone gave Angie their attention. She took Finn's hand.

"The story you and your mom told us is awful. You both survived terrible circumstances and came out the other side. But there's no question that us being photographed together from now until the end of time—"

"Yes!" Luna said, slapping the table.

"—will mean that your father may find you. And since we're going to have you in our lives as well," she said to Nachelle and Carmina, "you may get found too. And that means we have to be proactive."

"What do you have in mind?" Carmina asked when neither Finn nor Nachelle responded.

"An all-out publicity attack. We show up at your father's house with the press in tow. We make a grand show of reuniting you and your mom with your sisters, we make it clear that we'll be living in L.A., and we say that your father only wants the very best for his family, and he's given his blessing, etcetera."

"And he won't say that's not true because he won't want to lose face on camera." Finn nodded slowly, clearly considering it. "But then we're out in the open for him to come after us later. All of us." She nodded toward Luna.

"But Luna is the one who reminded me about all the crazy things we deal with. We have bodyguards, twenty-four seven. We have a gated property. We hardly ever go anywhere there aren't cameras. Frankly, I don't think he'd take the chance, because he'd be the first suspect on any list if anything did happen to us." Angie looked between Finn and her mom. "Waiting and hoping nothing happens isn't going to help the girls, and it'll always be like waiting for the shoe to drop. Confront him with the world watching, and maybe we can put this to rest."

Finn's jaw worked and her eyes narrowed as she thought, and

her mom looked equally thoughtful. Pablo shuffled in, yawning, and smiled gratefully when Susan pressed a mug of coffee into his hands.

"Why don't we leave you to talk it over?" Angie said. "The rest of us can go watch a movie."

Luna jumped up and headed for the stairs. "I get to pick!"

Helen and Susan followed her, arguing that they got some say in the options.

Carmina looked at Angie fondly. "Finn is a lucky woman. I think she's met her match in you."

Angie looked over her shoulder as she was leaving the room and smiled at Finn. "I love you."

Finn touched her chest over her heart. "I love you too."

Pablo sat on the couch opposite Nachelle and Carmina. It made sense that he be in on the decision-making, given that he was the one who'd been in proximity to her father the most. Finn's family would make the decision that affected the rest of their lives, and Angie would be there after, no matter the outcome.

As Angie snuggled into the sofa and Luna started the movie, she ruminated on the plan. It wasn't perfect, but she wanted a life with Finn that was free of fear, free of shadows of the past. Love demanded light, and she wanted to bring that light to their future.

Chapter Thirty

FOR THE FIRST TIME in years, there was no fight or flight mode raging through Finn's system at the sight of her father. That might have to do with the paparazzi vans and their crews surrounding her. But mostly it had to do with having Angie on one side of her and her mom and Carmina on the other. Beside them, Pablo stood tall, his jaw tight and arms crossed. They'd discussed whether or not it was wise for him to be at this showdown given that he lived in the DR and would have to deal with the fallout, but he'd insisted. She was his family, and he wasn't about to not be there for the moment she took back control of her life.

Her father stood at the door, his expression shuttered as she walked toward him, her head high, her shoulders back. She was done with fear, and it was time he saw that he no longer had any control. She studied him as she drew closer, and she saw an old man with gray in his stubble, flecks of gray in his hair, and lines around his eyes. Far from the monster of her nightmares, now he was an old gym towel, nothing but a rag that once was useful.

Finn smiled as she leaned toward him, and she turned her face as though to kiss his cheek so the cameras couldn't see it when she whispered, "It's over."

She stepped back and took Angie's hand. "This is Angie Davis. My girlfriend. And of course, you remember Mom and her girlfriend, Carmina."

His expression never faltered, but she was close enough to see the tightening around his eyes and the rage that flooded through them.

She and Angie turned so the cameras could see and hear them

fully. "When we received word that you wanted my sisters to come live with us in Beverly Hills, I was ecstatic but not surprised. You've always been the kind of father who wanted the very best for his family, and Angie has said she's happy to see that they get the education they need for whatever life it is they want."

"Of course, they'll have to get used to the cameras on them all the time," Angie said, laughing sweetly.

"Ms. Montoya, are you the daughter of Marco Rodríguez? Why did you change your name and move away?"

Finn made sure her shoulders stayed relaxed and the smile stayed in place, even though she felt her father stiffen behind her as he radiated fury. "My father and I discussed my desire to make it on my own, without the family name to pave the way. Only hard work and dedication would show me how to make my way in the world, and he supported my decision to leave and start fresh. As you all know, that paid off." She grinned, knowing full well the reference to her success would only serve to enrage him more.

"And what about your mother, Ms. Montoya? She was declared dead many years ago."

At this, her mom stepped forward. "We do not believe in divorce, and my ex-husband was an important political figure. However, I fell in love with someone else, and we agreed that it was better for his career and our families if it was believed I was dead. That way I could live my life, and he could find a woman who truly loved him."

Finn's stomach turned at the picture they were painting of him, as a doting father and understanding but ambitious husband. But this way, he'd have to play the part or look like the abusive, angry, vengeful man he really was, and that would be political suicide. This way, there were no accusations he could deny, and he'd have no choice but to leave them alone.

Finn's sisters came forward, each of them carrying a suitcase that Angie's bodyguards had helped them hurriedly pack while their father was busy at the front of the house. They edged past him, and their body language said more than words ever could as they shrank away from him, keeping their eyes down until they were well past him. With the plan in progress, Pablo had managed to get her sister, Celia, alone in a shop. She'd confirmed that she had no desire to marry the man her father had chosen, which meant Finn didn't have to worry that she was ripping her sister from a life she actually wanted.

And then all cameras were on the family as they hugged their mom and cried.

Finn's father took the moment to hiss in her ear, "You little bitch. How dare you defy me this way? How dare you and Nachelle take my girls from me? You will pay for this."

She glanced back over her shoulder at him, surprised at the lack of emotion she felt. "They aren't *yours*. None of us were ever *yours*. And they're going to have amazing lives far, far away from you. And if you so much as breathe in our direction, I'll make certain the press is there to record every word. If anything happens to any of us, you can be damn sure it will be traced right back to your doorstep."

Angie looked back at him as well. "We've given you the opportunity to look like a decent human being. We suggest you run with that. We'll leave you alone, you leave us alone, and we're all happy."

His jaw worked, and it was clear he was considering his options. Finally, he said, "Don't ever disgrace this country with your presence again. You're all dead to me," and then turned away and slammed the door behind him.

It was over. Finn nearly laughed out loud at the pure, empty space in her soul that had once contained all the fear and anguish of her past. She could fill that space with the beauty of her family now.

She put her arm around one of her sisters, and the whole group walked back toward the car. Angie and Finn answered the questions thrown their way in order to keep the press from becoming unruly, and waited until her mom, Carmina, Pablo, and her sisters were all in the limo before they waved at the press and got in themselves.

There were plenty of tears and short explanations given as they made their way to the airport. They boarded Angie's private jet, and Finn couldn't help but look around for any of her father's thugs waiting to thwart their escape. But there was no one there. Just the people she loved, about to start a new adventure.

Her sisters were awestruck as they boarded the jet and got settled in, and Helen, who'd waited on the plane, was already in motion making sure they were taken care of. Much to Luna's aggravation, she'd been left at home because they weren't about to bring her into a dangerous situation. When Finn saw her by the pool, they'd had a long talk, and it turned out Luna was afraid something would go wrong and they wouldn't come back, that she'd be left alone. Finn had hugged her hard and told her it would never happen. She'd pinky sworn it, in fact. She smiled as Angie sent a text, letting Luna know they were already on their way back.

Finn sat with Angie in the back and watched the organized chaos as they got ready to leave the DR, possibly forever.

"You okay? I thought that went amazingly well." Angie stroked Finn's hand, her expression one of concern.

"It did. A little too smoothly, really, but your plan to ambush him that way worked in our favor for sure. If he'd had any notice of us coming, he probably would have hidden my sisters away somewhere we'd have never found them." She kissed Angie's hand and hoped what she felt was clear in her eyes. "Thank you for this. Not just for understanding, but for helping me fix things."

"I suggested a plan. It was you and your mom who had to be brave enough to make it happen." Angie looked down the aisle at Finn's family. "Will your sisters be okay?"

"Eventually. It takes a long time to get past the kind of abuse my father was spectacular at, but once they know they're really safe, they'll start to heal. Thank you for offering them the guest house behind your place. It's good they can stay together but have their own space while they come to terms with their new life." As the importance of what they'd done set in, her heart felt like it could burst. "You showed me the way, Angie. Falling in love with you gave me the strength to do my own healing."

"And loving you means I get the happy ever after I wasn't sure really existed outside the movies." Angie smiled as one of Finn's sisters laughed and pointed at something outside the window. "Luna will love having a big family. And our parents can share their stories about us as they get used to their new lives too."

On the flight to the DR, they'd discussed the possible outcomes of their plan, and they'd convinced her mom and Carmina to come to California and start a new life, where they could spend time with Finn and her sisters and never have to look over their shoulders again. Pablo, too, would be starting over in California, and since he'd be living at Finn's house, he'd have plenty of time to build the life he wanted. Finn had gone from being utterly alone to having a beautiful woman in her bed, a great new kid in her life, and her mom and sisters, whom she'd never thought to see again, living nearby. Not to mention her oldest and closest friend, who'd always looked out for her. It was surreal in the best possible way.

"That day you walked into the coffee shop was the best day of my life." Finn's eyes watered at the beauty of what was ahead. Possibilities spread into the future like sunbeams and it was so beautiful, it made her soul ache.

"The best day of your life *so far*," Angie said, a wicked gleam in her eye. "I like a challenge, and I think I'm going to see how many times I can make you say that again."

Finn laughed, and her soul was lighter and sweeter than it had ever been. Her heart had led her home.

Epilogue

Two years and lots of stick figures later

Luna flopped onto the sun lounger next to Finn. "I used to hate having a lot of people around."

Laughter and music filled the air. "And now?" Finn asked.

"I still don't like being around a lot of people I don't know," Luna said, smiling as a toddler ran past, giggling wildly as Finn's sister chased him down to keep him from falling in the pool. "But I like my new family being here a lot."

Finn tousled her hair. "I'm glad to hear it, because nothing short of a bomb would get them out of your life."

"Drastic." Luna grinned and tapped at Finn's notebook, leaving a wet mark. "I bet you don't let them see the stick figures you draw of them."

Finn grinned and slid the notebook under her towel. "And if you want to stay my favourite daughter, you'll never show them."

Luna stretched and gave Finn a mischievous look. "As long as I stay your only daughter, we're good."

Angie sat on the edge of Finn's chair and handed her a glass of iced tea. "Show them what?"

Luna pushed up from the chair. "Hopefully, you'll never know." She gave a dramatic villain laugh as she left and headed to the barbecue.

Finn shook her head. "Fifteen and already a master at blackmail. We're in for a wild ride."

"Please." Angie scooted herself between Finn's legs so her back was resting against Finn's chest. "That's the most well-behaved teenager on the planet. With her internship at *National Geographic* this year, we'll be lucky if we hear anything that isn't to do with dead people or ancient civilizations."

Helen had retired, again. Now that Luna was a full-blown teenager, they'd decided she no longer needed a nanny, nor did she want her own personal assistant. Fortunately, Helen still came to the house often to visit with everyone. She regaled them with stories of Tibetan temples and fortune tellers in back alleys. She was proof that it was never too late to take up a quirky hobby. She'd sent her apologies for missing Finn's premiere, but she was busy backpacking in New Zealand. The photo she sent of the hotel made it clear she wasn't roughing it.

Barb sauntered over, her bright blue sarong catching the breeze and making her look like a walking commercial for whatever she was drinking. "Finn, I'm in love with Pablo, and we're going to have a million babies. Hope you're okay with that."

Finn laughed. "I don't think you'll find a better, more infuriating man to have those million babies with. You have my blessing, but you may have to trade in your lesbian card." She nodded imperiously, making Barb laugh.

"I'm so glad you're taking time off right when I'm sticking around too." Angie shaded her eyes as she looked up at Barb.

"Who knew you'd take a sit-com role and marry your soulmate?" Barb sat on the lounger next to them and was quickly joined by Pablo.

"Who knew Finn would leave her hermit hole in order to become someone's soulmate?"

"Finn, my car is blocked in. Can we take your truck for a supply run?" Susan called out, her arm around the girlfriend she'd proposed to six weeks ago.

"As long as you bring it back without any extra bodily fluids anywhere in it, yes."

Finn's mom shot her a warning look as she bounced a toddler on her knee, and Finn looked away before she started laughing.

The moment they'd all arrived in LA, her mom had dived into her matriarch role with relish. They'd settled her sisters at Angie's, Finn had bought her mom and Carmina their own home nearby, and Pablo had taken over Finn's house when it was clear she was pretty much already living at Angie's anyway.

Two of her sisters were attending college, and one was taking cooking classes at the local culinary school, where Susan had taken her under her wing. Pablo had started his own upscale interior design company, and Finn had been surprised at how innovative and creative he was. It was good to know people could still surprise her, even the ones she saw every day.

"Are you ready for the world premiere of your movie, Finn?" Carmina asked as she pulled up a chair.

"Can anyone ever be ready for that kind of thing?" In truth, Finn hadn't had a lot to do with the film. Someone else had written the screenplay, and she'd talked them through parts of it, and although she'd been invited to the studio to watch some of the filming, she'd declined. This was someone else's creative baby based on hers, and she only hoped it didn't look like a Frankenstein version, haphazardly sewn together to create something monstrous.

"It's going to be amazing," her mom said. "And even if it's different, you've still inspired a new story in the world, and that means something."

Finn's entire family had been almost overly supportive of her work from the moment they'd begun living their new lives. Her mom and sisters told everyone they knew about Finn's books, about the movie, about how beautiful and amazing Angie was. After so many years of solitary living, there were times it was overwhelming. Those were the times she sought out Angie, and they drove to the overlook where they'd first made out so long ago. There, they talked or sat in silence and simply enjoyed the feel of each other's presence. Unlike Finn's relationship with her family, Angie's had yet to progress much further than a few dinners a month. They still relied too much on talking about Angie's career instead of trying to get to know her as a person, and Luna disliked the suggestions they made about her changing her appearance so she could "fit in better." She and Angie had discussed it and decided that although they were family, they wouldn't go out of their way to include them in gatherings.

The only dark spot had been when they received news of her father's death. A heart attack, according to the papers. But Pablo's sources said there were questions about how natural it was. Questions which had been neatly swept under a rug that Finn and her family had no interest in looking beneath. None of them attended the funeral, and there was no question they all breathed a little easier with him gone.

Finn huffed when Angie elbowed her in the stomach slightly.

"Hey, stud. Focus on the now." She leaned back to kiss Finn's cheek.

Finn tightened her hold around Angie's waist. "Now is the only thing that matters."

What's Your Story?

Global Wordsmiths, CIC, provides an all-encompassing service for all writers, ranging from basic proofreading and cover design to development editing, typesetting, and eBook services. A major part of our work is charity and community focused, delivering writing projects to under-served and under-represented groups across Nottinghamshire, giving voice to the voiceless and visibility to the unseen.

To learn more about what we offer, visit: www.globalwords.co.uk

A selection of books by Global Words Press:
Desire, Love, Identity: with the National Justice Museum
Aventuras en México: Farmilo Primary School
Times Past: with The Workhouse, National Trust
Young at Heart with AGE UK
In Different Shoes: Stories of Trans Lives

Self-published authors working with Global Wordsmiths:
E.V. Bancroft
Addison M. Conley
AJ Mason
Ally McGuire
Emma Nichols
Helena Harte
Iona Kane
Robyn Nyx
Simon Smalley
Valden Bush

Other Great Butterworth Books

Stolen Ambition by Robyn Nyx
Two worlds. Two women. One chance at love.
Available on Amazon (ASIN B0BS1PRSCN)

An Art to Love by Helena Harte
Second chances are an art form.
Available on Amazon (ASIN B0B1CD8Y42)

Call of Love by Lee Haven
Separated by fear. Reunited by fate. Will they get a second chance at life and love?
Available from 1 May 2023

Cabin Fever by Addison M Conley
She goes for the money, but will she stay for something deeper?
Available on Amazon (ASIN B0BQWY45GH)

Zamira Saliev: A Dept. 6 Operation by Valden Bush
They're both running from their pasts. Together, they might make a new future.
Available from Amazon (ASIN B0BHJKHK6S)

Of Light and Love by E.V. Bancroft
The deepest shadows paint the brightest love.
Available from Amazon (ASIN B0B64KJ3NP)

The Helion Band by AJ Mason
Rose's only crime was to show kindness to her royal mistress...
Available from Amazon (ASIN B09YM6TYFQ)

That Boy of Yours Wants Looking At by Simon Smalley
A gloriously colourful and heart-rending memoir.
Available from Amazon (ASIN B09HSN9NM8)

Judge Me, Judge Me Not by James Merrick
A memoir of one gay man's battle against the world and himself.
Available from Amazon (ASIN B09CLK91N5)

Printed in Great Britain
by Amazon

58322685R10149